William Browne Hockley

Tales of the Zenana; or, A Nuwab's leisure Hours

With an introductory Pref. by Lord Stanley of Alderley

William Browne Hockley

Tales of the Zenana; or, A Nuwab's leisure Hours
With an introductory Pref. by Lord Stanley of Alderley

ISBN/EAN: 9783337024154

Printed in Europe, USA, Canada, Australia, Japan

Cover: Foto ©Andreas Hilbeck / pixelio.de

More available books at **www.hansebooks.com**

TALES OF THE ZENANA

OR

A NUWAB'S LEISURE HOURS.

BY

W. B. HOCKLEY,

AUTHOR OF 'PANDURANG HARI.'

WITH AN INTRODUCTORY PREFACE BY
LORD STANLEY OF ALDERLEY.

IN TWO VOLUMES.

VOL. II.

HENRY S. KING & Co.

65 CORNHILL & 12 PATERNOSTER ROW, LONDON.

1874.

CONTENTS

OF

THE SECOND VOLUME.

THE
TALES OF THE ZENANA.

———

CHAPTER I.

THE BUTCHER'S STORY (*continued*).

THE negotiation of marriage between the son of Saruk and the daughter of Hurrees-Al-Alghar had indeed taken place, so that there seemed but little chance of success for poor Ashuk, who with a heavy heart proceeded to his uncle at Cambay. Young Ajeez, in the meantime, was studying hard all the tricks practised in mercantile pursuits, under his able and experienced father, to qualify himself for the situation of supercargo of the ship, which in a year or two was to be richly freighted by Saruk, and probably by Nugdee Hurrees, whom they much wished to persuade to risk a large sum of money. This was the speculation he was pondering upon when the unhappy widow applied to him for the loan of one hundred rupees. But, to the disappointment of Saruk, the old miser was not inclined so highly to appreciate piece-goods and cornelians as his neighbours, and finally refused to risk any part of his capital in the concern.

Although averse to the mercantile speculation, old Nugdee

gave a ready consent to the proposition of marriage between Ajeez and his daughter, to whom he promised one lac of rupees, provided Ajeez could command only half that sum. Saruk was therefore the more anxious to dispatch his son to Bengal in charge of a valuable cargo, in the hope that on his return, aided a little by himself, the boy might be enabled to place at the feet of the miser the fifty thousand rupees, for which he was to receive one lac and the lovely Kheir Neyut as his bride. Independent of present advantage, Saruk indulged in the hope that, on the death of the miser, Ajeez would undoubtedly become his heir. Thus do mortals lay out plans for their worldly advantage, and become so persuaded of the final success of them, that they are little able to bear a failure with fortitude and resignation to the will of Providence. So was it with Saruk, who dreamed not of the danger of the sea, or of the changing winds of heaven, and the equally fluctuating mind of old Nugdee ; but, above all, the interference of any other mortal on earth, by whose schemes the wishes of his soul could be overthrown.

Ashuk remained two years with his uncle at Cambay. In vain did this kind relative try to fix the youth's attention to business ; the sports of the chase, hawking, hunting, &c., together with the recollection of his beloved Kheir Neyut, entirely engrossed his thoughts. Under these circumstances his uncle was compelled to send him back to his desponding mother, delivering into his hands a letter containing a bill of exchange for four hundred rupees for the poor woman's use, with the intelligence that she must expect no farther assistance from him. He regretted the impossibility of fixing the mind of his nephew to business, and recommended Beewah to procure **for** him **a** junior situation in the Nuwab's troops, a soldier's life being evidently more suitable to the boy's disposition.

Beewah with pain beheld the return of her unprofitable son, whom she severely reproved. On comprehending the contents of the letter she felt the utmost gratitude for the present it contained, and caused an answer to be penned immediately, to thank the considerate donor. The first use she determined to make of the money was to pay off her debt to old Nugdee Hurrees; and for this purpose, accompanied by Ashuk, she proceeded to the miser's habitation. Just as they approached the outer gate they espied Saruk **and** his son Ajeez in the act of taking leave of **the old** fellow: both passed Beewah **and Ashuk,** casting looks of ineffable contempt on them. Nugdee Hurrees admitted the widow and her **son,** ushering them into the old shed as **before.** Having stated her business, Beewah presented her rupees; and the miser, having calculated the enormous interest, together with the cruel bonus, Beewah found she must dip very deep into the four hundred rupees received from **her** good relative.

The money being paid, Ashuk recommended his mother to demand a deed of release, and thus hoped to hear Kheir Neyut summoned to bring pen, ink, &c. The old miser having **no** objection to the demand, accordingly called out to his daughter to bring pen and ink, but, as before, refused to provide the paper. This detestable meanness was likely to deprive Ashuk **of** a sight of the lovely girl, who would probably have performed her task ere he should return with the paper. The anxious fair one, however, perceiving him about to quit the mansion, guessed the object of his errand, and delayed producing the ink until he returned. Thus Ashuk had the felicity of being once more near his beloved, who was grown more beautiful and captivating than ever. To speak to her, however, was impossible ; and he was meditating how he could find an opportunity of addressing her, when the wind blew away the half-written deed from the feet of the miser, whose attention was directed towards mending a miserable stump of a pen. Kheir Neyut flew to pick up the paper ; and Ashuk following for the same purpose, both met near the gate, screened by the shed from the eyes of Beewah and the miser.

'How fortunate is this, lovely Kheir Neyut ! How long is it since I beheld thee ! Say, wilt thou allow me an interview to-morrow night ?'

'We shall be overheard, Ashuk. My window is at a great distance from the ground.'

'Then will I climb up to it. Deny me not, or I shall die with disappointment.'

'For heaven's sake then, Ashuk, be cautious. Come at mid-night.'

This was all the lovers had time to say, as the miser called out for his paper, which receiving from the hands of his daughter, he leisurely and cautiously finished the deed of release, which he handed to the widow.

Beewah and her delighted son returned home, from whence the former repaired to court, in order to speak a good word for her son, and obtain for him if possible some junior situation in the army.

Ashuk, whose whole mind was devoted to Kheir Neyut, and the means by which he could ascend to her window, hastened to the shop of Hussun al Habul, a rope-maker, to whom he gave orders to prepare a rope of a certain length and thickness, direct-ing him to **place** several large knots **at** equal distances thereon, with an iron hook at one end of the rope, of **a** particular shape and size. The rope-maker comprehending his wishes, was desired to have all in readiness by the following evening, when he would call for **it.** Hussun **al** Hubul promising obedience in every particular, Ashuk took his departure. Beewah not having returned home, Ashuk strolled about the city, conversing with many of his friends and **old** schoolfellows : from these he learned that Ajeez **was in** a week's **time** to proceed with his cargo to Calcutta, in the very ship commanded by Fureeb Khash, the schoolmaster's son-in-law. **A** thought **now struck him :** that through the means of Adeeb **Khan** he might prevail upon Fureeb Khash to detain Ajeez much longer than was necessary, and thus afford him more time to arrange his plans for possessing himself of the fair Kheir Neyut ; he therefore called at the schoolmaster's house, whom he fortunately found disengaged. Adeeb **Khan** gave him a most hearty welcome ; said he had heard of his return with regret, and enquired to what profession he now intended to turn his thoughts.

'With your assistance, kind Adeeb, I mean to think of only one occupation.'

'And what may that be ?' enquired Adeeb.

'Love, Adeeb Khan ; for that I feel convinced **is the** only line into which **I** am capable of entering with heart and **soul.**'

'Oh, Ashuk ! Ashuk ! will wisdom never enter thy poor brains ?'

'Now pray, Adeeb, don't preach **to** me ; I am not in a fit condition to hear you; so, for love of Allah, cease. I tell you, if you aid me, I must succeed, and become a rich man to boot.'

'But how in the name of wonder can I assist you, Ashuk?'

The youth, having made the schoolmaster promise inviolable secrecy, related his tale of love, and the arranged departure of his rival in his son-in-law's ship; he then at once begged him to persuade Fureeb Khash to detain Ajeez, in order that he might gain time to prosecute his plans for the possession of the fair Kheir Neyut. The schoolmaster having no great good-will towards either Saruk or his son, and being extremely partial to young Ashuk, ever since his spirited exertions in his defence, at last promised to sound his son-in-law on the subject, and desired Ashuk to call again in a day or two; Fureeb Khash being then in the city transacting business with the owners of the ship 'Futteh Mobaruk,' which was 'the name of the vessel he commanded. Ashuk pressed the hand of his old preceptor in gratitude for his kindness, and promised to call again in two days' time.

When the amorous youth entered his mother's house he perceived her wearing a countenance of joy and gladness, for she had, by expending her last rupee, contrived to get him appointed an officer in the Nuwab's body-guard—a situation highly agreeable to the youth, whose services would seldom be required, save when the Nuwab went out in state, and would secure him a permanent residence near his beloved Kheir Neyut. Ashuk spent the rest of the day in parading about the city, mentioning his appointment to all he met. When the evening set in he failed not to demand his rope from old Hussun al Hubul, which was all ready for him an hour before midnight, and made exactly as he desired. When he conceived his mother to be fast locked in the arms of sleep he softly arose, and unbolting the door, which he cautiously closed after him, ran down the street, and arrived at the spot where he had deposited the rope, and proceeded to the lane at the back of the miser's house; having provided himself with a long bamboo pole, by means of which he safely fixed the hook at the end of the rope to the bar of the window above him.

The moon, although behind a cloud, afforded him sufficient light to perceive with delight that the centre bar of the window had been removed. 'She intends to admit me!' cried the youth in ecstasy. 'Ah! I see her at the window; now, then, love assist me!' Saying which, he scrambled up the knotted rope. He had nearly reached the top, when the moon burst forth from behind the cloud, upon the window, where he espied, not the lovely Kheir Neyut, but the wrinkled visage of her father, with several men armed with swords and sticks. In an instant he slid down the rope and rushed from the lane. What could be the meaning of this? Had Kheir Neyut deceived him? It was impossible she could have been so treacherous; it must be the act of the rope-maker, who had probably watched his footsteps; to him, therefore, he determined that instant to repair and upbraid him for his ill-natured officiousness. The rope-maker had retired to rest, and, alarmed at the violent knocking at his door, was a considerable time before he durst venture to open it. As soon as Ashuk beheld the trembling Hussun al Hubul, he commenced loading him with abuse. The rope-maker was long ere he could comprehend the meaning of all this; and when he did, solemnly declared his innocence, swearing positively he had not quitted his house that night.

'Then you must have betrayed me to some one,' cried the enraged Ashuk, and was beginning to beat poor Hussun al Hubul, when his wife interfered, saying, 'I fear, sir, it is I whom you must blame; but indeed I was not aware I should injure you. This day, my husband having finished your rope full of knots, I went to the smith's to procure an iron hook such as you directed, and, in his absence, young Ajeez, the merchant, came to purchase ropes and lashings for his goods about to be sent to Cambav. Observing your very curious knotted rope, he enquired for what pupose and for whom it was intended. I replied it had been made by your order, but for what purpose I could not tell; and I declare I mentioned the circumstance to no one else on earth.'

'That was quite enough, thou babbling fool, to ruin me,' said Ashuk, angry and mortified.

The old woman begged a thousand pardons, which, however, were far from being granted—so incensed was her customer. Ashuk proceeded home, dejected and out of spirits, anticipating a seizure by the police in the morning, or perhaps that very night.

Whilst the youth is momentarily expecting the punishment for his rashness, it will be proper to explain the suspicions which were awakened in the bosom of Ajeez, who, having been informed that this extraordinary rope was for Ashuk, determined to watch his footsteps most narrowly. He accordingly saw him come for the rope, convey it to an old shed, and then return. At an hour before midnight he again saw him enter the shed, remove the rope, and proceed with it to the lane at the back of the miser's house.

The idea of Ashuk presuming to love Kheir Neyut never once entering his imagination, he concluded the daring youth was actually about to rob old Nugdee Hurrees; and being himself greatly interested in preserving the miser's hoarded gold, hastened to the front gate, where he knocked and called most loudly. Nugdee would seldom at night hear any summons at his gate; but the incessant violent kicking and bawling of Ajeez induced him to descend and enquire who was there. Hearing the voice of Ajeez, he opened the gate, and was soon made acquainted with the danger that threatened his house and property. The miser stood breathless with fear, and seemed quite at a loss how to act; but Ajeez calling to his recollection that no time was to be lost, he opened the gate, and proceeding to the house of a poor tailor, who lived opposite, he begged his assistance for the love of Heaven, for that robbers were about his house. The tailor, accompanied by his son, quickly appearing, Nugdee promised them a reward should the thief be secured. Having no doubt but the rope described by Ajeez was intended to be made fast to the window of his daughter's apartment, which looked into the lane, the miser, accompanied by Ajeez and the tailors, armed with swords and clubs, entered her apartment, and bade her retire to another room, for that robbers were about the house.

Kheir Neyut trembled for poor Ashuk, and was at a loss to account for the discovery of his intention to escalade the building; at the same time she was pleased to find his actions were imputed to a wrong motive, although either way, whether he was supposed to come for love or money, she could scarcely indulge in any hope of his escape. Determined to prevent her father or his attendants from injuring Ashuk with their formidable weapons, the alarmed girl, although ordered to retire to another part of the house, went no farther than the door, which she kept ajar, so as to enable her to see all that was going on in the room. Hearing the rustling at the window, she thus concluded her lover had discovered her father and his assistants in time to enable him to effect his retreat. The miser expressed his concern at thus losing his victim, and was now most anxious to get rid of the tailors, they having remained far too long in the interior of his mansion to please him; and he entertained fears that, whilst attempting to secure a thief from without his house, he was affording golden opportunities to fellows within it. The tailors, however, begged to remind Master Nugdee of his promised reward.

'Reward, indeed!' cried the old man. 'Where is the thief? I promised a reward on the apprehension of the robber, but you stupid fellows have suffered him to escape, and now, truly, have the audacity to ask for a reward! No, no! go home, my worthy fellows, and next time be more quick in your movements.'

'So we will, Master Nugdee, when you catch us again on the same errand; but, by Allah! your house may be robbed and burned, ere we attend a second time to your cries for aid.'

The dissatisfied tailors were accordingly turned away without the least recompense for their trouble, leaving Ajeez to consult with the miser what was best to be done.

'Of course,' said he, 'Nugdee, you will lodge a complaint against this daring robber?'

'I don't know that I shall,' replied the miser. 'I am not so fond of paying fees to the Cotwall, and after all see the fellow escape punishment; and if he does not get off, what good shall I get by seeing him hanged?'

'But he may be fined, Nugdee,' said the revengeful Ajeez.

'Ay, boy, and the fines go into the Cotwall's pocket. I shall get none of them. But hark ye, Ajeez, as you value my good-will mention not the subject in public; it can do no good, and may only put others up to following Ashuk's example.'

'But, sir, the tailors will assuredly spread the report.'

'They may do so; but they know not who the thief is, and that is all I am anxious about, for you know Ashuk is now an officer in the body-guard; and as we have not actually caught him, he may deny the fact, and involve me in much trouble. I shall have the whole guard enter my house, dig up my gold, and march off with it! So for these reasons, I command you, mention not the circumstance.'

Ajeez, aware if the idea of the body-guard's appearing in the sacred mansion of the miser had once entered into his brain, all he could say would be of no avail, left him therefore, promising not to mention the affair even to his own father.

Nugdee Hurrees, although determined not to take any public measures towards the apprehension of Ashuk, quickly commenced making serious alterations in his house, to provide against any similar attempts in future. He blocked up the window of his daughter's apartment, and sent her to a room which looked into the courtyard, so that she **was** compelled **for ever to give up the** idea of **again** beholding Ashuk in the back lane. Kheir Neyut, **however,** was delighted at hearing her father's wise determination **not** to prosecute her lover, and perfectly agreed with him in his idea of the danger of involving himself in trouble with an officer **of** the guard, **as well as the** useless sacrifice of money **in** the shape of fees at the Cotwall's office.

Ashuk, in the meanwhile, lay on his pallet fully expecting the **house to** be surrounded **by** police-officers, and was in **the** morning agreeably surprised **to find how** mistaken **he had been.** His mother desired **him to** dress and prepare to **be** introduced to the Nuwab, from whose **hands he was to receive his sword** and take the usual oath **of** fidelity. Ashuk, delighted beyond measure, prepared accordingly ; and **as his** mother had purchased for him a new red turban with a rich border of gold, and borrowed **a** Cashmire shawl to **tie round his** waist, he indeed cut a most imposing appearance, being tall, handsome, and graceful.

The youth was accordingly introduced at court, where he and **his mother were almost** ruined by the various fees demanded of **them by** chobdars, peons, mace-bearers, and other persons who guarded the sacred musnud. The provident Beewah had been fully aware of the demands which would **be made,** and had borrowed **money,** sold **and** pawned almost everything she was possessed **of.** The Nuwab seemed pleased with young Ashuk's appearance and bold manners, declaring he much resembled his father, whose services he should never forget. Ashuk received his sword most gracefully, took **the** necessary oath in a firm, collected voice, and then withdrew, gratified by the attentions of all about the court, who saluted him, saying, ' Salaam, Ashuk, Sahib ! Sahib, Salaam ! Khodawund, Salaam !' and **all** such epithets **as** officers about the Nuwab's person were accustomed **to** hear.

On his return home he expressed his gratitude to his mother for the expense she had incurred for his sake, promising to give into her hands his first **three** months' salary. The doting mother, clasping him to her heart, declared her entire satisfaction at **his** conduct, and expressed hopes of his future advancement. Beewah having **heard** nothing farther of her son's infatuation for the miser's daughter, indulged **in** the hope that he had entirely forgotten her. But in this idea, however, she was greatly mistaken ; the flame burned more furiously than ever, not **a** moment passing without the recollection of Kheir Neyut entering his mind.

The next step towards completing the consequence of Ashuk was to procure for him a horse—the body-guard being all mounted. There being no immediate necessity, however, Ashuk determined to postpone the purchase of one until the expiration of the first three months, when his salary would be entirely at his own disposal ; trusting to the generosity of some kind friend to lend him one, should he, in the interim, be required **to** attend the Nuwab on any parade or excursion. The youthful guardsman **now** strutted about the city, assuming the airs and consequence of his situation. All made their salaam to him ; and such is the effect produced by rank and fortune, that **even** Saruk, the wealthy merchant, made his bow to the young officer as he passed his house. As Ashuk returned homewards he chanced to overtake old Nugdee Hurrees, who also made him a very low obeisance.

' **Happy to see** you, good sir,' said Ashuk.

'So am I,' thought the miser—'outside my house.'

'Indeed, Master Nugdee, I know not how to express my gratitude to you for your kind assistance to my poor mother.'

'What an impudent rascal!' thought Nugdee; 'the fellow who would have robbed me only last night, to dare to face me and converse with me in the street!'

'It is some time since we have met, Master Nugdee,' continued Ashuk; 'I should be delighted, would you allow me to call occasionally and enquire after your health.

'Oh, sir!' replied Nugdee, 'pray don't give yourself so much trouble: my health is always good—never sick in my life; so you know there is no occasion to enquire about me. Rely on it I am always well; and if anything does affect me, 'tis a visitor coming to talk about nothing. If you have any business, indeed, I will with pleasure meet you at my banker's in the city; but pray don't trouble yourself to come to my house.'

'Why, Master Nugdee, your house is somewhat nearer to mine than your banker's; therefore there will be if anything more trouble, and certainly less pleasure, for me to repair thither, and undoubtedly much more inconvenience to yourself.'

'Oh, pray don't mind my inconvenience, sir; I am ever ready when business demands my presence.'

'Well, then, why object to admit me into your shed, if not into the interior of your house?'

'Interior of my house, young man! Allah forbid! No, sir, it is not my custom—so farewell!'

'Nay, Master Nugdee, suffer me to call now and then, I pray you.'

'Why, to tell you plainly, young **man, I object** to your visits above all others.'

'Indeed! Why?'

'Why, because you select strange hours and places **to** pay me your visits. Now do you comprehend **me?**'

'**Not** I, indeed, Master Nugdee. **Pray** explain yourself. I never even entered your house at any time; you **took good care** of that.'

'Ah, **indeed did I,**' said the miser; 'and shall **be** doubly cautious in future. The window is blocked up, young man.'

'Window blocked up! What **window?** Do you mean to insinuate that I am a thief?'

'Why, replied old **Nugdee,** '**it certainly** looked very much like it.'

'**I** tell you what, Master **Nugdee,**' said Ashuk; '**we must** come to an understanding in this business.'

'**My** worthy friend,' replied the miser, 'all the understanding I wish to come to is this—never come near my house again, either by day or night, and we shall be the better friends, rely on it.'

'Well, now, Master Nugdee, the understanding I wish to come to is this—if you have any charge to make against me for coming through your window, either by night or by **day,** I desire you will instantly accompany me to the Cotwall's court, and there make your complaint ; or, if you do not do **so,** go down on your knees and beg my pardon, and explain all your ambiguous hints, so injurious to my honour.'

'Well,' thought Nugdee, 'I have heard of impudent fellows, but this young man beats all that were ever read or heard of.'

They had now arrived at the miser's great gates, and Nugdee was applying the key to the same, when Ashuk prevented him, saying, 'You won't escape thus, my friend. I demand an explanation, either here or before the Cotwall. By Allah! I will drag you before the Nuwab.'

'Oh, mercy!' cried the terrified miser; 'it was not you: now I am quite sure it could not be you; yet it was very like you, I must confess.'

'What? Who was like me?'

The alarmed Nugdee related all the events of the preceding night, when Ashuk expressed his surprise that a man of his good sense should heed the malicious reports of Ajeez, his decided enemy, and one with whom he had been at variance from his childhood.

'Consider, sir; I never had an opportunity of entering your mansion; how was it likely, therefore, I could expect, even were I so wickedly inclined, to come directly at your hidden treasure without risk of discovery? I must own I feel hurt at your unjust suspicions.'

The miser now really began to believe he had been mistaken, and that Ajeez had been mistaken also; he therefore most humbly craved the young officer's pardon, congratulating himself on his caution and prudence in not prosecuting Ashuk, as advised by his informant, Ajeez.

The miser and Ashuk now parted better friends, though the latter could not obtain permission to enquire occasionally after the old man's health, Nugdee persisting in declaring he was always well, and always should continue so; that knocking at his gate for the purpose of enquiring **after him would only be** attended **with** trouble and inconvenience **to both parties ; saying** which, he opened the portal, made a salaam, and then shut **out** poor Ashuk from all hope of gaining a friendly footing in **that** dwelling, wherein, **of all** others, he most wished to be **admitted as** a visitor.

CHAPTER II.

THE BUTCHER'S STORY (*continued*).

ON the following day Ashuk repaired to the schoolmaster, who he hoped had consulted with his son-in-law, Fureeb Khash, captain of the good ship 'Futteh Mobaruk.'   Adeeb Khan, perceiving Ashuk approach his school, which happened at the time to be occupied by the boys, signed him to enter into the interior of his dwelling ; and this he did in so significant a manner as to plainly inform Ashuk he had good news to communicate.

'Well, Adeeb, have you seen the captain?' eagerly enquired the youth.

'I have, Ashuk; and for a promise of a reward, should you succeed in marrying the miser's daughter, he will do all you require of him.'

'Thanks, my friend,' said the anxious boy; 'I certainly will promise to reward him, and will commit my promise to writing.'

'Gently, my friend, not so hasty with your pen. Fureeb Khash, although my son-in-law, is not a man to be trusted with written agreements. I have pledged myself to see him satisfied, and that is sufficient; and rely on it, if he once gets Ajeez on shore, there he will leave him.'

'Ah ! but how is this to be managed, Adeeb?'

'This we must leave to my son-in-law, who is a crafty fellow, and will probably stop at some place on pretence of scarcity of water, induce Ajeez to accompany him, and there leave him to find his way to Calcutta as well as he can, where he will make many apologies for the urgent necessity he was under, owing to the tides and winds, for leaving his sagacious supercargo to shift for himself.'

'Admirable!' cried Ashuk. 'I will not only reward him, but you also. I feel I must succeed.'

'Farewell, Ashuk!' said Adeeb Khan; 'but be careful not to be seen conversing with the captain on any account. They sail in three days' time. Ajeez is already gone to Cambay, and my son-in-law joins him to-morrow. Farewell!'

The delighted Ashuk now tormented his imagination by framing plans to obtain an interview with Kheir Neyut, and daily passed the firmly-closed portal of her father's house, hoping some accident would one day cause him to be admitted into the court-yard, or once more into the shed. One day, as he passed the gate, he perceived an old woman carrying a basket containing perfumes, sweetmeats, scissors, &c. She knocked at the miser's gate, and Ashuk determined to ascertain from a distance the result of her application. No one came to the gate until the old woman had thrice repeated her summons, when old Nugdee him-self appeared, and seeing the old woman with her wares, bade her in a loud and angry voice 'begone, and come again on the follow-ing day, as he as well as his daughter were at present engaged in business.'

The poor woman retired, promising to come again on the

morrow. Ashuk followed her to a small **shop at some distance**, an idea having struck him by which he might gain admittance **into** the miser's stronghold. 'Good woman,' said he, taking up a small phial, 'what is the price of this bottle of essence?'

'One rupee, sir,' she replied.

'I suppose you get a pretty sum out of the miser's daughter, don't you?' '

'**No, truly,** poor lady ; **she** has not much money **at her** command ; **but** she in general purchases something when I call, **which** is once in every month.'

'What sum do you expect she will lay out with you to-morrow, **as** I heard her father desire you to call again at that time?'

'**Indeed, sir,** I cannot exactly say ; perhaps two rupees.'

'Now, then, my good woman, I will give you five rupees to **let** me go in your clothes, with your basket, in your stead ; and more-over, give you the value of whatever may be selected from your **stock.'**

'Five rupees, sir ! why, **what a** sum ! and all for nothing ! I **am** sure, sir, you are welcome to take my place ; but my clothes **are** very shabby ; and besides, are not you afraid of being de-tected ?'

. '**No,** my good woman, there is no fear of that. You are fortunately rather taller than the rest of your sex ; and if I stoop and counterfeit your voice, **I** think I must succeed.'

'Well, then, be with me, sir, to-morrow, at the proper time, and **I** will instruct you how to proceed, when you shall have gained admittance, for much depends on the manner in which you offer your goods for sale.'

Ashuk promised **to** be with her in time, and begged her, should anything prevent his coming, to **defer her** visit to the miser's until he should again consult with her.

Nothing occurring to prevent his repairing to the old woman's shop, Ashuk presented himself before her at the appointed time, having previously paid a visit to the barber's, to be cleanly shaved. This was an operation which subjected him to little or no inconvenience, being too young to have a beard which would cost him any pain to part with. The old woman was waiting his arrival, and quickly dressed him in her tattered garments, hanging her basket around his neck. '**Now,** sir,' said she, '**remember, when** the miser admits you, say not a word, but proceed to a shed on the right hand of the gate, and there quietly seat yourself; such is my custom. You will probably have to wait some little time ere the lady comes to you, but you need fear no interruption from old Nugdee Hurrees, who allows his daughter to select her purchases by herself, so that you may enjoy the lady's company as long as you please.'

Ashuk, being thus instructed, proceeded to the abode of his beloved; and having repeatedly knocked at the gate, **he** began to fear the miser was not within, but **at** last the portal was cautiously opened by old Nugdee himself, who, seeing the woman, petulantly cried, ' Come in with you, you old plague; always coming to worry me **out** of my property.'

The fearful Ashuk hobbled towards the shed, where he quietly took his seat. Old Nugdee called out **to** his daughter, desiring her to be quick and make her purchases, as he would not suffer people to remain long within his walls. Kheir Neyut, little dreaming of the pleasure that awaited her, descended to the shed, saying, 'Well, Fatimah, what articles have you brought to tempt me?' Ashuk presented her with a comb, the price of which the lady demanded, fixing her eyes at the same time on the countenance of the vender, who could not refrain from smiling. This betrayed him, and he was about to speak, when the maiden cried, 'Hush! for Heaven's sake! My father has long ears. But how durst you venture in this disguise?'

'Oh, my beloved!' said Ashuk, in a low tone, almost amounting to a whisper, 'what would I not venture to obtain a moment's conversation with thyself?'

'Truly, Ashuk, I will not conceal from you the pleasure this interview gives me, and we must contrive to make it as long as we can, for rely upon it you will not be admitted with your basket before another month passes away.'

Ashuk now declared, over and over again, how deeply her image was interwoven with his existence, and proposed to concert some plan by which they might escape from the power of her father.

'It is impossible, Ashuk; I can never consent to elope from my father's house. But this depend on: I will wed no one but yourself, and look forward with horror to the arrival of Ajeez, who flatters himself he will obtain my hand.'

'Fear not his speedy return, fair Kheir Neyut; I have taken care you shall not be troubled with his presence again for some time.'

'Heavens! Ashuk, you alarm me! I hope you have proceeded to no violence.'

'I have not,' replied he; 'but nevertheless it will be longer than he expects or dreams of ere he will visit Ahmedabad again, and before that time I hope to call you mine.'

'Alas! Ashuk, I fear your hopes will not easily be realised. We must wait patiently; and I need not add, could you obtain my father's consent, my happiness would equal your own. Strive, therefore, by all means in your power to become friends with him.'

'Alas! Kheir Neyut, I have done so to no purpose. He declined *my* visits above all others, on account of the alarm he experienced on the night I purposed to have enjoyed an hour's conversation at your window; and I fancy he is but only half-convinced I was not the man who dared to escalade his mansion.'

Here the lovers were interrupted by the voice of old Nugdee calling to his daughter, enquiring what she could be doing all this time. 'Be quick and buy what you require,' said he, 'or I shall soon be with you. That old hag has been here too long already.'

'We are just concluding our bargains, father,' said the artful girl, as again, heedless of her father's warning, she returned to the old theme; and so delightful were the moments thus snatched by the lovers, that they seemed as if they could have conversed for ever. So intent were they, that they perceived not old Nugdee approaching the shed, and he actually had seized Ashuk by the neck ere they were aware of his presence.

'Come, be off, old woman,' said the miser; 'you have out-stayed your time already.' So saying, he pushed Ashuk towards the gate, which he instantly opened, saying, 'Begone, and don't show your face here again for this month to come.'

'Call again next month, good woman,' cried Kheir Neyut, 'and bring what I require.'

When Ashuk had gained the street he congratulated himself on his very narrow escape, and proceeded to the real vender, where, having thrown off his disguise, he returned home, well-satisfied with the success of the day.

A few days after the above exploit, as Ashuk was sauntering about the city late in the evening, a poor maker of bows and arrows accosted him, saying he had for sale a splendid bow and a set of arrows. The bow, he said, was made of a single buffalo horn, and the arrows of the finest reeds. Ashuk desired the man to produce the wonderful bow, with an arrow or two, for the purpose of trying it, as there was yet light enough for the occasion. The man hastily repaired to his own house; and as quickly returned, bringing the bow and two arrows. Ashuk desired him to remain at his mother's house until he returned, intending to go without the city walls and give the bow a fair trial ere he determined on purchasing it. There being no friendly tree to serve as a mark, Ashuk walked forward for some time, and seeing a large owl, let fly one of the arrows at it, which with pleasure he perceived struck the bird and remained in it, the animal still flying, though with some difficulty. Ashuk, anxious to bring home a proof of the excellence of his bow and his own skill, pursued the owl, expecting every moment to see it fall at his feet. The almost exhausted bird at last fell and Ashuk was sure of his prey, when once more recovering strength it soared aloft and baffled the youth's attempt at seizing it. The ardour of the youth had led him much farther than he had intended; but, certain he should at last seize his game, he still **followed,** until he felt convinced the bird **had** fallen **into a tope of** mango and neem trees, and fancied **on** his approaching them **he** heard it rustling amongst the branches. He entered the tope and searched all around, but in vain ; no owl could he discover. Whilst so employed he fancied he heard some one crying in great distress ; **and leaving** the knot of trees, perceived a boy, the son of some poor cultivator, weeping bitterly. Seeing Ashuk, the boy enquired if he had seen his kid, which had strayed away, declaring he durst not return home without it, as his father would be angry and beat him.

'Indeed, my little fellow, I have not **been** so fortunate **as to** meet your kid ; but have you seen an owl with an arrow sticking in it fall anywhere near you ?'

'**No,**' said the boy, 'but I heard a rustling **in one of the** mango trees, just before you came up.'

'Then,' said Ashuk, 'come with me into the tope and assist **me** to find it, and I will afterwards aid you in finding your **kid.**'

'Oh, sir !' said **the** boy in great alarm, 'pray excuse my accompanying you into the tope ; and surely you will not yourself think of going there **at this hour ?**'

'Why not, boy ?'

'Are you, then, a stranger in these parts, sir, that you know not therein is an enchanted well, which only one person has been ever rash enough to approach ?—and dearly did he pay for his curiosity.'

Ashuk now for the first time began **to** think in what direction he had been running, and found the boy **was** indeed correct. He

was close to the spot so avoided by mankind—at once the
wonder and terror of all far and near ; and many a warning had
he himself received in his infancy never to venture near the enchanted well, concerning which there were strange reports. The
Hindús believed that it was the abode of Parvati, the wife of
Mhadeo, who guarded her in the shape of a fiery dragon ; and
this story had its origin a hundred years ago, from the circumstance of a small white bull, such as Mhadeo is represented to
ride upon, being found grazing among the trees of the tope,
saddled, but without a rider. The Mahomedans, on the other
hand, believed the well contained a fairy ; but there were many
who asserted it was the habitation of all the evil spirits, and that
Iblis himself there held his court. Under these terrific ideas no
person would on any account venture near the tope, much less
approach the well. Ashuk now remembered having heard his
mother relate the fact that a Hindú once ventured to peep into
the well, and had been in consequence reduced to a state of
idiocy, from which he never recovered ; that he would scream
violently at night, and arise from his bed declaring he had been
visited by the fiery dragon of the well. These fatal effects of
curiosity and rashness were quite sufficient to deter others from
following his example, and travellers would go miles out of their
way to avoid the dreadful spot.

Ashuk considered, however, that there could be nothing very
alarming, as he had himself dived a considerable way amongst the
trees in pursuit of his wounded game ; but seeing the terror of
the boy, he did not insist upon his following him, but strove
all in his power to find the poor lad's kid, but to no purpose.

The boy declaring he durst not return to his father without **the** kid, as he should certainly be cruelly beaten, Ashuk very kindly offered to accompany him, for **the** purpose of appeasing the angry cultivator, and making him promise not **to** chastise his son.

The boy was much pleased, falling at the feet of Ashuk, calling him his deliverer and preserver.

Arrived at the village where resided the boy's father, Ashuk quickly explained to the man the circumstance of the lost kid, begging him not to · **beat** the **boy, and** promising to make good the loss, provided the animal was not found in two days' time.

The cultivator promised not to punish his son, and thanked Ashuk for the trouble he had taken in the business.

Ashuk then expressed his fears that it would be late ere **he** returned home, and enquired the distance to the city.

'**It** is six coss,[1] sir,' said the cultivator.

' Six coss ! ' exclaimed Ashuk.   ' But four, surely ? '

'**The** short way is indeed only four, sir; but as you will not venture near the enchanted **well** at this time **of** night, I **fear you** have a good six coss before you.'

'Not venture, **my good man !** Indeed but I shall, and probably rest under the trees.'

'Oh, sir ! now cried both the cultivator and his wife, '**for** the love of Ishwur, do not be rash ; consider the consequences ! Remember the poor man who lost his senses ; pray, therefore, go home the long way.'

[1] Twelve miles.

' **Not I,** indeed !' replied **Ashuk.**   '**I** fear no evil spirits.'

' If you fear not them, sir, recollect the rage of Mhadeo ; all our villages, far and near, will feel the effects of his anger.'

' Well, my friends,' replied Ashuk, '**but I** shall not disturb either Mhadeo or his wife Parvati by resting awhile under the trees.'

' **Oh yes, sir !**   Although at the botton of the well, which is ten thousand feet deep, the **god will be** sensible a mortal is near, and will surely visit you with his vengeance.'

' But remember,' said Ashuk, ' I believe not in either Mhadeo **or his** wife **Parvati.**'

' True, sir; **but you** believe **in** fairies; **and it is the** firm opinion of the Mahomedans one is certainly **at the** bottom **of** the **well ;** and if not, that **it is** the habitation of all the evil spirits.'

' **What is your opinion,** my good man ? ' enquired Ashuk.

' Why, **sir, I firmly** believe Mhadeo, in the shape of a fiery dragon, guards the well ; and that it is certain death to encounter his eye, which they say is ever directed upwards.'

' Well, my friend, it is getting late, and will be midnight ere I **arrive at** the spot ; but I have not quite made up my mind about visiting the place of which you stand in so much awe.'

' **Pray,** sir, do be advised—go the long way home.'

' Perhaps I may,' said Ashuk.   ' Farewell !'

' Ram, Ram, Mharaj!'[1] said the cultivator, as he turned into **his** hut.

Ashuk, **with a** quick pace, journeyed homewards, meditating

[1] ' **Your** humble servant,' or ' Your most obedient.'

whether to take the advice of the cultivator or not, and turned not his head either to the right or to the left. Ere he had determined what to do **he** found himself at the very spot, and impelled by curiosity entered the tope. Something fluttering over his head, which he fancied must be his wounded owl; he quickly ascended the tree from whence the noise appeared to proceed. The tree was not sufficiently near the well to allow of his peeping into it ; but as he was reaching amongst the branches he thought he perceived flashes of light issue from its gloomy depths. Bold as he naturally was, he nevertheless now felt a sensation of fear enter his breast. Had any timid Hindú been in his situation he would doubtless have dropped senseless to the earth.

The darkness of the night, the dead silence of the awful spot, the unaccountable flashes of light, which shed a momentary gleam amidst the trees, were sufficient to make even a stouter heart than Ashuk's tremble, and he repented his rashness. The light became stronger and stronger, and at length a dark figure, covered with red stripes, appearing anything but human, emerged from the well. It stood, and turning towards the tree on which was perched the terrified Ashuk, emitted from its mouth a flash of fire more fierce than any he had before witnessed. Ashuk shut his eyes through fear, and when he again ventured to open them the figure was nowhere to be seen. The youth determined to wait a full hour to ascertain whether the demon would return; but the time expiring without his reappearing, he softly descended the tree. His alarm, being somewhat abated, **was** succeeded by curiosity. ' Surely,' thought he, ' now the demon is gone there can be no danger in just peeping over the brink.' He hesitated, however ;

but curiosity at last prevailing, he crept gently towards the well. Not **a sound** did he hear, save the rustling of the **trees in the** night wind; all was dark and gloomy, not a star was visible through the **leafy** canopy above him.

The well had a low wall around it; under this crouched the trembling Ashuk, not daring for some time to look over it. At last, ashamed of his weakness, he suddenly thrust his head over the wall, but soon withdrew it, falling insensible on the ground, for his eyes encountered the **fiery** dragon. Two glaring meteors were its eyes, its golden wings were extended as if in the act of flying upwards, whilst its ponderous jaws were opened, as if ready **to** devour his prey. As soon as Ashuk recovered from the shock he had received he rushed from the tope, gained the fields, and stopped not until he arrived at his mother's house. Beewah had long awaited the return **of her son'**; and still hoping he would speedily arrive, had not retired to rest. It was with delight, therefore, she heard his well-known voice demanding admittance; but, **on** opening the door, how was that delight changed into alarm on perceiving the terror-stricken countenance of Ashuk, who fell to the earth gasping for breath! In vain she enquired the cause of his extreme agitation. 'Have you been attacked, Ashuk, robbed, or engaged in any quarrel? The bow-maker has in vain awaited your return, and——'

'Oh!' cried Ashuk, 'curse **the bow** and arrows, and the maker of **them** also. Leave me, my mother; nay, stay, lead me to my bed. I am ill and fatigued.'

The poor widow was unable to fathom the cause of this alarm **in** her son, but forbore to harass him with questions concerning it, determining, however, to know the whole truth in the morning. She, therefore, silently conducted **the youth to** his bed, from which he **arose** not until late on the following morning, having passed a miserable night, dreaming of fiery dragons **and** hideous demons. He determined to keep secret from every **one,** even his mother, the events of the preceding night, not willing **to** confess either his temerity or his fears. When Beewah, therefore, begged to be informed of the cause of his alarm, he confessed he had been greatly agitated, but begged her not to enquire farther, as he had sworn not to divulge the cause; he concluded by extorting a promise from his mother not to mention **to** the bow-maker or any other person his late return and alarm. Beewah, although sadly disappointed at not being informed of the whole mystery, readily gave her promise to be silent on the subject.

Ashuk pondered deeply on the events of the preceding night, and severely rebuked himself for his cowardice, feeling convinced **that** but for the long catalogue of horrors he had heard from the cultivator he should not have been guilty of so much unpardonable weakness. After turning the subject over **in** his mind he came to the determination of visiting the well in broad daylight, and was proceeding thither when the bow-maker stood in his **way,** begging to know how he liked the bow.

'**It is** a good one,' said Ashuk, 'and I shall keep it, provided the price be not too high.'

'**It** is only fifteen rupees, sir, and the **arrows** are half a rupee each.'

'Very well; then **send me a dozen** arrows, and I will pay you at a future time.' The man, making a salaam, retired, leaving

Ashuk to pursue his way towards the place of terror. He arrived at the tope of trees, which, notwithstanding the sun was at its height, was gloomy and uninviting; not a soul was near, so carefully was the spot avoided at all hours. Drawing his sword, he entered the place, determined to fight either man or dragon, and to cut down even Mhadeo himself, should he offer any opposition. He approached the well, into which, after a little hesitation, he ventured to peep. He saw the dragon in its place, having, however, now but one fiery eye, and that by no means so brilliant as on the preceding night. Strongly suspecting a trick from this circumstance, he determined to ascertain the disposition of the monster below, and called out loudly. No answer, no noise, save the echo of his own voice, was returned. Finding the dragon so tame, he ventured to throw down a small pebble, which he directed with so good an aim as to see it fall on the head of the beast, which nevertheless moved not. He then selected a heavier and larger stone, which also alighting on the animal's skull, the single fiery eye became suddenly dark as the other. 'Ah! ah!' thought Ashuk, 'if I can so easily extinguish the brilliancy of the dragon's eye I shall have but little difficulty in annihilating him with my sword, and will at all hazards descend.'

The well having large stones at equal distances protruding from its sides, for the purpose of forming steps, and made, most probably, by the people who first built it, Askuk, by their means, with caution and without any opposition, descended. When within reach of the animal he drew his sword and made a thrust at the monster, when what was his surprise to find his formidable enemy composed only of paper!' He now more than ever reproved himself for his fears, and hastened to examine the figure which caused so much terror throughout the district. He found a very ingeniously contrived dragon, with gold-paper wings, and a head so constructed as to admit of two small lamps being introduced behind it, so as to illumine the monster's glassy eyes, one of which, it had appeared, had gone out, and the flame of the other was nearly exhausted, when probably the shock received by his second stone had displaced the trembling wick, so as to cause it to fall, and thus divest the figure of its greatest terror.

Having now fully convinced himself of the imposition which had been so long practised on the world, he began to conjecture the object of it. There must be some chamber, some secret recess, containing probably some fair lady; if so, he determined not to rest until he should discover it. Behind the dragon was a large square flagstone, similar to those with which the bottom of the well was paved, as it was perfectly dry, not having the slightest appearance of having contained water for many years. The stone behind the dragon appearing immovable, Ashuk felt assured that without a light he could effect nothing.

He therefore ascended, intending to provide himself with a lantern or torch on the following day, fearing a second visit on the same day might attract notice and create suspicion.

Arrived at home, his mother was rejoiced at beholding her son once more cheerful and free from care; she therefore refrained

---

' The natives, especially the Mahomedans, are very expert at forming birds and beasts of divers-coloured papers, stretched over a thin bamboo frame-work. At the Mohurrum, one of the greatest festivals, numbers of these paper animals are made and carried in procession through the city.

from questioning him on the forbidden subject. The following day, Ashuk, having provided himself with a lamp and a torch, with materials for striking a light, proceeded about two hours earlier than before to the enchanted well. He found the dragon's eyes most brilliant, the lamps having been trimmed by the guardian of the place, for, owing to his early appearance at the place, the oil had not been expended. Who could the person be that acted in this mysterious manner? and what could be his object? The former was a point he should probably not easily discover, but the latter he trusted would soon come to light.

Ashuk descended the well, and lighting his lamp at the dragon's eyes, found at the bottom of the flagstone, which was ingeniously let into the side of the well, two iron wedges, which carefully removing, the stone slipped from a groove above, and was thus easily displaced, presenting to view a dark cavity, the pent-up vapours of which, escaping at the aperture, nearly extinguished his lamp. He entered, and found himself in a small stone chamber, and by the light of his lamp discovered in one corner, not a beautiful woman, as he had come prepared to find, but sundry bags, which doubtless contained treasure. He quickly untied one, and found it full of gold bars; he did the same to a second, and a third, and all contained gold bars like the first, about six inches in length, and half an inch in breadth. His foot now struck against something, which he discovered to be a pair of scales, and in an opposite corner were others of a larger size, with weights, &c., fixed to a low post in the earth. The delighted youth knew not how to proceed so as to elude the suspicion of the nocturnal visitor of the well. To carry away one of the bags would certainly create alarm in the owner's breast, who would in consequence remove the treasure elsewhere; besides which, all the bags were numbered, counted over, and probably weighed occasionally. After deep consideration, therefore, he took a bar of gold from one of the bags and placed it in the small scales, to ascertain its real weight; which being done, he carefully treasured the remembrance of it in his mind, replacing the golden bar whence he had taken it; and before he fastened up the bags he had opened took about a dozen of the bars, to ascertain by the scales if they were all of equal weight. He found one bar corresponded with another in weight, shape, and size. Having tied up all the bags as before, he retired, and fastened the stone door with the two iron wedges, leaving no possible trace of any stranger having entered the place. Arrived at the brink of the well, he found all as quiet as the grave, and quickly retraced his steps homewards.

'Mother,' cried Ashuk, as soon as he entered the house, 'I require about ten rupees—can you accommodate me?'

'No, truly, Ashuk, I have not so much in my possession; but to-morrow, you know, you will receive your pay. Cannot you wait until then?'

'No, mother, I want them immediately, being ordered to Kaira on duty.'

'To Kaira, Ashuk? For what reason?'

'That I know not, but shall receive my instructions on my arrival there.'

'Well, son, you must borrow a horse, and perhaps the same friend will lend you the money. Go, therefore, to Doolubdass, the shroff; I have had much dealing with him, and doubtless he will oblige you by the loan of both horse and money.'

Away went Ashuk to the shroff, whom he found at home, and at once stated his wants. Doolubdass advanced the money, and ordered his horse to be got ready. Ashuk, thanking the shroff, promised to call in about half-an-hour for the horse, having some business to transact before he started. . This business was to beg leave of absence from the captain of the guard, to proceed to Kaira on private affairs. Permission being granted, the joyful Ashuk was soon mounted on the shroff's horse, which safely conveyed him to Kaira, a large town, not very far from Ahmedabad. He arrived in the evening, and halting at a Durhm Salleh, procured provender for his horse, and proceeded forthwith to the bazaar, in search of a dealer in lead, whom he soon discovered, and from whom he demanded as many pieces of lead, of a certain weight and shape, as he could purchase for six rupees, desiring they might be ready for him in the morning. The lead-mer chant promising obedience, Ashuk returned to procure some food for himself.

The wary youth had experienced from the rope-maker how ittle the people of his own city were to be trusted, and thus planned the journey to Kaira for the purpose of procuring what he required. Having provided a stout bag, he called for his lead early on the following morning, and found about twenty pieces all ready for him, for which he paid the full value, and rode away at a rapid rate towards Ahmedabad, hoping soon to exchange them for a purer metal. Arrived at his own city, he returned the horse to its owner, with many thanks, and proceeded to his mother's house, from whence he repaired to the Nuwab's treasury to receive his salary.

Beewah, ever curious, but doomed never to have her curiosity gratified, enquired the nature of the duty Ashuk had been employed upon.

'It is a secret, mother, and must not be divulged.'

This was quite enough to silence poor Beewah, who was too much delighted to find her son entrusted with affairs of importance to desire to pry into the secrets of the government.

On the following day, when sure of no interruption, Ashuk repaired to the well, and having entered the treasure-chamber, opened eighteen bags, selecting from the bottom of each one bar of gold, supplying the deficiency with a bar of lead, reserving two of the number procured at Kaira as patterns by which others could be made, as he determined to appropriate nearly the whole of the treasure to his own use. With eighteen bars of gold in his possession, Ashuk quitted the enchanted well, regarded by the superstitious inhabitants with so much terror. Arrived at his mother's house, he considered how he should dispose of the wealth he had with so much trouble obtained. Who the sufferer could be he was at a loss to conjecture; nor did he now trouble himself to solve that point, but meditated how to convert his gold into money, calculating the exact value of each bar. After considering for some time, he decided that the safest way would be to obtain leave of absence to visit his uncle at Cambay, and there effect the change. Permission being granted, he selected nine of the bars to take with him, leaving the remainder buried under the floor of his apartment, not mentioning a word on the subject to his mother. At Cambay, having first paid his respects to his uncle, he went to a shroff's shop, where, on producing one of his bars, he found it valued at fifteen gold mohurs, or two hundred and twenty-five rupees. Having disposed of all his bars at different shops, he found himself possessed of more money than he could conveniently carry about him, and was compelled to take bills on Kaira for half the sum, converting his silver rupees into mohurs, for the better convenience of carrying about him. When, therefore, on his way back he presented his bills at Kaira, he became so laden with money as to feel considerably fatigued ere he reached Ahmedabad. Proceeding to his apartment, to deposit his load in the secure spot under the floor, what was his vexation at not being able to discover his nine bars of gold which he had left there concealed; in an agony he enquired of his mother if anyone had been into his room.

'No, my son,' she replied, 'no one save the ratcatcher and his boy, whom I employed to destroy the rats, and under the floor in your room they found three large ones.'

'They did indeed mother, and thrice that number.'

'No indeed, Ashuk, they told me only three, which they produced, and very large ones they were.'

Ashuk, not wishing to explain all to his mother, said no more on the subject, but heartily cursed the ratcatcher and his boy, who had discovered his dear treasure. Fortunately he had a treasury to resort to which he believed to be inexhaustible, and he therefore made up his mind to the present trifling loss. In order that the owner of the gold should not suspect him by seeing him become suddenly rich, he continued to live on as before, and even borrowed money to purchase a horse, which was now become actually necessary, as he should be obliged to make sundry trips to the adjacent towns. Whilst at Cambay, he took care to procure fifty pieces of lead, which, with some other articles, he gave into the hands of a porter, who brought them safe **to his** own house in Ahmedabad.

Ashuk paid another visit to the well, and selected fifty more pieces of gold, taking care to supply their places with lead, always leaving a few golden bars at the mouth of each bag, in case the owner should by chance peep into them. Thus, by degrees, did he possess himself of nearly four lacs of rupees, the half of which he converted into money, which, together with the bars of gold, he buried in the garden of his mother's house, under a beehive, trusting to those industrious guardians for protection. Having now removed as much of the bulk of the gold as he deemed safe, he directed his attention towards the discovery of the owner and guardian of the well, and for this purpose lay in ambush one night, intending to dog the footsteps of the black man with the fiery mouth. He saw him emerge from the knot of trees, and followed him silently at a distance into the city. His figure, he thought, resembled that of Saruk, the merchant.

'O Fortune!' said he, 'hast thou indeed thrown into my hands the wealth of that proud man, whose son was to deprive me of my adorable Kheir Neyut? **If so I** thank thee, doubly thank thee, for now I have the golden key to the door of felicity, and I, instead of Ajeez, shall wed the lovely girl.' That he might be certain, however, that the man whose footsteps he so narrowly watched was indeed Saruk, he kept yet closer to him, and perceived, on nearing the city, the mysterious man take off his sable-garb and fold it into a bundle. As far as the darkness of the night would allow him to discern he was convinced the person was certainly not a young man, and yet he appeared not so like Saruk as he did previous to throwing off his disguise. Determined to observe whither he went, he dogged him so silently and cautiously that he felt certain he had not been observed, and at last saw the nocturnal visitant of the enchanted well enter the house of Saruk, the merchant.

''Tis indeed him !' cried the youth to himself. 'Now am I revenged on his insolent son, and more than on an equality with himself.'

A day or two after this discovery, Ashuk, thinking it prudent to become friends with the man he had robbed, paid a visit to Saruk, and kindly enquired after his son.

'Why,' replied the merchant, 'I am rather alarmed at not having heard a syllable from him since his departure, but still hope all is going on well.'

'Impossible it can be otherwise,' said Ashuk ; 'but have the owners of the ship heard no tidings of their vessel ?'

'None whatever ; and I have this day enquired of Adeeb Khan, the captain's father-in-law, but he has received no letter from him, so we must wait patiently.'

Ashuk often visited Saruk, who was pleased at this attention of the young officer, though bearing no good-will towards him in his heart. Many days elapsed, and Ashuk once more penetrated into the secret chamber of the well. He perceived in the centre of the place a large bag, apparently recently deposited there ; it had a ticket suspended from the string which fastened its mouth, on which were written the words, ' Saruk Sahonkar, rupees 5,000.' Nothing was now wanting to convince him who it was he had been plundering. Prudence whispered him to leave the bag untouched, and also not to withdraw any more golden bars from the other now scantily-supplied **bags, and** for once he returned home empty-handed.

Once every month did Ashuk personate the old woman, the vendor of essences, &c., and was always admitted by old Nugdee Hurrees, and had the felicity of conversing **with his beloved** Kheir Neyut ; but all his vows and ardent protestations of everlasting love failed to persuade her clandestinely to quit her father's roof and put herself under his protection. Thus passed month after month, without any intelligence being received of Ajeez **or the** noble Fureeb Khash, captain of the good ship 'Futteh Mobaruk.' One day Beewah received intelligence of the approaching death of her brother-in-law at Cambay, at which she as well at Ashuk **were** deeply grieved. The latter instantly proceeded to Cambay, to pay his **last** respects to his dying relative ; he arrived ere the vital spark **was** extinct, and though speechless, with pleasure he perceived his uncle appeared **to** recognise him.

He died, and without a will, and it **was** generally supposed Ashuk was his heir; but alas ! **no** money **was** to be found, although the merchant was known to be possessed of great wealth. Ashuk, far from contradicting the report of his accession to his uncle's property, encouraged it as **much** as possible, and returned to Ahmedabad, giving out that he had become enormously rich by this unexpected death of his near and **dear relative.** His mother believing this to be true, rejoiced at his good fortune, and blessed the memory of her good brother-in-law, who had thus generously acted. Ashuk was now no longer afraid of sporting his wealth; he bought a spacious mansion, kept servants, and made a great display in the city, not from the succession to the property of his **uncle, but from** the proceeds of the enchanted well. **No** longer **did** he assume the character and habit of the **old** essence-vender, **to** enable **him to** see his beloved Kheir **Neyut; he boldly visited the miser ;** and now finding little or no difficulty in gaining admittance, he at once solicited the hand of his lovely daughter.

'Your offer, young man, comes too late,' said **Nugdee ;** 'my promise is given to Saruk, **who daily expects** his son, and **I dare** not break my promise.'

'But, my dear **sir,**' said Ashuk, 'what can have become of the youth? Why does he not return and claim his bride?'

'Why, that I don't understand,' said the miser : 'I fear all is not right. **However, I** shall wait the end of the year from the time of his departure, and if he then appears not, why you shall have my daughter, provided she consents to the change. But allow me **to** congratulate you on your recent good fortune : **I** suppose you will have no great difficulty in laying down half a lac on the wedding-day, to convince me **I am** giving **my** daughter to a staunch money-man?'

'**No** difficulty whatever, sir,' replied Ashuk; 'the money shall be ready whenever you demand it.'

'Ah! this **is** something like indeed;' said Nugdee, 'money down! ready money! without going to Bengal in a crazy ship, to scrape it together from the sale of piece-goods and cornelians. Would you had been so rich six months ago! However, have patience. I much doubt whether Ajeez will ever return.'

Ashuk was of the same opinion, but was much perplexed to account for the schoolmaster not having heard from his son-in-law, and entertained serious apprehensions for his safety.

About a month after the above conversation with the miser Ashuk paid him another visit, and was thus received.

'Ah! my wealthy friend, you are too late, all chance is gone: young Ajeez arrived last night.'

'Returned? Impossible!' cried Ashuk. 'Why, the captain is not come back yet, nor the ship either; how is it possible, therefore, that Ajeez is here?'

'He flew, I suppose, on the wings of impatience,' answered Nugdee; 'but, from all I can understand, not very successful.'

'Indeed! And will he not be able to command the half-lac of rupees?' eagerly enquired Ashuk.

'Can't say; time will show,' said the self-satisfied miser; 'but go home, and rest assured the young merchant is returned.'

Ashuk instantly repaired to Saruk's house, and congratulated him on the arrival of his son, who soon after making his appearance, Ashuk addressed him in a friendly manner, hoping he had experienced a pleasant voyage.

'By no means so,' said Ajeez, 'a wretched and most unprofitable one.' This was all he could learn from Ajeez, but he soon heard the whole truth from Adeeb Khan, who had proceeded to Saruk's house the instant he heard of the return of his son.

'Oh, Ashuk!' cried Adeeb Khan, 'my unfortunate son-in-law has rather overdone the business, for it seems when in the Bay of Bengal, on pretence of a scarcity of water, he ran his ship towards the Andaman Islands which lie on the eastern side of the bay; ignorant of the shore and place altogether, his ship struck, and filled with water; and all the cargo, together with every soul, save the captain, Ajeez, and two sailors, were lost for ever. These four shipwrecked men contrived to gain the shore, where they were received by the woolly-headed inhabitants of the islands, who danced, sung, and wallowed in the mud, so delighted did they appear at the event which caused others so much grief. Here my son-in-law and his companions remained nearly two months, and were treated kindly by the natives, who seemed extremely unwilling to part with them. At last my experienced son-in-law contrived to fit up a large boat, in which the unhappy Ajeez and the two sailors accompanied him to Calcutta, where a ship being on the point of sailing for Bombay, Ajeez instantly took his passage in it, leaving my son-in-law to act as he thought proper. Fureeb Khash, I have no doubt, apprehends little advantage in returning hither, there being now no chance of his being again employed by the merchants in this part of the world, so that it will probably be very long ere I again behold him. Thus is Ajeez returned without his cargo or money, and Fureeb Khash left behind without ship or friends.'

'This is indeed a most melancholy piece of news,' said Ashuk. 'But was not the cargo insured?'

'No,' replied Adeeb; 'Saruk was too avaricious, and had too much confidence in both ship and captain.'

' Then, Adeeb, it is not probable they will be able to produce the half-lac of rupees required by Nugdee Hurrees.'

' I know not how this may be; Saruk is rich, very rich, so do not trust to the present misfortune which has befallen them.'

' Ah!' thought Ashuk, ' so Saruk himself thinks, **but he** will soon be undeceived.' To his surprise, a day or two **after** the above conversation with the schoolmaster, Saruk paid a visit to Ashuk; he had called, he said, to beg the favour of his presence on the following day, at the house of Hurrees Al Alghar, to **witness** the contract between his son and the fair Kheir Neyut.'

Ashuk **was** somewhat startled at the request, but conceiving his presence might prove advantageous to himself, accepted the invitation. Another motive urged him to be present: he anticipated the secret satisfaction of beholding Saruk's boasted wealth appear in the shape of lead, and witnessing the miser's rejection **of** his son, when he would then himself step forward and secure the prize. Ashuk was ready at the appointed hour, and was called for by Saruk, accompanied by his son Ajeez, and a tribe of shroffs and Sahoukars, for the purpose of pronouncing the value of **the** gold he was about to lay at the feet of Nugdee Hurrees.

The miser received the cavalcade of wealthy worthies into the interior of his mansion, where stood Kheir Neyut, more like a victim than a bride.

' Come along, my friends,' said Nugdee; ' I have my money **all** ready, only produce yours, and the agreement is then fulfilled.'

The porters who carried the bags of Saruk were now desired to place their precious burthens on the floor, around which quickly squatted the keen-eyed shroffs and witnesses, amongst the latter of which was Ashuk, seated at the right hand of Saruk, eagerly looking forward to the opening of the bags. Nugdee was not idle; he repaired to sundry strong chests, from which he selected several bags of gold, which he threw on the floor with violence, which caused the shroffs to start at the grateful sound. Nugdee having gazed with secret satisfaction on the pile of bags before him, and enjoyed the homage and admiration he saw beaming in the eyes of the spectators, perched himself on the summit of his little hill of wealth, crying, 'Now to business! Now, Saruk, produce your cash!' The shroffs untied bag the first, belonging to Saruk, from whence fell golden ornaments, bars, silver, gold mohurs, and other valuables, the precise value of which being ascertained, and Nugdee himself having frequently rubbed the gold on the unerring touchstone, the second bag was taken in hand. 'Now, then,' thought Ashuk, 'now comes the lead.' But alas! bag after bag was opened, and to his mortification the contents turned out to be of the purest kind.

'Now, then,' cried Saruk, 'let us see your hoard, Master Nugdee.'

'Very well,' cried the satisfied miser, seizing one of the bags from under him, which, in order to create an imposing spectacle and dazzle the eyes of his beholders with a shower of gold, he untied, and holding by the bottom let fall, not gold, but heavy lumps of dirty lead. To paint the visage of Nugdee is impossible; the despair which came over that countenance, which but a few moments before shone with internal satisfaction and delight, was like a dark cloud passing over the sun; his lip quivered, his hand shook, his whole frame was paralysed, **his eye** alone remained fixed on the direful lead, as if he hoped his agonising gaze would transmute it into gold. Indeed, the surprise of the whole company, especially Ashuk, nearly equalled that **evinced** by the miser, and a dead silence ensued. Kheir Neyut, **who stood** at a distance, alone felt for her father; she witnessed the agony **of** his mind, and was prepared to fly to his aid, should he sink under his disappointment.

At last Saruk broke the awful silence, saying, 'Try another bag, brother Nugdee ; perhaps you will find therein a purer metal.' Slowly did the miser draw from under him bag No. 2, from which fell, as **before,** lead, heavy lead, mixed occasionally with a **few** bars of gold. He tried the **remainder,** and found the contents **of** all to be the same. The groans and sighs of old Nugdee would have moved **the** hardest heart, but to paint the astonishment depicted on the countenance of Ashuk would have baffled the **skill** of the most eminent artist. To think that he had been robbing, not Saruk, as he had imagined, but Nugdee himself, was a circumstance so full of wonder, and altogether so singularly unexpected, that anyone amongst the company, could they have found leisure to withdraw their eyes from the miser, the lead, and the gold, **and** cast them upon Ashuk, could not have failed reading in that index to the heart a confession of a full knowledge of the mystery.

Hurrees-Al-Alghar's wish for life **was now** banished from his breast; his money, his dear gold gone, what pleasure did existence hold out? He covered his face with his hands, through which **the** tears were seen to trickle. When somewhat composed, Saruk sympathised with him, and said 'that circumstances being so unfavourable, he hoped he would not be angry or surprised if he declined the marriage of his son with Kheir Neyut ; not but that he should have been proud of the alliance, had affairs turned out more pleasing to both parties.'

This was the fatal **wound to** the pride, nay, to the peace of the miser, who had **for** some time indulged in the fond hope that, if either, he should be the man to decline the match, on the plea of the poverty of the opposite party. **To see** the bags of Saruk, therefore, **filled with** the purest ore, whilst his contained but lumps **of lead ; to hear the** merchant decline the match on the very plea he himself **had expected to be** compelled to urge, were mortifications which sunk deep into the heart of **poor** Nugdee. Whilst meditating how to answer the speech **of Saruk,** Ashuk came forward, saying : 'Since the worthy merchant declines the honour of an alliance with you, **sir, may** I beg to express **the** ardent love I bear your daughter, and to state my readiness to espouse her, and lay down the sum required ; and beg your acceptance of as much again, to compensate you **in** some measure for the grievous loss you have sustained ?'

The miser raised his eyes, saying, 'Be it so, Ashuk ; call my daughter.'

Kheir Neyut, who at a distance had witnessed the whole scene, **was,** although concerned for her father, delighted **at the** loss being urged **as a** plea for breaking off her match with **Ajeez,** whom she most cordially detested. In obedience to her father's commands Kheir Neyut stepped forward, and the miserable old man, with tears in his eyes, thus addressed **her :**

'Kheir **Neyut, I** once was worth more than **four lacs** of rupees; a villain has stolen it from me, and I am now a beggar! A guardian angel steps forward to my assistance, and claims in return your hand in marriage. Come forward, Ashuk.' The youth advanced. 'This, Kheir Neyut, is the man **to whom** I trust you will not object to be united.'

'**My** dear father,' answered the maiden, 'you know I have ever bowed to your will in your prosperity, and God forbid I **should** now become disobedient **in** your adversity! Here, **therefore,** Ashuk, is my hand.'

The delighted youth seized the extended hand, which he pressed to his throbbing bosom, his eyes manifesting the delight which his lips could not give utterance to. Saruk and Ajeez had, long ere this took place, collected their gold and departed, **having** no farther business to transact. Nugdee appointed the following day to settle the money matters; and thanking Ashuk for his kind offer of giving him half a lac of rupees to compensate for his losses, he observed that perhaps he was not utterly ruined, as he suspected, and promised on the morrow to give him his final answer, whether his circumstances would render it necessary to avail himself of his liberal offer.

Ashuk repeated his readiness to assist the poor miser, and then turned towards Kheir Neyut, with whom he enjoyed unrestrained conversation, whilst Nugdee was picking up the few gold bars which remained for him. Ashuk, perceiving the old man toiling away, offered to assist him, and in so doing discovered on the floor the bag of money which he had remarked in the stone chamber of the well at his last visit, having thereon the memorandum, 'Saruk Rs. 5,000.' This, no doubt, was a sum laid on one side to form a part of the lac to be put down on the occasion of the marriage. Having stayed some time enjoying the company of his beloved Kheir Neyut, Ashuk took his leave, being assured he should again meet Nugdee on the following day.

As soon as night had set in, the desponding Nugdee proceeded to the well, whose horrors had so long been his safeguard, but which at last failed in their effect, some daring villain having certainly found his buried treasures. 'Surely,' thought he, 'all my gold is not stolen;' and with the hope, though a very faint one, of finding the remaining bags, as he could have wished them, full of gold, he entered the stone chamber. Alas! he found each remaining bag as replete with lead as those he had opened in the presence of Saruk. Selecting the few gold-bars which lay at the mouth of each bag, he rushed from the place, overthrew in his haste the guardian dragon, and ascended the well, never more to return to it.

It has been stated that people were at a loss to discover how the miser, from being a common street-sweeper, first amassed a sum of money by which he became so very rich. The fact is, that he and another man, whilst travelling through a forest, discovered about eighty thousand rupees buried under a tree; this they removed, determining to share it between them. Nugdee, however, having selected a place for its concealment, proposed to his friend to allow the whole sum to remain there, and that every rupee each might pick up should be added to this fund; and when it had increased to one lac they should divide it, and not before.

The foolish man consented; and one day, when he visited the spot, found the money vanished. He of course suspected his partner, Nugdee, and was proceeding **to** his house to accuse him of the fraud, when that arch-knave met him, **saying,** ' Oh, brother, how could you serve me such a trick ? **I** went this morning to place a few rupees in our hoard, and find you have removed the whole. I prithee give me my share.'

His simple partner declared he was then seeking Nugdee to make the same complaint to him; and after much sham grief on the part of the latter, it was decided that some thief had found their money and walked off with it, although the fact was Master Nugdee himself was the robber.

Having thus fraudulently possessed himself of his own and his friend's share of the treasure, Nugdee, with a bullock, on whose back he placed the money, **made** all possible haste towards the city, passing by the enchanted well. It **being the** rainy season, **a** violent storm compelled him to take shelter under the trees which surrounded it. The miser was greatly alarmed at finding himself in the vicinity of the place of terrors, and stood silent under a large mango tree. Finding himself unmolested, he by degrees approached the well, and actually ventured to peep into it; but no horrid form meeting his eye, all fears vanished, and leading his bullock to the brink, he descended the stone steps. **Arrived below,** he found no water, but a regular paved place, having on one side a cavity **of** considerable extent. A thought then struck him that this place, above all **others,** would be best calculated to protect his treasure, and he determined to revisit it in order to contrive some door to conceal the cavity.

Accordingly, when the storm had abated, he drove home his bullock laden with gold, which he deposited in his house with other small sums, and on the following day again repaired to the well. Having in his early days been accustomed to gain a livelihood by aiding masons and bricklayers, he was sufficiently master of the art to fit up the chamber in the manner in which Ashuk found it, and when completed he therein deposited his golden store. The superstitions of the people, he imagined, would be a powerful safeguard to him ; but to add to the horrors of the place, he framed the dragon of paper, which he nightly illuminated, and was rejoiced to hear how alarmed the unfortunate Hindú had become on daring to peep into the well, as his rashness would doubtless be a warning to everyone else. For thirty years not a rupee was missing, and probably, but for the daring spirit of Ashuk, the chamber and its contents would never have been discovered.

One night, about a year after Nugdee had deposited his gold in the well, he fancied he heard some one among the trees as he was quitting the tope. To terrify whoever should be so rash, he ever after made it his custom, whenever he visited the well, to put on a suit of black, with red stripes all over it, placing in his mouth a burned stick or bit of charcoal, which, as he breathed, emitted the flashes so alarming to Ashuk. It so happened that on the very night Ashuk dogged the footsteps of the sable guardian of the well old Nugdee had appointed to meet Saruk at the house of the latter at a late hour, on particular business, and thus was Ashuk deceived as to the real owner of the gold, firmly believing he had found his way into Saruk's, not Nugdee's, treasury, which he had always understood was within the wall of his own house in the city.

Finding himself almost a beggar, Nugdee Hurrees repaired to

Ashuk's house, who, knowing full well the state of the remaining bags in the stone chamber, had prepared the money he had promised the almost heart-broken old man, who received it with many thanks. The wedding of Kheir Neyut and Ashuk was soon after celebrated with much expense and magnificence. Amongst the guests none showed so much real delightas poor Beewah, who at last had lived to see her son become a great man ; and when he with his bride passed her, and reminded her of his former declaration, that Ajeez should never wed Kheir Neyut, and that he would prevent it, she replied, 'Ay, boy ! you may thank your good fortune, not your own caution and prudence, which has thus verified your assertion.'

' I may, indeed, mother, if you knew all,' said Ashuk in a whisper, leaving Beewah mute with astonishment.

Hurrees Al Alghar recovered not from the effects produced on his mind by the loss of his dear gold ; his health and strength gradually failed him, and he at last took to his bed, where, lingering for many months, he bade adieu for ever to the riches of this world, leaving all he was worth to Ashuk and his wife, Kheir Neyut.

Ashuk was one morning agreeably surprised by receiving a visit from the schoolmaster, accompanied by Captain Furreeb Khash, who had just arrived. They enjoyed a laugh at the difficulties he had involved himself in to serve Ashuk, who made him a most handsome recompense, by which means the captain in a short time obtained another ship, and in a few years realised a handsome independence. Ajeez married a girl not approved of by his father, who in consequence dismissed him from his firm, so that the stupid fellow, in attempting to trade on his own account, was ruined, and left Ahmedabad for ever; whilst Ashuk and his wife lived happily together, had a numerous progeny, and were beloved by every one.

The butcher here concluded; and the Nuwab, declaring he was much pleased with the tale, suffered him to depart, appointing the following day to hear the fifth story.

The remaining persons having assembled as before at the Deewan's palace, the lot fell upon Sooe-bin-Taunchnee, the tailor, who was accordingly ordered to be in attendance on the following day, when, the Nuwab and the ladies having assembled, the tailor commenced the story contained in the following chapter.

CHAPTER III.

THE TAILOR'S STORY.

IN the city of Aurungabad, many years ago, there lived a Moolah, named Ghoosah Khan, a man of so irritable a disposition that there were few who could boast an intimacy with him. He was tall and thin, with a most forbidding countenance, strongly marked with the small-pox, by which fatal disease he had been deprived of an eye. On his chin grew a thin shabby beard, whilst the hair on his upper lip completely covered his mouth. In his dress he was slovenly and dirty, and throughout his establishment, which consisted only of one son and an old Mahommedan servant, named Suliman, economy was most rigidly maintained.

The Moolah was at this period about fifty years of age, though to appearance a much younger man. His wife had long been numbered with the dead, and it had been the wonder of the whole city how the poor woman contrived to live as long as she had done, the temper of the Moolah being so violent and insufferably irritable. After her death the Moolah never sought a second wife, probably because he imagined his search would be attended with considerable trouble to no purpose. Ghoosah Khan was reputed wealthy, although **no one** knew where to find his gold. Some there were who entertained suspicions not very favourable to him, ascribing the possession of riches to supernatural causes, whilst others openly expressed their belief that he dealt with Iblis himself, who occasionally visited him. Whether it was owing to his riches, his situation, **or his** temper, certain it is that everyone beheld the Moolah **with awe,** and were particularly anxious to avoid giving him cause for displeasure.

At **no time had a** priest possessed **so** much influence in Aurungabad as Moolah Ghoosah Khan was allowed to enjoy; all the inhabitants, from the Nuwab down to the peasant, bowed to **his opinion,** and the mosque at which he performed service was **morning** and evening crowded to excess. Mothers consulted with the Moolah regarding the marriage of their children, and men **took his** advice on affairs of secrecy and importance. Amongst the inhabitants none **were** so wretched and led so melancholy a life as poor Nazook, the Moolah's son, on whom his wrath was wont to fall, right or wrong, so that the youth actually looked forward with pleasure for death to remove this furious father, who was so great **a** clog to his happiness and comfort. Whilst he lived, however, Nazook was compelled to behave with respect, fearing his father would otherwise disinherit him, or die without revealing the spot where his treasure was concealed. There **was one** person in the city to whom the Moolah bore a mortal antipathy, and this was a Khoosh Nuvees,[1] named Dubeer Khan.

It once happened that the Nuwab requested an extract from the **Koran, or from some** law-book, to enable him to form a

[1] **A** fine writer.

correct judgment on an important case before him. In order that he might be sure of a correct exposition of the law, he employed the Moulvee and the Moolah Ghoosah Khan to furnish him with the Futwah.[1] Accordingly the Moolah, having carefully written his extract, coupled with his own idea and construction of the law, took it to a celebrated fair copier and ornamental writer named Dubeer Khan, desiring him to write out the Futwah in the most ornamental style possible. The Moulvee also employed this famous writer on the same occasion, and both were laid before the Nuwab, when the Moolah, seeing the two copies, fancied the Moulvee's was written far better than his, and consequently bore in his heart so great a hatred to the Khoosh Nuvees, that for many days poor Dubeer Khan durst not venture abroad. Several months after the offence taken at the conduct of the writer, Nazook was called into his father's apartment.

'Nazook,' said the Moolah, 'it is high time for you to look out for a wife; but as I have no reliance on your choice, I have determined to demand for you the hand of Zooma, the daughter of our respected Cazee. Do you presume to look dissatisfied, you audacious boy? Look pleased, sirrah; smile, I say, or by Mahommed you shall rue your conduct!'

The poor lad tried to smile, but, alas! the nature of the communication, together with the black looks of his father, produced only an idiotic grin, which unfortunately was construed by the Moolah into holding him in derision.

'What, sirrah, you laugh at me, do you? Is it come to this ! Ho, Suliman, come hither ; be quick !'

[1] Exposition.

The old trembling attendant entered, making a low salaam.

'Indeed, my father,' said Nazook, 'I had no intention of being disrespectful to you. I tried to smile in obedience to your commands; but alas! when the heart is sad it is difficult to dress the countenance in smiles.'

'And what, pray, makes your heart sad, you pampered, ungrateful boy?'

'The subject of your conversation, my father, has grieved me. I cannot wed Zooma; I love another.'

'Don't speak another word, you villain! My breath is going.' ('I wish it was gone,' thought Nazook.) 'I say, be silent; you will else drive me into one of my rages, which, you know—oh! 'tis coming on, I feel it—I cannot stay, and yet am spell-bound to the spot. Bring me some water, Suliman. That viper will be the death of me.' Having moistened his lips with water, the Moolah was somewhat more composed; and after some little time said, 'Who is it you pretend to love? Speak, I command you.'

'As you have commanded me, father, I must obey. I love Zeinab, the daughter of Dubeer Khan, the Khoosh Nuvees——'

This was quite enough. Down fell the Moolah, groaning, kicking, and clenching his fists like a maniac, calling down the vengeance of Mahommed on his son. Old Suliman, knowing how to manage his master, recommended Nazook to let him have his rage out, for that, like the most furious fire, must sooner or later abate. The fit, however, was of longer duration than the sagacious Suliman had ever before witnessed, and it was some time ere the distorted countenance of the Moolah resumed its habitual aspect. He breathed hard, foamed at the mouth, and was convulsed with rage; so much so that Suliman sent for a doctor, on whose arrival he **found** his patient stretched out, not moving a muscle. The doctor examined the Moolah, and shook his head.

'Well, doctor,' cried Nazook, 'any hopes?'

'None,' cried the Hukeem; 'he is already dead.'

'Why, man,' said Nazook, 'that is the very——' But checking himself, and pretending to shed tears, continued in a melancholy tone, saying, 'Is my dear father really dead?'

'We have indeed lost our learned Moolah,' replied the doctor.

'Fetch a sheet, Suliman,' cried the youthful **Nazook. 'You** may depart, doctor. Go and tell the sad news.'

The Hukeem made a salaam and retired, whilst Suliman and Nazook began to tear off the deceased's coat and turban, leaving only his trousers, and then bound him up in the sheet. Suliman was then dispatched to arrange the funeral, which was ordered to **take** place the same evening. In the meantime Nazook ransacked the house to discover a will, which after some time he found, and in it read with pleasure he was named as the sole heir to the deceased's property; but unfortunately there was no mention made in the will where the property was to be found, so that Nazook saw himself heir to nothing save the old empty house over his head. Certain, however, money was somewhere concealed within its walls, he sent for labourers and bricklayers, determining to pull the whole house down in search of the hidden gold; but fearing the workmen might discover it during his absence at the funeral, he gave orders not to admit them until his return, leaving old Suliman in charge of the mansion.

The funeral took place, and the remains of the furious Moolah were then thrown into a shallow grave, without a single tear being shed on the occasion; and although Nazook, at the time of the interment, made repeated exclamations of 'Allah, oh, Allah! Allah! oh! Ackbar,' &c., yet, when the earth had completely hidden the remains of his father, he turned round to his friends, saying to one, 'God is merciful! My friend, I hope to have the pleasure of your company at dinner this evening. I mean to do the thing handsomely.' 'Mirza Raheen,' said he to another, 'you will honour me with your presence; we will have a nautch! I know you are fond of a dance, and old Bucktanee[1] has a choice Taefu,[2] you know.' 'Most respected Dubeer Khan, father of the lovely Zeinab, I beseech you spend the rest of the day with me.' All promised attendance, and Nazook hastened home to quicken old Suliman, who had lived many a year in that house without dressing a single dinner for company. He therefore began to urge difficulties, but Nazook silenced him with repeating his orders for a grand entertainment.

Many persons out of employment, seeing the disposition of Nazook, crowded round his mansion offering their services; he accepted many, and gave them their particular offices. Six he appointed running footmen, two to be servants under old Suliman, three cooks, four musalches,[3] twelve palanquin-bearers, and a clerk or writer. Water-carriers, water-coolers, hookah-burdars, and chobdars, were added to the list; so that what with the bustling obsequiousness of these newly-hired vagabonds and the

---

[1] An old woman of that name who kept dancing-girls.
[2] A company of dancers.   [3] Torch-bearers.

noise of the workmen breaking through the walls and staircases to discover the treasure, the poor old Moolah's house resembled the interior of a fort after capture by an enemy.

The clerk was called to take an inventory of what could be found, whilst Nazook repaired first to one set of workmen and then to another, anxiously enquiring if they had found any treasure; but alas! how mortified was he at receiving the repeated answer of 'No, sir, not yet,' from each party of labourers. At last he set them all to work on a very thick stone wall under a narrow staircase; and as it would be midnight ere the task would be completed, he appointed a chobdar and two peons to stand by, with orders from time to time to report progress to him.

Old Suliman and his cook, in the meanwhile, were not idle, and the dinner hour arrived, and with it the guests, at the head of whom advanced Dubeer Khan, the writer. A kid roasted whole smoked before the delighted Nazook, and was soon, by the help of wooden spoons and fingers, divided amongst the party; a large pilau formed the centre dish, whilst sweatmeats, curry, rice, and milk were all piled one above another. Some of the guests had wooden platters, whilst others were content with plantain-leaves; and it was astonishing to behold with what avidity they hauled about the dishes, and thrust their fingers into the rice and ghee which formed part of every dish. In the midst of the feast the chobdar on duty at the thick wall appeared, when a dead silence ensued.

'My lord,' said he, addressing Nazook, 'the workmen have come to a thick plate of iron.'

'Work away,' cried Nazook; 'down with the iron plate, and suffer **none** to enter the place, but await my coming. **Ah, my** friends,' said he, turning to the company, 'we shall have many a feast now; the walls of the old house shall ring again with the noise of the puckwaz.[1] **Ho, there**! are the Taefus in attendance?'

'They are, **my lord.**'

'Then clear away, **and** bring water and hookahs; and hark **ye, let** us have plenty of pawn and betel-leaves, with cloves, cardamums, and so forth.'

All these delicious spices were soon brought; and the company arranging themselves at the upper end of the room, the nautch commenced. The doors being thrown open, crowds of uninvited persons flocked into the hall, which, far from being disagreeable to the young heir, highly flattered his consequence, and he bowed and smiled **to all** around him. . **Men** of **the first** rank now assembled, congratulating Nazook on his accession to the property, interlarding their joyous greetings with sighs of condolence for the loss of his revered parent, the learned Moolah. All this time Nazook was under great alarm lest the treasure should not be found, in which case he would be puzzled to pay for the present entertainment, much less be able to continue this splendid style **of living.** At length the chobdar, the welcome herald of felicity, stalked **in** amongst the dancers, crying, 'The wall and iron door are nearly broken through, my lord.'

'Lights, bring lights!' cried the transported youth. 'Come, my friends, come and witness my wealth.'

[1] The small drum which invariably accompanies the dancing-girls.

The hall was now deserted by the **company,** who crowded after Nazook down narrow staircases and through deserted rooms until they arrived at the spot where the workmen were in the act of removing the iron plate. Nazook, seizing a torch, viewed with delight all obstacles to possession of his wealth removed.

'Now, then, my friends,' said he, already having one **foot** in the narrow cell, and holding at arm's length a flaming torch, 'now, then, look forward to happiness and pleasure; the gold shall not lie idle, rely upon it.'

'Wah! wah!'[1] exclaimed the approving mob, who crowded around the aperture.

'Wah! wah!' **cried** those above, who filled every step of the narrow staircase.

Nazook entered the small chamber, but soon **retreated,** uttering a fearful shriek, which resounded through the vaulted passages. Some who also ventured to peep to ascertain the cause of alarm screamed aloud, whilst others fainted through fear. The people on the stairs hastily retreated, whilst those from above vociferated, 'For the **love of Allah!** what is it? Tell us, **or** you shall not come up.'

'Make way!' cried the poor tremblers below. '**By** Allah! we have seen the old Moolah's ghost perched on his strong-box.'

'Water! water!' was now the cry; 'Nazook is dying!' And die he might, for at the mention of the Moolah's ghost the whole assembly with one mighty rush quitted the house. Old Bucktanee and her nautch-gils, fearing they should be left behind, clung to the shoulders of the terrified **men,** and were thus borne from

[1] A common exclamation of approbation or surprise.

the mansion. In the attempt at a speedy exit, lamps, hookahs, and fans were broken and overthrown, whilst the newly-hired servants of the heir appropriated to their own use, in their flight, every article of value they could lay their hands upon.

Poor Nazook, who had indeed by the light of his torch beheld the gaunt figure of his father, wrapt in his winding-sheet, perched on the top of a huge treasure-chest in the centre of the chamber, after some time recovered, and called for Suliman; but Suliman had fled, and it was now high time for him to follow his example. His knees tottering under him, he ascended the stairs, expecting at every step to be pulled backwards by the ghastly one-eyed Moolah. Arrived safe, however, at the top, he closed a door, hoping thus to shut out even the remembrance of what he had seen; but its hollow sound reverberating through the now desolate mansion added fresh terror to his mind. What a scene presented itself to him! His late festive and brilliantly-illuminated hall was now a perfect chaos, wherein he alone was the hapless tenant.

Without a light to guide him, he stumbled first over one thing and then another, until he became quite bewildered. At last he felt a window, which he opened, and called aloud for help; upon which some few stragglers in the street, who hovered about the house talking over the recent alarm and confusion, screamed violently, running away, crying, 'The ghost! the ghost! the Moolah!'

In vain did Nazook endeavour to convince them that he was not the Moolah, but his son, alive, and anxious to get out of the house; the more he called the louder they screamed. At last he beheld lights approaching the mansion, and congratulated himself on his approaching liberation ; he felt out the entrance-door, and gained the courtyard which surrounded that side of the house next the street. Just as he approached the great gates of the courtyard, what was his mortification at hearing the sound of hammers, **nails,** and chains on the outside, accompanied by the clamour of blacksmiths and carpenters consulting on the **best** way of fastening up the gates of the haunted house! All poor Nazook's screams for aid were drowned by the ponderous strokes of **the** sledge-hammers and the noise of the crowd without ; and, vexed and mortified, he threw himself on the ground, wailing and weeping bitterly.

'What ungrateful villains !' cried he, **as** soon as **he was** convinced the gates were **so** secured as to resist **his** utmost efforts to open them. 'What do they imagine has become of me ? That they should fly from my father's ghost **I am not** surprised at— **God** knows I am equally anxious to escape it—but surely they might have considered me. Doubtless they think my father's spirit has pounced upon me and borne me away to the other world. **Oh,** woe is me, that know the contrary ! though Heaven only knows how soon the **icy** hand **of** my father may grasp my throat, now that I am immured in the same place with him. Oh, ungrateful people ! thus to leave me exposed to the horrors of the place, and certainty of starvation.' Thus was the remainder of the night spent by the truly wretched youth.

On the following morning the unhappy heir to misery alone once more approached the gate, **which** he found had been nailed and screwed up so tight as to banish all hopes of escape by that way. He returned, trembling with alarm, into the interior of the

building, and found his way to the kitchen, where, to his joy,
heaps of uncooked rice, dhal, and flour, with the remains of the
last evening's feast, met his eye. He ate sparingly, not knowing
how long he might be doomed to linger within the walls of the
detested mansion. Towards evening he ventured to ascend the
terrace of the house, hoping to espy some friendly person in the
city or on the adjacent buildings, who, seeing him, would vouch
for his being alive. Here he remained until dusk, not having seen
a soul to whom he could apply.

As he was about to descend he fancied he saw a figure glide
across the courtyard ; and, looking again cautiously over the pa-
rapet, to his horror he beheld the ghost of his father, enveloped
in his winding-sheet, with slow and measured step approach the
gates of the courtyard and attempt in vain to open them. The
figure then retraced its steps, and entered the interior of the dwelling. Nazook remained riveted to the spot, in an agony of mind
not to be described. He at length arose, and having secured the
door of the terrace, determined to spend the night there; for,
although hungry and thirsty, he durst not venture to descend to
the kitchen, where lay his slender store of provisions.

It is now time to account for the mysterious reappearance of
the Moolah, who, although concluded by Nazook and the sagacious Hukeem to be dead, was only in a swoon, into which his
ungovernable rage had thrown him. How long he would have
lain quietly in his grave cannot be known ; but when it began to
grow dusk he was alarmed by feeling something scratch his face,
and at the same time received a severe bite on his toe, which
roused him from his trance, and he began to wonder where he

was. At first he imagined he **was in** his bed, with a quantity **of** clothes over him, but could not conceive why his head was bound up so tight ; he struggled and bit through the sheet which covered his face, and after writhing about with all his strength, and making **a** hole for his single eye, discovered, to his horror, that he had been buried alive, and that he must attribute his escape to two large jackals, who, according to their practice, had scented out the new-made grave, and by their biting and scratching had awakened **him** from his death-like slumber. These never-failing attendants **on** burying-grounds **the** Moolah actually saw in the act of running away in fright, so unaccustomed were they to see their prey rise and stand upright from the grave. The indignation and rage of the Moolah may be better conceived than described. On his **son** he bestowed curses and bitter reproaches, **and hastened, with** his winding-sheet round his shoulders, towards the city, to convince **him he was yet** alive, and prepared to punish him for his brutal **and** unnatural conduct. He passed through the streets unnoticed **until he** came **to** his own residence, which, to his surprise, he beheld illuminated, and crowded inside and out with visitors of every description. **He** heard the strokes of the workmen, and shrewdly guessed the nature of their employment. Alarmed for his money, he pushed through **the** crowd, whose ideas were running on the living only, dreaming naught of the presence of the dead, and found his way to a low private portal within the courtyard, which he opened, and then quickly descended to his treasury by a secret entrance known only to himself, meditating how he could best protect his loved gold. He had just reached the chamber as the workmen were removing the iron plate in the wall, and had scarcely time to seat himself on the chest, when Nazook with his torch entered, exclaiming, 'Now, then, my friends, the gold shall not lie idle!' The Moolah was about to speak, when the scream of his son and the shrieks of the crowd around him convinced him his appearance had had the desired effect; he therefore kept his seat, assuming all the horrors of the grave. The rest has been already mentioned.

The Moolah, when left alone, began to consider how he had best proceed. The torch of his son lay burning on the ground: snatching it up, he ascended the narrow staircase. Not a soul stood in his way—all was still and silent as the grave from which he had been so providentially rescued. Wandering through the house, he found some rice and remains of a pilau, which he eagerly devoured, and retired to his treasury, there to spend the rest of the night. In the morning he arose, and once more ascended the stairs; but fancying he heard some one moving about, retired, not wishing yet to discover himself; for, should one timid person at first behold him, he much feared he should not be able to convince the world that he really was a living man, and no spectre from the other world; he therefore meditated an appearance in some public place, and trusted to chance to further his intentions.

At night he once more emerged, and entering the courtyard, proceeded to the gate, debating whether he should, at that hour, show himself in the city. What was his astonishment, however, at finding the gates strongly fastened on the outside! He had not a doubt but that this was the act of his reprobate son, who had spread reports injurious to him and the building through the city. In the midst of wealth it seemed he was doomed to starve, and once more returned to his treasury, meditating how to escape from the **fate** which awaited him. **Near the** broken wall lay a crowbar, and he bethought himself how this might aid him. He remembered that next to him, on the side not protected by the courtyard, there lived **a** grain-merchant, who had, **he knew,** gone **a** long journey, and would scarcely be returned; he therefore applied the crowbar **to** the wall which divided **their** houses, hoping to enter the residence **of** the merchant, and thus effect **his** escape.

He soon effected **an** aperture, and listening attentively, found the house quiet—not a sound **met** his ear; but, in order that he might be quite certain the house was unoccupied, he waited for another night, keeping his ear from time **to** time close to the aperture. He could hear nothing but mice and rats, by which he concluded he had broken into the merchant's granary, which he **knew** was apart from his dwelling-house. Determined, however, not to be too hasty, he resolved to wait **till** the following night.

CHAPTER IV.

THE TAILOR'S STORY (*continued*).

WHILST the old Moolah was hammering away at the wall of his house, his unfortunate son, hearing the hollow reverberation of the crowbar issue from the direction of the treasury, became more and more alarmed, fully expecting each blow would be succeeded by some horrible vision, or that his father's spirit would grasp him by the neck. Flying to the terrace, therefore, he there crouched up in one corner, covering his face with the skirts of his coat, not daring to cast his eyes around him. There being no end to his fears, he imagined that the ghost as well as himself might find his way to the terrace. Like a hunted hare, therefore, did he descend the staircase, and concealed himself behind a door. Again, not conceiving this a place of sufficient security, he proceeded cautiously towards the kitchen; and, at last, so much did fear take possession of him, that he determined on spending the night in the open air in the courtyard.

Still, wherever he went, the hollow sounds from below struck upon his ears; and when at last they ceased he became more terrified than ever. Morning, however, beaming once more, cheered his spirits, and he proceeded again to the kitchen, where, snatching some **raw rice, he entered** a small room, the door **of** which he fastened, determining **at all hazards to attempt his** escape that night, intending not **to stir from his present retreat** until the **sun** should for **some** time sink into **its western hemi-**sphere.

The Moolah in the meanwhile had made so much **good** use of his crowbar as to effect an entrance into the merchant's store-rooms. He soon groped his way to the habitable part **of the** house, where he rested himself; when, as **he was ruminating how** to escape, a back door slowly opened, and a female cautiously entered. The Moolah, fearful of **a** discovery, covered himself with his sheet, maintaining a profound silence. The woman said, in a soft voice, '**I am** here before you; but **be** quick, or my husband will return.' **In** her hand she carried a lamp, and enter-ing an inner room, called to the Moolah in the merchant's name, saying, 'Come, Ganem, why treat me thus?'

The Moolah arose for the purpose of retreating by the back **door,** but the rays of the woman's lamp falling on his counte-nance, she gave a piercing shriek, and instantly sank to the earth. The Moolah, heedless of her condition, fled, and gaining a narrow lane, determined to proceed to his own mosque, and there wait until morning, when he would convince the inhabitants that he was indeed alive.

The shrieks of the woman in the merchant's house brought several neighbours to the spot, who, on hearing from the terrified creature of the spectacle she had witnessed, were all struck dumb with fright, and one by one sneaked off, so that the poor woman was left entirely alone, until her husband, who was an oil-seller, arrived.   He, burning with anger at her infidelity, **and** regardless **of the** fright she had endured, commenced with **a thick strap** to **endeavour** to bring her to her senses,—but, **alas!** soon discovered his blows **were** bestowed upon an inanimate object.   The sight of the dead Moolah, together with the consciousness of her shame being made public, had so worked upon her weak intellects, that **she** swooned **and died.**

Whilst **all this turmoil** and confusion was going on the merchant **himself arrived, and the** enraged oilman, finding he had in vain **applied the** strap to his poor wife, set to work on the merchant, **whom** he most soundly belaboured.   How far and to **what lengths** he would have proceeded cannot **be** surmised, had **not the police** interfered **and** released the merchant from his fury.   **The** merchant, it **is true, had** taken a fancy to the oilman's wife; **and on this** night, returning from Ahmednugger, whither he had **been on business,** passed by the oilman's shop, and gossiped with his wife.   He made himself so agreeable, and displayed so large **a bag of silver,** that the weak woman could not resist his offers.

As he had several other places to go to ere he returned home, he gave her the **key** of the back door, desiring she would, at the hour of eleven, proceed to his house and await his coming, saying, ' Probably I shall **be** at home to receive you.'   Seeing the Moolah, therefore, in the house, the woman naturally concluded it was her paramour, and was induced to act in the manner already related.

The idea of the Moolah's spirit actually walking the earth now became firmly impressed **on the** minds of the inhabitants; and as Nazook, his son, had not emerged from the haunted **house,** they concluded he had fallen a victim to the vindictive disposition of his father's ghost.

In the morning the Moolah, **whose very** name **was now** sufficient to make every pious Moslem in the city shudder, took his station in the mimbah of the mosque where he had been in the habit of reading prayers. The first who approached was the person who, since his interment, had officiated in his stead.

No sooner did he cast his **eyes on** the mimbah than **he** dropped down insensible. Ghoosa **Khan** descended for the purpose of dispelling the fears of the officiating priest; and, raising him up, cried, ' For shame, brother, thus **to** give way to fear; you see I am not dead; therefore arise and go forth and undeceive the inhabitants.'

By this time several persons had approached the mosque, but beholding the acting priest, half-sitting, and half-lying, **with** Ghoosa Khan hanging over him, instantly took to their heels, crying, ' Allah protect us! the ghost has seized our poor priest!' Ghoosa **Khan was** deeply hurt at this ungovernable superstition and foolish alarm of all the people, and actually wept aloud.

The officiating priest, now recovering himself, ventured to open his eyes, which he cast fearfully around him; and seeing Ghoosa Khan in tears, began to entertain doubts **as** to his being a spirit from the other world, and, in a low voice, ventured to pronounce his name.

' I am here, brother,' answered the afflicted Moolah; ' why **am** I shunned? Indeed I am a living man, and hope to continue so yet a few years longer. See, feel my hand, behold my face, convince thyself of the truth of my assertions.'

'Indeed,' replied the priest, 'I have been, I perceive, unnecessarily alarmed; but tell me, where is your son? I fear you have committed some violence on him.'

'No, truly, brother, I have not beheld my ungrateful boy since his employment of treasure-hunting in my house, and would I had been spared the sight.   Is he not at large in the city?'

'No, indeed, we have all believed that you or your spirit had dragged him to the other world.'

'I am surprised at the superstition of the populace,' said the Moolah; 'but now hasten, I beseech thee, and undeceive them. Tell them I am here alive and well, and ready to assist in the search for my wicked son, of whose fate I am ignorant.'

The priest being now satisfied he had conversed with a mortal, and not a spirit, left the mosque, and proclaimed aloud that Moolah Ghoosa Khan was alive, and commanded everyone to repair to the mosque, where they might see and hear him read prayers.

The populace, having at last ventured near the mosque, were all fully convinced the Moolah was indeed living, and that he never had been dead.

The Nuwab, hearing the report, now summoned the Moolah, who related how he had found himself in the grave attacked by jackals, and the inconvenience he had suffered in consequence. These events were related by the Moolah with so much gravity and solemnity, as if the fate of the empire depended on his being dead or alive, that the Nuwab, although he endeavoured to check all inclination to laugh, could **not entirely** command his risible faculties, for **which** breach of good manners he atoned by ordering great attention to be paid **the** Moolah, **and** granting his permission for him to take possession of his house **once more.**

The Moolah, now followed by a crowd of persons, approached his dwelling, whose gates were so well secured. **The same** persons who had fastened it up were now called to open it **again,** which, in a short time, they effected.

In the courtyard stood the alarmed Nazook, whose attempts to escape had proved fruitless, and hearing the joyful sounds **of** hammers **on the** outside of the gate, concluded **the** inhabitants were anxious **to** come to his rescue. **He** therefore stood in the middle **of the** court, to welcome his deliverers; **but how** was he astonished **on** beholding his father enter the gates, attended by many hundred people, none of whom wore countenances **of** terror! The angry Moolah stood before the affrighted son. ' Explain, sirrah,' said he, 'how and for what purpose thou hast dared to attempt the commission of murder, and wish to become a parricide.'

Nazook declared he thought his father had really been dead, and the opinion of the doctor justified him in the belief.

' Young man,' said the Moolah, ' I have witnessed your disposition—fain would you that **I** in truth **had** been dead, but Providence has ordained it otherwise. It would have been more decorous to have kept my body awhile above ground, ere you so joyfully solemnised my funeral. **Your** object was **a** quick and hasty accession to my property; but, that in future I may not be subject to your avaricious inclinations, **I** here declare, before all assembled, that I for **ever** disinherit **you**; **and so** odious **are** you in my eyes, that henceforth this house **is no** longer a place of shelter for you. Depart, sirrah, and never let me see you more!'

Nazook, having been **so** solemnly disinherited, attached not much value either to **the shelter of the** old house **or** the society **of** his furious parent; **he** therefore left the house without uttering a single word.

· At this moment **arrived Daeeb** Khan, the **nephew of** the Moolah, who **had** been dispatched **by** his **father from** Ahmednuggur to enquire into the strange reports which had reached him regarding the death and sudden reappearance **of his** brother, **Ghoosa** Khan. The young man **had ever been** accustomed to **look**' upon his uncle with profound respect, and therefore now embraced him **with** tears **in** his eyes, expressing the delight **he** felt **at once** more beholding him.

The Moolah, pleased **to perceive there was** one person at **least** who rejoiced in his resurrection, invited his dutiful nephew into his house, which, **he** expressed a hope, might in future be considered his home. Daeeb was delighted, as he had but little doubt but that **he** should now become the declared heir of his uncle, poor Nazook **being** entirely cast away.

The Moolah **was now** become more rigid than ever, but very wisely abstained from giving **so** much latitude **to his** rage, his recent burial having served as an excellent warning **to** him.

Nazook, in the meanwhile, called upon **Dubeer** Khan, the **Khoosh** Nuvees, but was received coolly by the writer, although as cordially as ever by his lovely daughter. The former, having heard of Nazook's expulsion from his father's house, was now not over-anxious **to bestow on him the** hand of **his** fair daughter, Zeinab ; yet, as he was not entirely without hope **that** he would one day be reinstated **in the** Moolah's favour, **the** cautious Khoosh Nuvees did not altogether banish or forbid the youth his house.

Nazook **was** sadly distressed for money, having parted with everything of value he had ever possessed ; and by the assistance **of** Dubeer Khan he contrived to procure a situation under the Nuwab's sheristadar, **or** secretary, which rendered him tolerably comfortable ; **and. the** Khoosh Nuvees was at length persuaded to give his consent to **the** marriage **with** Zeinab, which **in due** time was performed.

The Moolah, **as it may be imagined,** directed **his attention to** his treasure as soon as he felt himself once more firmly fixed **in** his own mansion. He had ascertained that the strong-box was **firmly** locked, and that his son, Nazook, had never disturbed its contents. Searching for the keys, however, he could nowhere find them. Old Suliman must know something of them : he sent to his house to enquire, first, why his servant had not appeared before him; and secondly, to desire he would inform his master where to find his large bunch of keys. He was amazed, however, to hear that neither old Suliman nor his family were in the city ; that they were gone **no one knew** whither. He now reflected that at the time of his indisposition the keys were fastened to his girdle ; and the idea struck him **that** they had most probably been buried with him, and if so, by searching in the grave he might possibly find them.

For this purpose he proceeded to the burial-ground, and commenced a vigilant search ; but, alas ! all to no purpose. 'Some one,' said he, 'must certainly have got them ; and if so, my money is by no means safe.' The only method seemed to be to remove the money and conceal it elsewhere, and thus disappoint whoever should be in possession of his keys. For this purpose he sent for a smith to force the locks ; when, to his agony and grief, the chest was empty—not a single bag of gold remained. The afflicted Moolah beat his breast, cried and groaned most piteously ; so much so, that his lamentations reaching the ears of his nephew, he flew to ascertain the cause, and comfort his dear uncle; but when he found his dear relative was become a beggar, and that he should be heir only to empty boxes, the dutiful nephew sneaked out of the house and returned to Ahmednuggur, reporting to his father the disappointment.

Moolah Ghoosa Khan now really fell sick, and after a lingering illness, in good earnest died. Having made no will since the one discovered by Nazook, which the cunning youth had carefully preserved, he remained still the lawful heir, and took possession of the house. Money there was none, and Nazook more than half-suspected his cousin Daeeb Khan had robbed his father of his loved gold.

It was about two years after the decease of the Moolah, when one day, as Nazook was walking in the street, a man came up to him, and giving him a letter, hastily departed. Nazook opened the letter, and found, to his surprise, it came from Suliman, his father's old servant, informing him that if he would instantly set out to meet him he would learn something greatly to his advantage. Nazook lost no time in obeying the wishes of the writer, and soon arrived at Hyderabad, where he found Suliman indeed dying, **but not yet** speechless. Suliman **in a** low voice said he had sent for him to divulge a great secret, and do an **act** of justice, which was to restore to Nazook the gold **of** his father, Ghoosa Khan.

Nazook expressed his surprise, but Suliman said, '**Listen, my** young master, and I will explain all. Many years ago I happened to discover where my master kept his money, and determined, when an opportunity offered, **to rob** him ; this opportunity, from my master's extreme caution and watchfulness, never came until the day when we both thought he was **indeed dead.** You were anxious to remove the dead **body, and I to** possess the **keys of** the treasure-chest, which I perceived hanging to my master's girdle. You left me at home to **take** charge **of** the house whilst **you** followed your father's remains to the grave. As I had long determined to rob my old master, I hesitated not to plunder **my new one ;** and **ere** you returned **from** the funeral contrived to empty the strong-box of all its contents and convey them to my own house close by. The reappearance of the Moolah induced me to fly, and I have since settled in this city, where **in a** par-ticular spot **is** buried the money which by right is **your own.** Promise to provide for my **wife, and I** will direct you **where it is** to be found.'

Nazook promised to make his **wife a regular** fixed monthly allowance, and the aged Suliman directed him where to find the wished-for gold. Soon after this Suliman died, and Nazook, well-laden with rupees, returned to Aurungabad, where, as he had promised his friends, he gave many **a** nautch, uninterrupted by his father's ghost, and was in consequence extolled by the whole city.

The Nuwab made no remark on this story of the poor tailor, but arose, intimating his intention of being present next day to hear another tale; and in consequence Moyedin summoned all the remaining persons of the palace ; and the lot falling upon Tambadass, the coppersmith, he on the following day appeared, and commenced his narrative as follows.

CHAPTER V.

THE COPPERSMITH'S STORY.

IN the Island of Bombay lived an inoffensive Brahmin called Donga Sette. At this period the island was entirely in the possession of the Portuguese, who, bigoted to their own religion, strained every nerve to make proselytes of their Hindú and Mahommedan subjects. The tyranny they exercised for the accomplishment of their purpose baffles all description. Their first attacks were on Brahmins and Moolahs; conceiving, could their conversion be effected, the lower orders would unhesitatingly tread in their footsteps. The rainy season had just terminated, and produced a verdure delightful to the eye throughout the island. The cocoa-nut trees, which almost touched the walls of the fort, gracefully waved their verdant branches in the refreshing breeze ; the cattle with avidity sought out each green spot to graze upon, and the cultivator joyfully anticipated his coming harvest of rice and other grain.

At such a period the surrounding country appeared enchanting : the dusky brown of the mountains, those barriers of the Maharatta country, on the opposite side of the harbour, was changed to the lively green, o'er which wildly skipped the joyful goats ; whilst the anxious mariner, preparing his favourite bark again to plough the ocean, were scenes which ought to have inspired delight in every heart. Unfortunately a fever raged through the island, which served the Portuguese as a pretext for prosecuting their plans of converting all classes to Christianity, declaring the fever to be a judgment from Heaven on the idolatrous Hindús and perverse followers of Mahommed.

In this idea they sent their officers to all parts of the island to summon the principal inhabitants, whom they threatened with ruin and destruction if they refused to change their religion. Firm, however, to the faith of their forefathers, almost all openly avowed their horror of the religion offered them in exchange for their own. Consequently the work of ruin commenced : the lands of the Brahmins were confiscated, and the merchandise of the Mahommedans was subjected to enormous duties, which threatened to annihilate trade, whilst many principal men were sentenced to imprisonment. Notwithstanding Donga Sette had been included in the list of sufferers, he lived as if regardless of the tyranny practised upon him ; and not only existed, but appeared to thrive, whilst others were reduced to actual starvation.

Donga Sette was a stout broad-shouldered man, inclined to corpulency, which, to the mortification of his persecutors, seemed rather to increase than to diminish. Several hundreds of the poorer classes, unable to weather the storm of cruel tyranny, compelled to external appearance to renounce their tenets, became Portuguese Christians ; whilst many Brahmins and learned Moolahs, reduced to beggary, laid down and died, cursing with their last breath their bigoted unrelenting government. In this state of affairs—when **disease** and starvation **with** giant strides stalked through the little island, when trade became stagnant, and in consequence provisions were almost impossible to procure—how Donga Sette Brahmin contrived to grow fat and maintain his dignity, became a subject of no small wonder to the Governor and his counsellors.

The council were **in** full debate on this extraordinary **man**, when **a Jew,** known by the name **of** Ismael Yahoodee, solicited an interview with the Governor. His request being granted, he was admitted to the council-board, and there proposed that **a** strict search should **be** made **in the** Brahmin's house, **where** doubtless vast treasure was concealed. **Ismael** had **more than** once advanced large sums to the government, and to the Governor himself: he **was** therefore honourably received, and requested to **be** seated. **At** this period, money being much wanted by **the** government, they scrupled **not to** approve and put in practice Ismael's plan. A large body of police, accompanied by the Jew, therefore, sallied **from** the **fort to** the humble dwelling **of** their victim.

The Brahmin's house was situated amidst the cocoa-nut trees in the small village of Geergaum—those trees once his **property,** that soil once his own. Here he lived with his wife **in** peace, employed in study and in charity, beloved by **all who knew** him. When evening spread **her** shade around, the worthy Brahmin might be seen instructing a herd **of urchins,** to whom he preached **most** wholesome lessons of morality; then, having dismissed his youthful audience, he would sally out and search for objects of compassion, on whom, with heartfelt pleasure, he bestowed his charity. His evening lecture had but just concluded, when the Portuguese police, followed by the Jew, surrounded his humble dwelling. Accustomed to such unceremonious visits, the Brahmin, folding his arms, stood aloof, casting a look of ineffable contempt on this Christian rabble, gathering up his garments, fearing lest they should be polluted by a touch.

There was something truly dignified in this reception of the Brahmin's unwelcome guests; the proud manly look of an innocent, injured man, inspired the myrmidons of tyranny with an awe which effectually shielded the person of the Brahmin from violence or insult. Even Ismael, the Jew, shrunk from the penetrating eye of the worthy Brahmin, and the leader of the party stood for sometime motionless ere he produced his search-warrant. The Brahmin, casting his eye over the paper, pointed to the interior of his dwelling, but deigned not to utter a word, sedulously covering his mouth with his shawl, to evince to the Portuguese his dread of contamination from their breath. It was by such signs of contempt and horror of the presence of the Christians, which Donga Sette seized every opportunity to display, that caused him in particular to be remarked as the most obnoxious to the government.

The searching party, obedient to their instructions, ransacked the whole house; and although aided by the crafty Ismael, whose shrewd piercing eye allowed no corner to escape his observation, they discovered naught save a few old books and manuscripts in the Sanscrit language, and therefore abandoned the search. Donga Sette was quietly seated in his verandah, and allowed the party to leave his dwelling, maintaining the same silence with which he received them. Ismael, the Jew, was **the last to** retire ; he caught the eye of the injured Brahmin, and saluted him with a mock reverence, pronouncing the words 'Ram, Ram, Mharaj,' in a tone so peculiar, **and** accompanied by **a** movement of his **keen** grey eye so fraught with meaning, as to cause the Brahmin **no** very pleasurable sensations.

The Jew marked the alarm depicted on the Brahmin's countenance, notwithstanding his evident attempt to disguise it. Joining the body of police, the Jew affected to lament their disappointment, and instructed the leader how **he should** report **to the** Governor.

'We will leave this to you, master Ismael,' said the officer ; 'it was by your suggestion **we** were employed in this business, **and** it is your affair to report upon the issue of it.'

'I should have no objection,' replied the Jew, 'had I not business of importance to attend to at a distance ; on my return I will visit the Governor.'

'No, no, my friend, this **won't do** ; come with us you shall ; attempt to do otherwise, and by all **our** blessed saints I'll run my sword into thy miserable body, and it's hard if I cannot obtain absolution for killing a Jew.'

Ismael perceiving resistance useless, silently followed the guard to the castle, and was quickly ushered into the presence of the Governor. The haughty ruler at **a** glance perceived a failure, and in no very courteous manner expressed his displeasure and his demand for money. Ismael perceiving a storm gathering around the already clouded brow of the Governor, promised to advance a certain sum, which after a given time was to be doubled. The Governor, somewhat pacified, bade him begone, and to beware how he deviated from his promise. To raise the first amount, it was necessary for the unhappy Israelite to journey towards Salsette, where resided his partner in trade, and in whose hands a large sum of money had been lately deposited. For this purpose he obtained the proper passports, and, wrapping his cloak around him, commenced his journey on foot.

The Island of Salsette is within a few hours' walk of Bombay; but Thanah, its chief town, whither the Jew was proceeding, a good five hours' journey. Night was fast approaching when Ismael set his foot on Salsette. He repented his hasty proceeding, and wished he had postponed his journey to the following day; for the island being infested with tigers, whose roaring repeatedly saluted his ears, caused him to tremble with agitation and alarm. The night was unusually dark and gloomy, a few stars only shed their feeble light in heaven's spacious canopy, affording little or no assistance to the benighted Ismael. The rainy season having terminated so lately, the path was muddy, and the ground so uneven as often to cause the traveller either to stick fast, or miss his footsteps altogether, and plunge him in the rice-fields on either side, inundated as they were with the rains, which had been this year unusually heavy.

This was the case with poor Ismael; the impenetrable darkness, the howling of wild beasts, his own age, and want of nerve and activity, all operating at a moment when he was picking his path through the most difficult part of the road, caused his foot to slip, and precipitated him into an overflowing rice-field nearly up to his middle in mud, whilst he feared to attract the notice of the wild beasts by attempting **to** call aloud for **aid.** The miserable old man, who fancied he was sinking every moment deeper and deeper, gave himself over as lost, and prepared to die. The Jew's preparation for coming dissolution, however, **was** not of that repentant nature that it ought to have been; for instead of praying for forgiveness from heaven for all his enormities, he banished from his recollection his usurious habits and sundry extortions, bewailing only his hard lot, and cursing the avarice of **the** Governor, through which he had been brought to his present predicament.

Moreover, heavy were his regrets at dying without having attained the key to some concealed treasure, which chance had revealed to him was by only one method **to be** obtained; **but** which, in consequence of the inactivity incident to old **age, he had** been prevented securing, though almost within his grasp. Even at this time he had schemes already planned for obtaining **the** philosopher's stone, which could not, he imagined, fail to ensure success. To find, therefore, himself, his secret, and his deep-laid plans, all fast sinking in the mud of **a** rice-field, was a mortification to which he found impossible to resign himself patiently. What the Jew intended to have done, and what **scheme** was floating in his brain, and how he became informed of any treasure existing within his grasp, shall presently be related, when the unfortunate man is extricated from his perilous situation.

Finding lamentation of no avail, Ismael, in silence, brooded over his hard fate. Hungry, thirsty, his limbs and his faculties benumbed, suffering from terror of approaching death in the horrible shape of suffocation, or in the more appalling one of a tiger's jaws, no helping hand to save him, the situation of poor Ismael may be better conceived than described. The silence which, partly through policy, and partly through necessity, he continued to preserve, enabled him to hear the blundering footsteps of some traveller like himself. As he approached the fatal spot, the Jew distinctly heard the tones of the traveller's voice, indulging in a woful soliloquy, and sobbing most bitterly, as he plodded and picked his slippery path. Ismael wished, for his own sake, to guard the stranger against the danger he had fallen into; and, judging from the voice, he was arrived at or near the broken path where he had himself stumbled, called as loud as he was able, desiring the traveller to be cautious.

'Oh! brother,' cried he, 'for heaven's sake, take care of yourself, and come to my assistance, or I shall surely perish.'

The stranger was alarmed at hearing a voice proceeding from he knew not where, but rejoicing at the certainty of a fellow-creature being near the spot where he imagined he stood alone, demanded where he was, and how he could assist him?

The Jew, for the purpose of guiding him to the spot, floundered and splashed about in the water, crying, 'Here, here! give me your hand; but take care of your own footsteps, or we may both be drowned.'

The traveller, using all the caution in his power, and feeling his way with his hands, after some time and difficulty touched the hand of the half-drowned Israelite. Ismael, having at last found something to hold by, grasped the traveller's hand with all the strength he was master of, and implored him to extricate him from his perilous situation.

The traveller, after great exertion and imminent risk of himself tumbling into the water, succeeded in aiding the Jew to emerge from what he, at one time conceived, would have proved his watery grave.

Ismael no sooner felt his foot on dry land, than he overpowered the traveller with thanks, and the warmest expressions of gratitude for his assistance, and enquired whither he was journeying. The stranger replied he was proceeding to Bombay from Thanah; but that as it was immaterial to him when he reached that place, he would, if the Jew pleased, attend him to a small village about a mile forward, where he could dry himself, and be sheltered for the night.

Ismael cheerfully accepted the kind offer, and both cautiously picked their way to the haven of rest mentioned by the traveller. Having arrived safe at the village, they knocked and cried aloud at the door of one of the cultivator's hovels, and with difficulty succeeded in arousing the sleepy inhabitants. Being at last admitted, on promise of a liberal reward, the cultivator prepared a fire with some fagots, by which the **Jew** soon dried himself, and proposed to his companion they should rest where they were until the morning.

Having safely extricated the Jew, whilst he and his friend are enjoying a sound repose at the cottage, it may be a fit opportunity to explain how the crafty Ismael gained information of vast treasures being somewhere near at hand.

Ismael for many years was a wanderer; he had no fixed place of abode. On the death of his father he had succeeded to some property, chiefly in goods and merchandise, but very little ready money; he was indefatigable in his endeavours to accumulate wealth, and conveyed his goods throughout the country to such markets as he imagined would be most advantageous to him. He lent money on exorbitant interest, where he knew he could successfully apply to the strong arm of the law in case of non-payment. Growing old, and having amassed much wealth, he settled amongst the Portuguese at Bombay, where he soon became notorious for his riches, and had more than once assisted the Governor with loans of some magnitude. Hearing of a famine in the Deccan, Ismael, whose storehouses were well stocked with all sorts of grain, sallied forth with heavily laden bullocks towards Poona, where his profits were, as he had calculated, immense. As his cattle were to return unladen, his watchful eye was unnecessary, and he therefore sent them forward, following himself on a sorry tattoo, or pony. Towards the close of evening, the Jew found himself near the celebrated cave at Carli, and never having examined this extraordinary specimen of human ingenuity and labour, he determined to ascend the wooded mountain where it is situated.

Securing his pony, therefore, he ascended the hill. He was utterly amazed at the extent of the cavern, and at its astonishing height and construction of the roof, being coved, and supported by twenty-one pillars on each side, and terminating in a semi-circle. The capitals of the pillars, surmounted by elephants with their riders, together with the wide aisle without the columns, the time, and the lonely situation in which Ismael found himself, inspired him with an awe which hitherto he had been a stranger to. In turning round to depart, he fancied he heard a low hollow moan issue from one of the cells to the right, which probably had been used as the residences of the priests and their families. He paused ; again the moan struck upon his ear so distinctly, as to convince him imagination had not deceived him.   Curiosity prompted him to advance towards the cell, the low door of which was ajar, and enabled him to perceive the flickering of a miserable lamp.   He was on the point of entering the cell, when he distinctly heard a voice cry, in a soothing tone: 'Peace, Baba ; rest, holy man ; you will recover.'

A hollow voice, as if speaking from the grave, replied : ' 'Tis all over with me ; the hand **of** death **is on me, I feel its icy grasp.** Talk to me no more of life, **mine is at an end ;** but whilst speech is allowed me, let me give you information **which, if** attended **to,** will amply reward you for your care and charity towards me.   **I am** the last of twenty-four holy Goseins, whose whole lives **have** been spent in accumulating money.   (The Jew crept closer to the **door.) We bound** ourselves, by a solemn oath, to deposit our gains in one particular place, secured by—— (Here the sick man's voice failing him, left the listening anxious Jew in an agony of fear lest death had snatched him away in the middle of his grand disclosure.   The Gosein resumed his narrative, however.) The treasure is concealed in the cavern on the Gharipoori Island, near Bombay.   Search the fourth pillar on the left hand side, at its foot ; raise a stone, and you will find an iron box with a key in **it.**   Open **it** on your return home.   Within is **a** book—it is the Book of Knowledge, written in the Sanscrit language.   Study it well, obey its precepts, and the wealth is yours.'

Scarcely had the sick man uttered these words ere his friend and attendant burst from the cell, and turning towards the entrance of the cavern, perceiving not the cunning Jew, hastily departed, leaving the Gosein to die without him.

Ismael, desirous of gaining more information on so important a subject, and remembering his pony, which he knew would convey him to the wished-for place long ere the Gosein's friend on foot could get there, glided into the cell and grasped the Gosein's hand.

The sick man, his eyes closed, his countenance wasted away, and his tongue parched, feebly returned the pressure, and continued, in a low and almost inaudible voice, his benevolent instructions, as he imagined, to his attentive charitable friend. 'Be sure,' said he, 'to possess yourself, my friend, of both the keys of this iron box; the one, I told you, was in the lock, the other you will find in a small niche to the right.' (Here his voice failed him; the Gosein gave a convulsive shudder, groaned, and expired.)

Ismael, convinced his informer was no more, quickly followed the former person's example, and hurried from the cavern. Having descended the mountain, he sought his tattoo, which, however, had slipped his bridle from the stump to which his master had fastened him, and was grazing at some little distance. The angry Jew, grudging this loss of time, quickly mounted his pony, and turning his head towards Bombay, made him feel the weight of his stick pretty handsomely.

As he continued to urge on his tattoo, he fancied he heard the sound of horses' hoofs immediately preceding him. The night was not so dark but he could see his way, though trembling for

his neck at every step of the pony.   **Some one** was preceding him
he was convinced, for he distinctly heard the neighing of a horse :
to overtake the man he felt to be impossible ; nor was he anxious
to do so, lest **he** should be detained **or** impeded in his progress.
With difficulty did the anxious Jew get his tired pony **to** descend
the Ghaut and arrive at Campowli, the name of the village at the
foot of it ; to go farther was impossible, his tattoo was jaded, and
himself shaken and sorely **tired.**   With such a golden harvest
before him, however, on his own bodily fatigue he bestowed not **a**
thought ; and leaving his tattoo with the potail[1] **of the** village,
procured a fresh one, and once more started on his way.

At Chowk he did the same, and reached Panwell three hours
before sunrise ; here, alas ! ponies or horses would have been of
little use, for his way laid across the sea, and he loudly called for
a boat.   He was informed that the only one had been hired by a
Brahmin about three hours ago ; added to which, the tide would
not then serve, were there a fleet of boats to be had.   What a
disappointment **to** the greedy Jew !   The certainty, however, that
by his expeditious travelling he had been sufficiently beforehand
with the Gosein's friend, alone consoled him for this unavoidable
obstruction to the path of wealth, and he inwardly chuckled as he
pictured to himself the woful countenance of the man, on discovering the iron box to be flown.

Ismael, in order to seize the first boat which might arrive,
remained fixed to the water's edge until morning beamed.   **A**
fishing-boat soon appeared with the coming tide, and the Jew
lost no time in striking a bargain **with** the fisherman to convey

---

[1] Head man.

him first to the Island of Gharipoori, and from thence to Bombay. Gharipoori [1] is a hill whereon is a small village, through which the Jew hastily passed, and commenced his ascent of the mountain through romantic passes, o'ershadowed by wood or walled by rocks, until he arrived at the cavern. Having lately come from Carli, Ismael was not so much struck with the appearance of Gharipoori as he otherwise would have been. It seemed at first all darkness ; but he gradually became reconciled to the gloom, and proceeded into the vast chamber, whose entrance is nearly sixty feet wide and length the same, and fully twenty in height. The whole he found supported by massy pillars, carved in the solid rock. Anxiously did he cast his eye on the fourth column on his left hand ; but ere he ventured to approach it, gazed in wonder at all he saw. Gigantic figures stood or reclined all around him ; and in the centre at the farther extremity, immediately opposite the entrance, he discerned the three-formed god of the Hindús—Brahma, Vishnu, and Seva. The Jew was lost in wonder how these works could have been brought to perfection ; and well he might, for to accomplish such a labour forty thousand men for forty years would scarcely be sufficient.

Having cautiously looked around him, and satisfied he was alone, the Jew approached the fourth column, at the base of which he discovered a small square stone, which with difficulty he removed, and thrust in his hand to seize the iron box ; but, oh ! how great was his dismay and vexation to find it was gone. Unwilling to be convinced of the fatal truth, he again inserted his

---

[1] Called by the Portuguese Elephanta, from the circumstance of a colossal tone elephant being placed opposite to the landing-place.

hand; he felt **to** the **left, to the** right, **but** nothing could **he** discover. **In** despair, he was about to cover up the place, when he remembered the dying words of the Gosein to himself, and searching more minutely to the right hand of the stone receptacle, discoverd the niche, in which was suspended on a nail, **a** small key of curious workmanship, which with avidity he grasped. Ismael doubted not, but that notwithstanding all his expedition **the** Gosein's friend had been beforehand with him and secured the box, which he still hoped would one day be his.

Ismael, vexed and disappointed, returned to his boat, desiring the fishermen to row hard to Bombay, which they accordingly did, and landed the Jew in safety. The Jew's wife had been anxiously looking out for his arrival, and when she perceived his haggard look and care-worn countenance, expressed her alarm lest he had failed in his speculations, **or** been robbed **on** his way home. **Ismael** assured her all had gone well, declared he was much fatigued by his journey (and well he might be), and desired her to prepare his bed and a cup of coffee directly. Vexation and disappointment effectually banished sleep from Ismael's eyes, and symptoms of fever greatly alarmed him; he took an opiate, which, however, instead of lulling his tortured brain, had a direct opposite effect, and he was seized with a delirium bordering upon madness.

A brother Jew, called a doctor, visited poor Ismael, and administered first one drug and then another without effect. The patient raved incessantly; his imagination seemed to dwell on some scene of horror which he, it was supposed, had witnessed in his travels; he spoke of the dying Gosein, cursed his friend for **stealing** money, then burst into a hysteric laugh, and sunk, overcome with the violent exertion. **Many long** days and tedious nights did Ismael pass, stretched on his bed of sickness, and long **was it ere** the fever left him : that he ever recovered was to his neighbours, who had witnessed his sad state, most extraordinary.

When completely recovered, Ismael, far **from** giving up all **idea** of the iron box, **determined** to become possessed of it. The first step towards **the** accomplishment of his wishes, **was to** ascertain in whose possession it was; and the second, **a very** material point ere he could reap any benefit from the contents of it, to learn the language in which the Book of Knowledge was written. That it was Sanscrit he had heard the Gosein declare, but he was utterly ignorant of this language, sacred alone **to the** Brahmins and religious and learned Hindús. That ignorance should **not** exclude him from the acquirement of wealth, the Jew, long ere he busied himself to discover who possessed the book, commenced the study of the Sanscrit language, to which he devoted one entire year, and with such earnestness did he prosecute his studies, that at the expiration of that period he could decipher the most ancient and difficult writings in that learned tongue. For some time he could gain not the slightest clue to direct him **how** to discover the possessor of the wished-for Book of Knowledge.

When, however, the public curiosity became excited respecting the unaccountable manner of living **of** Donga Sette Brahmin, notwithstanding every species of tyranny had **been** practised on him **by** the Portuguese Government—his lands sequestrated, his trees cut down, and every visible mode of living denied him— Ismael entertained **a** strong suspicion this man possessed the

Book of Knowledge, that grand **key** to inexhaustible wealth. In order that he might himself be certified of this fact, the Jew proposed to the Governor the searching for treasure **in** the Brahmin's house, not with any idea the crafty Brahmin would **be so** imprudent in these times **as to** bury gold in any part of the house, but because he, accompanying the searchers, would have an opportunity (otherwise impossible to have obtained) of ascertaining **whether** his suspicions respecting the iron box were well or ill founded.

Ismael, during the search for money, anxiously cast around his eyes to discover the longed-for box, which he determined to secretly possess himself of. The Brahmin's **retiring to the** outer verandah during the search afforded him a golden opportunity to carry his plan into execution. **In** the **centre of** the Brahmin's house stood his great idol, Gunputty, with the elephant's head ; and at its feet, to Ismael's joy, was a small iron box, which with avidity he pounced upon, but was again doomed to be disappointed. It was chained by a chain of steel, and secured by a strong padlock to the idol's leg. One point was only gained : Donga Sette was in truth the possessor of the Book of Knowledge ; and Ismael, pleased by the acquisition of this first step towards gaining it himself, left the Brahmin with a **mock** reverence and significant movement of the eye, as has been already related.

The Governor's demand for an instant supply of money, much to the Jew's discomfiture, for the present interrupted his plans ; and with the golden harvest in view, his concern at finding himself sinking in mud, death staring him in the face, and no help at hand, may easily be conceived.

CHAPTER VI.

THE COPPERSMITH'S STORY (*continued*).

EARLY in the morning the two travellers arose, each to pursue his respective route. The Jew, however, seeing his friend—a fine, handsome, active young Mahommedan—felt somewhat curious to learn the cause of his grief, which he had expressed on the preceding night by sobs and lamentations. Ere they parted, therefore, Ismael, with a pretended display of fellow-feeling and compassion, enquired what could have caused him so much distress ; and further, to induce his companion to be communicative, hinted his readiness and desire to render him any assistance in his power. The young man, without hesitation, gave the following account of himself :—

' My name is Alnusur ; my father was a respectable merchant, residing at Cambay ; I was his only son, and he indulged me in all I could wish or desire. The great object of my father was that I should marry, and become steady and attentive to business. To this I could offer no objection, but stipulated that the woman should meet my approbation in every respect, and that unless she possessed great beauty I would never consent to wed. My father in vain preached to me of the advantages to be derived from the beauty of the mind, not the person ; **I** shook my head and adhered firmly to my determination.   The reason why I thus stipulated was because **I** strongly suspected my father had his eye upon the daughter of a great friend of his, who happened to **be** my particular aversion, both on account of **her** excessive ugliness and incorrigible temper.

'I was ruminating on matrimony, when a palanquin, with its curtains closely drawn, attended by several servants, passed close by me.   I learned from the bystanders the sedan contained the beautiful Zaide, daughter of the Deewan and prime minister of his highness the Nuwab.   "What would I give," thought I, "to gain a sight of this lovely creature, of whose beauty report speaks so highly !"   Scarcely had I allowed this idea to skim through my brain, ere the litter, which I had kept my **eye** firmly fixed upon, by some accountable accident broke **down**.   I rushed to the **lady's** aid, and sedulously kept aloof the officious and inquisitive bystanders.   The attendants, indeed, were equally assiduous in their attempts to drive me from the broken litter ; but with great perseverance, and by evincing the greatest anxiety for the lady's safety, I was suffered to assist in raising her, and was rewarded by a sweet smile from the too lovely Zaide.

'I suggested she should enter a house until I could procure another palanquin, as it was impossible to make use again of the broken one, and equally **so** for her to walk through the streets. Zaide assented to the plan ; and having seen her safely lodged in a respectable merchant's house, I ran quickly to the nearest place where **I** knew a palanquin was to be had.   The bearers followed

me, and taking up the litter, I accompanied them to the merchant's house. Zaide thanked me for my zeal, enquiring to
whom she was indebted for such attention. I informed her
my name, and professed myself her slave at all times. Her veil
being now closely drawn over her face, allowed not of my
being gratified by a second view of her transcendent beauty, but
the melody of her voice almost compensated me for my disappointment.

'Returned home, in an ecstasy I rushed to my father, who was
busily employed in his warehouse. "Oh, father!" I cried, "I have
seen the woman whom alone I will wed." Ere he could speak, I
ran on with a string of epithets in praise of her beauty, with such
volubility that my fond parent conceived me mad ; when, however, I at length ceased, the expected question of "Who is the
lady?" burst upon my ears. "Who? Why, who can it be but
Zaide, the daughter of Harak, the Deewan?" said I.

'My father stood fixed to the spot, maintaining an awful
silence, which he at length broke by saying, "Oh, my son, what
has possessed you? Reflect on the haughty disposition of the
Deewan ; recollect also his thirst for gold, and his towering ambition. Think you he will ever consent to a union with his
daughter? I pray you drive all idea of the kind from your
bewildered brain."

'The more my father begged and prayed, and the more difficulty he pointed out to me, the more obstinately determined did
I become, until, won by my earnest entreaties, my father consented to apply to the haughty Harak. I fell at his feet, pouring
out my most grateful thanks, and buoying him up with the cer-

tainty of **success.** My indulgent parent accordingly promised **to** do all I could desire, but expressed his fears that all would be to no purpose.

'On the following day my father solicited an interview **with the** Deewan, leaving me at home in indescribable anxiety for the result **of** the visit. I had not long to wait; my father returned bathed in tears, declaring we were ruined irreparably, for **the** Deewan no sooner heard his presumptuous proposals than **he** fell into a dreadful rage, **and** rushed to his daughter's apartments, from whence he returned **convulsed with** wrath. **He** threatened us with everlasting ruin **if we** quitted **not** Cambay **in eight-and-**forty hours. He was prompted to this, probably, by having ascertained from Zaide her partiality **towards myself. What stung** my father to the quick was his abuse of us—he called us shop-keepers, pedlars, cheating dealers, and expressed his amazement **at our** audacity in dreaming of obtaining his consent to a union **with his** daughter, a descendant of **a** vizier, and connected with royalty itself. When my father's grief had in a measure subsided, he sent a petition **to** the Deewan to revoke his cruel sentence of banishment from Cambay; but this only exasperated the tyrant the more, and he repeated his orders in so peremptory a manner as to leave **no** hope of mercy in our bosoms.

'With a heavy heart did my father quit his native country and take **up** his residence in Thanah, on this island, where, being a stranger, he was looked upon with envy by the rest of the old-established merchants of the town, who effected his ruin, and he sickened and died, leaving me a beggar. I was lamenting the loss of my father, my mistress, and my means of subsistence, when your voice arrested my attention, and interrupted for a moment the melancholy train of ideas floating through my brain.'

The Jew expressed his compassion for the unhappy young man, and his hopes that he should be farther acquainted with him, for that possibly it would be in his power to render him assistance. He explained to him, therefore, the situation of his house in Bombay, desiring him to call there after two days' time; and as an earnest of his good intentions, presented him with a sum of money for his present exigencies. Alnusur was extremely grateful to his benevolent fellow-traveller; and promising to call on him at the time appointed, took his leave. Ismael, whose whole thoughts were occupied with one subject only, had enjoyed little or no repose during the night, and he determined to enquire into the circumstances of his fellow-traveller, in the hope that some recent affliction might have so reduced him as to render him a fit tool for the accomplishment of his purposes. Alnusur's melancholy history, therefore, was rather pleasing to the Jew than otherwise, and he determined on enlisting the youth into his service, and employing him in the difficult task of purloining from the Brahmin the wished-for Book of Knowledge. For this purpose did he appoint a meeting with him at his house in Bombay.

Having arranged his business at Thanah, and obtained the money for the Governor, Ismael returned to Bombay, and, agreeably to the appointment, waited for Alnusur, who, equally anxious, was punctual to the time agreed upon. Ismael drew him aside, and thus addressed him :—

'Young man, fortune has used you cruelly, but you have now an opportunity of reaping a great advantage. I will serve you by a liberal advancement **of** cash, and place **you** in the way **to** accumulate a handsome independence, provided you will steadily adhere to business, and make the most of your time and money.'

Alnusur had commenced overpowering the benevolent Jew with expressions of gratitude, when Ismael stopped him, saying : **'Stay,** young man ; you must earn these advantages ere you receive them. I have a task to perform, which my age and inactivity prevent my engaging in personally. You are young and strong, and can depend upon your nerves. Will you undertake the business ? '

' That,' replied Alnusur, ' depends upon the nature of **it ; and** I tell you frankly, if **it** be murder, **or——'**

' No, no, no ! ' interrupted Ismael, ' 'tis no such thing. Listen to me. There lives a man in this island who is in the possession **of** a book containing only a history of Jewish rites and ceremonies, **of** great importance to me, and of no use whatever to him. In **vain** have **I** attempted to bargain with the man for this small **book** ; the more anxious I appear to possess it the more tenacious of it is its ill-natured possessor.'

'This is indeed very strange,' observed Alnusur, 'and I think **I** should be guilty of no crime whatever in obtaining it for you. Would you instruct me how to proceed ? '

The Jew's eyes twinkled with delight, and he replied, ' I can direct you to the house wherein this book is preserved, but there are difficulties attending the seizure of it you are little aware of. The name of the man who has the book is Donga Sette, a Brahmin, living in the small village of Geergaum. He seldom quits his house, and when he does leaves such strict orders with his wife to admit neither friends or strangers during his temporary absence, **that** to gain a footing, even for a minute, is next to impossible.'

'Trust me,' said Alnusur; 'although I am a Mahommedan, I will gain an entrance to the Brahmin's mansion, rely on it.'

'Allowing you **do,**' continued the Jew, 'the book is as far from your reach as ever—he keeps it chained in an iron box, fastened to the leg **of a** huge ugly idol, in the centre of his house. Violence must **not be** attempted, for although the Brahmin is obnoxious to the Government, yet his **money will** obtain him justice.'

'Artifice,' said Alnusur, 'often effects what violence cannot.'

'**True,** young man,' said Ismael'; 'but it must be artifice most deadly deep which can succeed in the present instance, **for the** Brahmin keeps the key of the steel chain by which the box is secured **to** his idol, together with **the** key of the box itself, continually about his person, and when himself and his wife are both **from** home (which I believe happens only once a year) the key of his house also.'

'Could I but effect **an** entrance,' said Alnusur, 'a file might be of use.'

'Not at all,' said Ismael; 'no file, let its teeth be ever so sharp, will be able to cut the polished steel; therefore you must think of some other plan. It may be a year before you even get a clue to the slightest probability of success. I, if satisfied you are daily exerting your ingenuity in my service, will grant you a monthly allowance sufficient for your maintenance; but visit me as seldom as possible.'

Alnusur promised obedience, and swore to be zealously employed in the service of the **Jew, but** hinted the possibility **of** Ismael's failing in his promise to enrich him, in **the** event of his labours being crowned with success.

'Should I do so, could I be so base?' replied Ismael. 'You have always revenge in your power by betraying **me** to the Brahmin, who will not fail to bring me to justice.'

'True,' replied Alnusur; 'but recollect, in so doing **I shall** criminate myself.'

'As you please then, young man,' said Ismael. 'I have only **my** promise to give you; will you consent?'

'What sum am I to receive?'

'One thousand dollars, and a shop in the bazaar, all ready for you to commence trade.'

'Well, then,' replied Alnusur, 'when **you give me** the money I will deliver over to you the box.'

'Agreed,' replied the Jew ; 'and when **you** give me the box, provided the book is within it, I will give you the money and the **shop.'**

Both parties mutually understanding each other, they separated.

It may be supposed Alnusur's first step was to reconnoitre the residence of the Brahmin, which he did, not without wondering what could be the contents of this book for which the Jew offered so large a sum, and what could be the Brahmin's motive for retaining it. 'However,' thought he, 'this is no affair of mine, and I am determined to get possession of it somehow or other.' In various disguises did he attempt to gain a footing in the Brahmin's house, but all with no avail. **If** he went as a fakir or holy beggar, alms were never denied him, but liberally bestowed, by either Donga Sette or his wife, from the verandah of the house. **If he** went as a visitor only, he was desired to go **about his business.** Some repairs being necessary in the roof of the Brahmin's house, Alnusur, disguised as a bricklayer's labourer, contrived **to** get a peep into the house, **and** actually saw the iron box, chained, as the Jew had informed him, to the leg of the idol. Nevertheless he was far, very far **from any chance** of securing it. In vain did he rack **his invention to devise** schemes **for** the accomplishment of his purpose, and began to **despair of being able** to succeed. The **Jew also became** impatient, and gave with **an ill grace** the monthly allowance to his willing but inefficient agent. **As Ismael** had observed, a year had passed without Alnusur having advanced **a** step towards the fulfilment **of his** wishes.

The Brahmin, in the meanwhile, although little dreaming of **the vile intentions of** Alnusur **or the** Jew, lived as before, keeping **a vigilant eye upon the** iron box, and carrying the keys affixed by **a ring to his silver** kurdoorah, or waist-chain, day and night. **N**ot once **during the year did it** happen that Donga Sette and his wife were both at the same instant absent from home. At last a ray of hope **darted** across the brain of Alnusur. A Jatra, which happened only **once in** seven years, and at which every strict Hindoo attended to obtain absolution and purification from their sins, was now about to take place, and the mode which **the** idolatrous people adopted to ensure such absolution and forgiveness **is of so** singular a nature that it demands a full explanation. It was **this** strange ordeal everyone was called upon to submit to which suggested to Alnusur the possibility of his being able to turn it **to** advantage.

In the island **of** Bombay, about two miles from the town, rises a considerable **hill** stretching into the ocean and forming a sort of promontory. At the extreme point **of** this hill, **on** the descent towards the seashore, there is a rock, upon the surface **of** which there is a natural crevice, which communicates with **a** cavity, opening below and terminating towards the sea. **This place** is used by the Hindoos as a purification for their sins, which they pretend is effected by their going in at the opening above and emerging out of the cavity below. At the celebration of this Jatra crowds of persons of all ranks and castes invariably attend, and several await below the aperture **to catch in** their arms the purified Hindoo and break his fall on the uneven ground. There was a rude path by which those from above could descend to the seashore; and a constant running **up and down** takes place during the eventful day.

Early on the morning **of the** day of the holy Jatra, Alnusur posted himself near the opening of the rock above, and watched the process of purification, amusing himself by witnessing the timidity **of** some people and the confident boldness of others. Women as well as men subjected themselves to this looked-for purification, which many submitted to from mere impulse of curiosity, and many for the sole amusement of sliding through a hole. About the middle of the day came the persons Alnusur was most desirous of seeing, viz. the Brahmin, Donga Sette, and his wife. Alnusur, having ascertained the precise moment when the Brahmin would undergo the ceremony, hastened by the rough path to join the rabble below, who with outstretched arms awaited the coming **of** fresh subjects through the wonderful **crevice.**

Alnusur had planned the seizure of the Brahmin's keys whilst **he evinced** an earnest desire to save his victim from falling on the **rocky** ground below. For this purpose did he station himself foremost amidst the crowd below, anxiously awaiting the coming of the worthy Brahmin. Donga Sette, the last time he performed this ceremony, **had slided** down the aperture with no difficulty whatever; but he unfortunately forgot how very fat and unwieldy he had since that time become; consequently, to the no small amusement of the spectators, he stuck fast about the middle of the crevice and roared aloud for help. The rabble below, hearing peals **of** laughter from above, and seeing a man sticking **in the** hole, one and all, save Alnusur, rushed up the path, and were soon at the opening above. Alnusur with joy perceived his victim sticking almost within his reach; he peeped up the crevice **and saw** the Brahmin's shining silver kurdoorah and the wished-for keys hanging thereunto, but, alas! both out of his reach. That the poor man might not easily be extricated by the persons above, he gave him a tight pull by the heels, which fixed poor Donga Sette still faster in his narrow prison. The Brahmin roared with pain, and complained of the treatment he was suffering from some one below; but the noise, the shouting of the rabble above, effectually drowned his voice Still the keys tantalised Alnusur by swinging from the kirdoorah, just beyond his **reach.** The silver waist-chain being fastened by a screw in the front, fingers alone could loosen it. How Alnusur was to contrive so **as** to effect this he knew not; no time was to be lost, for he expected every moment to witness the bulky Brahmin drawn up by the people above. Donga Sette writhed and kicked about his legs most impatiently, although he little dreamed **of** the robbery about to be practised on him by an enemy below; had such an idea entered his head, he would doubtless have been absolutely frantic. Alnusur cast around his eye, and to his joy perceived two oars belonging to a fishing-boat; he instantly secured them, and taking off his turban, formed a sort of ladder by which he was enabled to reach the Brahmin's waist. The moment Donga Sette felt his sacred chain touched by a human hand he yelled and kicked so violently that Alnusur, on his slender ladder, was fearfully alarmed lest he should fall. Securing one of the Brahmin's legs with one hand with all the force he was master of, he succeeded in unscrewing the silver chain, and effectually removed it, with the keys attached; quickly descending, he untied his turban, which had served him for steps to his ladder, threw away the oars, left the silver chain on the ground below, and scampered off by a narrow path towards the town of Bombay. When at a distance, secure from pursuit, he examined the keys. There was one large one, which doubtless belonged to the house; a second, rather smaller, which probably fitted the padlock on the steel chain; and a third, smaller than either, of curious workmanship, which **he** doubted not belonged to the iron box. The latter Alnusur determined not to surrender to the Jew, hoping, by withholding it under the plea that it was not on the Brahmin's person, he would offer an additional reward for its recovery at a future period. Should the Jew, however, refuse to repay him at the present time, and insist on being possessed of the key, he intended to request a few **days' time** to procure it, and finally to **present** it **to** Ismael, magnifying the dangers he had encountered in purloining **it from the Brahmin.** With these intentions Alnusur quickly proceeded to the residence of the Brahmin. All persons being at the Jatra, no one impeded his progress, and he quietly opened the house-door. Entering the centre apartment, with joy did he perceive the iron **box** in its usual place; **he** fitted the key to the padlock, it turned, and the box was quickly concealed beneath his coat. Leaving the house expeditiously, he sallied onwards to the residence of old Ismael, who fortunately was within.

The Israelite saw by the sparkling of Alnusur's eyes he was the bearer of good news, and anxiously did he question him; **but when** the youth tapped significantly on the lid **of** the very box beneath his coat, the ecstasy **of** the Jew was unbounded. He embraced his trusty agent, and demanded the box. Alnusur reminded him of the reward. Ismael opened a strong box, took out the dollars, presented them, and received the iron box, which **he in** his joy pressed to his heart. As he turned to the window to examine it, Alnusur, gathering up **his** dollars, quickly left the house; he had scarcely gone twenty paces from the outer door, however, when he heard the voice of the Jew hallooing after him **most** lustily. Alnusur turned round, nodded, waved his hand, and signed to the anxious Jew his intention of speedily returning. Having deposited his dollars **in** a place of safety, Alnusur once more repaired to Ismael's mansion, and innocently enquired his commands.

'**The** key, boy, the key! where is the key of the iron box? Fool **that I was to** give you the money without demanding the key.'

' The key!' exclaimed Alnusur. 'Oh, you never told me about the key; my agreement was **to** deliver to **you** the box only.'

' Idiot!' replied the Jew. 'Of what use is the box without the key? Besides, we agreed that, unless the book was within the box, you should not be entitled to your reward; how am I to ascertain whether such be the case or not?'

' Break open the box, to be sure,' replied Alnusur, quite **un-**concerned.

' You **know not** what you say, young man; but **tell me,** attached to the key of the padlock of the steel chain, did not you perceive a smaller key?'

' No, indeed; by Mahomet there **was only** the key of the house, by which I obtained an entrance.'

' How did you contrive to get these keys?'

' That is no matter, worthy Master Ismael. I have had trouble enough, I can tell you, in getting the keys of the box, and your discontent, because the key of the iron box is not delivered to you, **I am** greatly surprised at. By Allah! I think it is lucky I secured my reward, **or** you would have withheld it, I am thinking.'

' Doubtless,' replied the Jew, 'your work **is** only half done. However, I promise you five hundred dollars in addition, if you will procure the key for me.'

' I fear 'tis impossible,' replied Alnusur; 'such an opportunity as I have had this day will never occur again. However, I will try, rely on it; but as it **is** the book you want, why not break open the box? What signifies the **key?**'

' **It** must not be done, boy. Go, **leave** me, and to your task once more. **Remember, the** shop I **promised is** still in my possession.'

'**Ay,** ay, Master Ismael,' said Alnusur; 'and were you an honest man, it ought now to be mine, according to your promise.'

To this the Jew replied only by repeating, 'The key, the key, **boy; go, go to your task** once more.'

Alnusur, congratulating himself on his own cunning, left the delighted Jew, and returned to his lodging.

Ismael, **it** will be remembered, was in possession of one of the keys; but anxious for both, suffered Alnusur to depart, under the idea **he** had no means **of** opening the box save by violence. When he first agreed with the young man he was so fully certain the key would naturally be delivered with the box, in the event of his being able to purloin it, that the necessity of making a separate stipulation for its production never entered his head; and so overjoyed was he at seeing Alnusur enter with the box, that he unhesitatingly paid the promised reward. That Alnusur actually had the key in his possession, and wilfully withheld it, never entered Ismael's brain; for, having surrendered the box, he could not possibly suppose, had the boy got the key, he could have any motive in refusing to surrender it. When Alnusur had refused to obey the Jew's call to return, Ismael contented himself with just **peeping** into the box; and seeing the wonderful book safe within it, closed it, expecting the return of his agent. Thus, after great patience and the aid of craft, did Ismael at length become the possessor of the Book of Knowledge.

CHAPTER VII.

THE COPPERSMITH'S STORY (*continued*).

THE unhappy **Donga Sette** having with considerable difficulty been extricated from the rocky crevice, instantly **placed his hand** on his waist, to **ascertain if** all **was safe.** The kirdoorah, alas! was gone. For the loss of this, however, he grieved but little ; but the keys, the sacred keys, being missing also, caused him much agony of mind. To his wife did he pour **out the** sorrow of his soul, and to the crowd did he loudly assert the cruel robbery **practised** on him, and lamented the loss of his silver chain in so **moving** a manner that many offered their assistance to recover it if possible. Some, indeed, consoled him with expressing their hopes **that** by a **strict** search below it would be found, as it most probably had fallen off the Brahmin's person. Donga Sette's wife accompanied a party of searchers to the seashore, and there, sure enough, she found the chain, but alas! the keys **were gone.** The Brahmin, **to the surprise** of the bystanders, exhibited no signs of delight on receiving his chain, for the loss of which he **had so** loudly complained; they little knew the real source of his grief. The fact was, he had rather indulged in a hope that the chain had attracted the **eye of** some thief who, having obtained it, would perhaps bestow no attention on the keys suspended thereon. The result of the search proving the direct contrary to be the case, cast a gloom of despair over the unhappy man's countenance unaccountable to the wondering multitude.

Both the Brahmin and his wife, long after the conclusion of the Jatra and dispersion of the multitude, continued groping about below the fissure; but alas! darkness coming on, with woful visages they abandoned the search and returned home. Arrived at his house, the Brahmin's worst fears were realised the instant he perceived his outer door open and the key within the lock. To the idol he at once approached; his iron box, so carefully guarded, was gone, and he threw himself on the floor in utter despair.

The first page of the book had informed him of the existence of two keys, on perusing which he instantly returned to the Gharipoori cavern in search after the second key, but owing to the Jew's visit to the same spot, was unsuccessful. Not in possession, therefore, of the second key, Donga Sette conceived it necessary to guard the box with more than ordinary vigilance, and would, but for the unfortunate Jatra, probably have retained possession of it for many years longer. Who could be the person now so fortunate as to have the Book of Knowledge? What enemy had robbed him of his invaluable treasure? And how, without money, was he to exist? These perplexities kept the worthy Brahmin wide awake the whole of this miserable night, and by the morning he was suffering from fever, which all the skill of his wife could not subdue.

Let it not be imagined that the Brahmin, knowing of the

repository of **wealth,** could, independent **of** the directory (the Book of Knowledge), at any time visit the delightful spot. Easy, indeed, would have been his descent to the hoarded treasure, but to retrace his steps, to be certain **of** a safe retreat, was, without the guide, without the golden book, next to impossible. **The means** of exit from the cavern were of themselves a difficult study ; for each particular day was a different mode of egress planned and appointed ; and so intricate on this head were the rules and instructions, and so dependent on the moon, the sun, and the stars were the sanctioned **days of** visitation to the cavern, that without the Book of Knowledge to visit the spot was, he knew, risking his **life.** The Brahmin regretted he had not employed himself in transcribing the wondrous pages—this might have now **proved of** the greatest utility ; yet, without the original, he consoled himself by **firmly** believing his success would have been uncertain **and of short** duration.

The crafty Ismael, on perusing the book, staggered as he **perceived** the difficulties attendant **on** the acquirement of his wished-for **gold. He had** imagined the **book** would direct him to a hoard **which he** might, if he pleased, visit every day, **and** extract as much **of** the precious ore as suited his convenience. That any caution or study was necessary to ensure his exit from the cavern he never dreamed **of.** Greatly, therefore, was he vexed and perplexed on perusing the intricate instructions, the solemn warnings, and the exhortations **to** practise all good works, and denouncements of ruin and evendeath should he neglect to follow **the** many excellent moral **rules** laid down in separate **chapters in** the Book of Knowledge.

In the first page, in large letters, was written: 'He who possesses this book let him preserve it in the iron box, and be in possession of both its keys.' Next followed the days sanctioned and appointed for visiting the treasure-chamber; the mode of entrance, and the difficulties, without strict attention to the book, of retreating. For each day a specified amount to be drawn was laid down, with heavy denunciations against a neglect of this rule. Next came chapters on every moral virtue, an obedience to which alone would crown the possessor of the book with permanent success. The very first chapter was on Charity, a virtue the Jew was an entire stranger to. At the commencement of this chapter, in large letters, was written, 'To turn a beggar from thy door is death.'

The second chapter was on Humanity, headed by these words: ' Pity the distressed, heal the wounded, comfort the widow, or thy gold shall be like burning coals unto thy fingers.'

The third chapter was on Patience, the fourth on Chastity, the fifth on Temperance, the sixth on Honesty, the seventh on Worship, and the Eighth on Frugality, all headed by a short sentence explanatory of their contents. Ismael shuddered on perusing these pages; he determined, however, to live according to these golden rules, which he thought he would study at his leisure, and or the present turn his attention to the means of entrance and exit from the cavern, and the day when he could dare to make his first visit.

Finding he should be under the necessity of waiting three days, he deposited the book in its iron case, and enclosed it in his strong-box. Scarcely had he done this ere Almusur visited him for the purpose of making some pretended report of his progress in securing the second key. The Jew, who had foolishly conceived he could do very well with only one key, evinced no great anxiety concerning the second, and repeated not his offer of reward to Alnusur, could he procure it. Alnusur, therefore, concluded he had succeeded in opening the box by some other means, and that consequently he had no hope, of reaping a second reward. Not willing to exhibit any signs of disappointment, he asked in a careless manner what language the book was written in. The Jew was on the point of informing him, when he checked himself, saying, 'How should I know until I have opened the iron box?'

'True,' said Alnusur; 'but as you informed me the book contained a history of Jewish rites and ceremonies, I thought perhaps .you might know in what language it was written.'

'What does it signify to you?' enquired the Jew. 'It is written, most probably, in some language which you do not understand, and never will; so farewell, young man.'

'Stay,' said Alnusur; 'where is my shop you promised me?'

'Where is the key?' replied the Jew.

'Oh, very well, Master Ismael; you may repent this deviation from your promise! Farewell, most upright Ismael.' The Jew waved his hand contemptuously, and Alnusur left the house.

Alnusur began to suspect that this wondrous book contained something more than a history of Jewish rites and ceremonies, and began to lay schemes for gaining possession of it. Congratulating himself on having one of its keys, he determined to watch the Jew narrowly, The first place Ismael repaired to was the residence of an old Brahmin, under whom he had studied the Sanscrit language, and whose farther instructions were now requisite ere he could comprehend several of the rules of the Book of Knowledge. Astronomy, also, he found must be attended to in a slight degree, and from his worthy preceptor he looked for every information on the subject. Alnusur watched the Jew to the learned Brahmin's house, and marked the time he remained there. When these visits became frequent, Alnusur, determined to learn the reason and purport of them, silently crept under the window of the house, and there distinctly heard both Brahmin and Jew singing and bellowing out whole verses of Sanscrit, and in conclusion heard the hour at night appointed for a lecture on astronomy. Alnusur, now convinced that the Book of Knowledge was written in the Sanscrit language, and that the study of the heavenly bodies also was indispensably necessary, set to work, under the tuition of a Brahmin, to perfect himself in both Sanscrit and astronomy.

The Jew, having devoted a whole year to his studies, and having now only the stars to attend to, and a few ancient words in the Sanscrit to comprehend, had, of course, the start of Alnusur, who was under the necessity of commencing a course of studies in a language and a science both of which he was entirely ignorant of. Nevertheless, the indefatigable young man, by the most persevering attention, made such great progress as to be able to read with tolerable accuracy in less than six months. So devoted was he to his studies, that he could spare not a moment in watching the footsteps of the **Jew,** who, studying the rules **of** the book, visited the Gharipoori **cavern** on **the** appointed days, and possessed himself of much wealth.

Donga Sette, in the meanwhile, busied himself **in** endeavouring to discover who had deprived him of his iron box, **the loss of** which had so sorely grieved him. It may be a matter **of** surprise that he did not watch at the cavern to ascertain in whose possession the book at present **was.** Donga Sette, in fact, **did proceed** several times to Gharipoori, and with true Brahminical patience ensconced himself for hours behind some one of the gigantic **figures,** which formed excellent screens for the purpose ; but all this while Ismael was prosecuting his Sanscrit and astronomical studies, determined to be perfect ere he ventured near the treasure-chamber ; hence Donga Sette became wearied by long and fruitless watchings, and in gloomy silence confined himself **to** his **house.**

As the loss of the Book of Knowledge was day and night **uppermost** in the Brahmin's thoughts, it is not surprising that he should **be** one night visited by **a** dream. He dreamed that Bhavanee, the consort **of** the God Mahadeo, appeared at the foot of his pallet, pronouncing his name three times distinctly. The goddess directed him to make a pilgrimage to the great temple of Jaggernaut, in Orissa, and instructed him as to the nature of the offerings he should make to the idol for the terrm **of** one month, at the expiration of which he would learn not only **who** possessed the Book of Knowledge, but by what means he might regain it.

This dream appearing to him three successive nights, Donga

Sette informed his **wife** of his determination to follow the instructions of the goddess Bhavanee, and intimated his intention **to** commence his long **journey** without loss of time. The poor woman in vain essayed to divert him from his purpose by urging the immense distance, and the difficulties to be apprehended on the road. Her spouse, bent on obeying the goddess, who had thrice condescended **to** appear before him, actually set out on his pilgrimage.

Ismael, who **had all along** dreaded being watched **by** the Brahmin **on** his **visit to** the cavern, **learned** with delight that Donga Sette had set out on a long journey, which would ensure his absence for some time, and leave him in uninterrupted possesssion of the mighty hoard at Gharipoori. **It** was the practice **of the** Jew never to hire the same boat twice, **and he** engaged but one boatman, who, with himself, was sufficient to row him safely **to the island.**

Thoroughly comprehending the Book of Knowledge, and the **means of** effecting both an entrance **to and** an exit from the cavern, Ismael boldly visited the repository of wealth, little dreaming his footsteps were narrowly watched by Alnusur, who, being now quite a Sanscrit scholar, commenced putting his plans into execution.

Many were the hours and days that Alnusur passed, with his eyes bent upon the Jew's door, and often did he tramp after the old Israelite, from one corner of the island **of** Bombay to the other. At last he watched him to the seashore, near the village of Mazagaum, where the Jew beckoned to a boatman, with whom he conversed. A boat soon approached the water's edge, and the boatman, showing signs **of** readiness, received on board **the** cautious Jew.

Ismael being seated **in** the boat, handled the oar with a dexterity which convinced Alnusur this was not his first attempt. The day was clear, and afforded a distinct view of all the islands in the harbour. Alnusur's anxious eye followed the Jew's boat to Deva Devi island, and he imagined it was there he intended to land; but straining his eyes, he perceived the little skiff skim round a point of land and make **for** Gharipoori, where it appeared **to** come to anchor.

Alnusur had often heard of the **famed cavern of** Elephanta, as the Portuguese called it, and the truth now dawned upon him, that therein was some repository of wealth, to which the Jew had been directed by the Book of Knowledge. Alnusur deemed it impolitic to await the return of the Jew, and therefore proceeded **to** his lodging. After turning in his mind various plans for watch-**ing** the Jew's motions in the cavern, he determined, as it was quite uncertain when he would pay his next visit, to proceed on the following morning early to the island of Gharipoori and recon-noitre the cavern, and take up his residence at the small village at the foot of the mountain, keeping a vigilant look-out for the Israelite's arrival, when he would ascend the hill, and conceal himself in some friendly niche in the cavern, from whence he would be able to observe every action, every motion of the wary Jew.

This plan was, as soon as morning dawned, put in execution; and Alnusur, ere the sun became powerful, reached the island and discharged the boatman. Quickly did he ascend the mountain;

the stupendous cavern **burst** upon his **astonished** sight, and he **stood lost in** wonder and admiration. **Feeling** within his bosom an indescribable glow **of delight, on** reflecting on his proximity to what his fancy pictured **to him** inexhaustible **treasure,** Alnusur darted into the cave, as **if** expecting that his very presence would **act as a** charm **to throw wide** the gates of wealth, when lo ! a huge **serpent of tremendous** thickness issued from **its** dark **recess,** hissed, reared its frightful head, **and darted across his path into a** gloomy **cell on the** opposite side of the cavern. The alarmed **Alnusur, on whose brow trickled a** death-like perspiration, hastily **retreated,** praising Allah for his protection in this time of danger. **At this period,** when superstition **held** sovereign **sway over the** minds **of all** classes, of whatever caste or persuasion, the appearance of the **awe-inspiring serpent was considered by** Alnusur as **ominous of some** pending danger, **and he for a** moment gave up **all intention of prosecuting his search.**

Upon returning to the village, however, all his former ambition, all his eager **thirst for wealth, returned** with their full force, and he endeavoured to banish from his mind all idea of danger. ' The **Jew,'** said he to himself, **' is** not harmed by the serpent, why should **I** then **fear? To-morrow will** I once **more** explore **the cavern.'** Not without an inward dread of witnessing something **even more horrible** than had met his eye on the preceding **day did** Alnusur **slowly** ascend the hill, carrying in his hand a stout **pole,** by which **he might** defend himself from snakes and other **reptiles.**

Nothing, however, interrupted his entrance **this** day ; yet when **in the** centre of the cavern, the only living being on the spot, a dead-silence reigning all around, and surrounded on every side by numerous colossal statues, whose hideous countenances, carved by expert sculptors, seemed frowning in anger upon him, Alnusur's fears **once more** overpowered him, and **he stood** trembling, **not** daring to lift his eyes from the ground. **When at** length he became convinced no danger was at hand he raised his pole, and advanced to the three-formed god, opposite **to the entrance ; he** searched above and below, but nothing like an aperture **or door** did he discover.

To await the arrival of the Jew was his only **chance, and lest** he should be **now** on his way, he determined **to return to the** village and patiently await **his** coming. **He** retraced his steps, passing the awful row of **gigantic** statues, which **he now** minutely inspected. Some were crowned with helmets, others with crowns rich in every device, and many with snakes **twisted** through their **arms,** which were attached to their unwieldy bodies. The visages **of the** figures, distorted into horrible and fearful forms, inspired **the** youth with inexpressible terror, and he hastily effected his retreat.

For many days did Alnusur look **out** in vain **for the coming** of old Ismael ; **no** boat had approached the island since he had resided there.

At length the anxious Alnusur one morning espied a fishing-boat, containing two individuals, one of whom evidently was the wished-for Jew.

Alnusur, convinced it was indeed Ismael, scampered up the hill, bearing his formidable pole, and entering the cavern, searched out **a** hiding-place, from whence, unobserved, he could watch the Israelite's motions. For this purpose he concealed himself behind the stupendous bust, the three-formed god, opposite the entrance of the cavern ; from hence he could command a view of the whole place, and doubted not success would attend him. He had not waited long in his friendly niche, when a slow and cautious foot-step approached. It was the wary tread of Ismael, the Jew, pro-ceeding towards one of the colossal statues, which stood entirely separate from the rocky side of the cave, upon a circular stone platform, nearly six feet in circumference. The Jew stood with his side towards Alnusur, who was enabled to see his every action. Taking from his cloak a small round piece of wood, about a foot in length, Ismael pressed it on the toe-nail of the right foot of the statue, which yielding to the touch, Alnusur perceived th statue and its platform gradually recede, exposing a cavity, through which the Jew prepared to descend. As soon as he had disappeared the image by a sudden jerk darted into its original place, leaving no trace of its having been disturbed.

Alnusur waited patiently in his hiding-place until he perceived the statue once more in motion, and the Jew appeared bearing in his hand a bag evidently well filled. By a pressure on the toe of the left foot the statue again closed over the aperture, leaving all as before. The Jew examined his bag, saying aloud, 'This is well; to-morrow its fellow shall be in my possession ; till then, most friendly statue, farewell !'

. Alnusur, after waiting a prudent time, to be certain the Jew would not return, emerged from behind the three-formed deity, seized his pole, which he had concealed in a convenient place, and proceeding towards the image, pressed the toe as he had seen the Jew do before him, and to his joy the platform receded, and presented to the young man's view a flight of narrow rough stone steps, by means of which he quickly descended. To his surprise the platform of itself closed-to with so sudden and strong a jerk as to shake the stairs on which he was standing.

Descending the narrow stairs, Alnusur, by a light which came from he knew not where, placed his foot on some uneven broken ground, scattered over with triangular pieces of stone, which lacerated his feet dreadfully, and he anxiously sought for a more comfortable footing. Becoming by degrees familiar to the cavern's light, Alnusur perceived this broken stony ground extended for many yards, and beyond it, a well-paved place, over which were scattered piles of silver in bars. Ancient coins, gold rings, and ornaments were numerous; but the piles of copper coin, with which the place abounded, astonished the delighted Alnusur. There were also bags containing precious stones, and gold coins dazzling to behold. Discovering a pile of small gold rupees, Alnusur counted over ten thousand; these he secured about his person in a long narrow bag, which he had taken care to provide himself with, and then prepared to quit the place. He ascended the narrow stairs, with difficulty maintaining his footing, they being rugged, uneven, and unprotected by any railing to prevent his falling upon the rocky ground below. Arrived at the top stair, he waited patiently for the accommodating statue to suffer him to retire ; but alas ! closed was the aperture, and all his attempts to escape ineffectual. He examined the lower part of the platform, which he found was studded with brass knobs of various sizes, surrounding a plate of ivory, on which was engraven in Sanscrit the following verse :—

> If of advice you stand in need,
> With care the Book of Knowledge **read** ;
> To learn from hence how you **should flee,**
> Read the book, and you will **see.**

' **This,** then, is the **Book of** Knowledge, **by** which **the Jew** succeeds !' cried Alnusur ; ' whilst I, wretch that **I am,** having imprudently **visited the place** without **so** useful a guide, am **doomed to** imprisonment.' Fortunately **he had heard** the Jew express his intention of returning on the following **day** ; his confinement, therefore, would not **be of very** long duration ; **yet to** appear before the wary Israelite in such **a place, and** at once **disclose to him** his knowledge of the secret, was **a** reflection **most** galling **to Alnusur,** who had flattered himself he had been **acting a** part with **a** caution and cunning **not to** be exceeded even **by the Jew** himself.

Alnusur conceived it would be advisable to remain silent until **Ismael should** cause the statue **to recede, when** he would make **sure of** effecting his escape **so quickly** as to leave the Jew in ignorance as **to the** individual who had **discovered** the secret. Tedious seemed the **time,** dreary was the apparently endless night, and wearied was the watchful Alnusur, ere the time came when he might expect the Jew. All was silent as the grave, not a sound saluted the ear of the alarmed Alnusur. Should the **Jew not arrive,** should he **not** return **for** weeks, a horrible **death awaited** him, for without the aid of Ismael egress from the cavern he felt **to be** impossible.

At length Alnusur, whose eye had been unceasingly directed to the brazen plate above him, which formed the entrance-door to the cavern, saw it slowly recede from its position, and two **thin** spare legs, which he at once recognised as the supporters to **the** body of old Ismael, cautiously seeking out the **first** stair. Now, then, was the time to prevent the fatal portal **closing on** him and leaving him to the mercy of the Jew. Grasping his pole, therefore, Alnusur rushed up the stairs ere the Jew had reached the third step, and in his haste to insert the pole between the sliding platform and the spring, which **was** ready to catch it with unerring certainty, overthrew the alarmed Jew, whose feet failing **him, he** was precipitated into the cavern below, whilst, to Alnusur's amazement, the pole (which he had imagined he so dexterously inserted to prevent the closing of the portal), **from the** weight of the colossal statue above the platform, and the immense force of the spring which controlled **it,** snapped **in halves, and he** was again a prisoner, though not a solitary **one.**

Alnusur's attention was now directed to the fallen Jew, who was groaning most piteously and calling for assistance.

' Who art thou,' enquired the sufferer, ' that has found thy way hither, and slain an inoffensive man, to whom alone this place belongs ? '

' Slain ! ' exclaimed Alnusur. ' Allah forbid ! **Rise,** Master Ismael, I pray thee.'

' **Ah !' cried** the surprised **Jew,** ' that **voice I** do remember. Tell me, is it Alnusur speaks ? '

' **The** same, good Ismael.'

' **Ah,** wouldst thou had suffered me to stick fast in the rice-field, than to have dragged me out to murder me in this place.'

' Murdered, Ismael ! What mean you ? '

'I mean, young man, that thou hast killed me. I have fallen on a sharp stone; its point has entered my skull. See! examine.'

Alnusur did so, and to his horror perceived the unfortunate man's head covered over with blood, which he found impossible to staunch. Alnusur's dejection at perceiving the miserable state of Ismael, the work of his hand, kept him for some moments silent, until he began to reflect should the Jew die before he learned the means of escape from the cavern, his own demise must be the consequence. Perceiving the Jew's breath growing shorter and shorter, therefore, he besought him to forgive him for being the innocent cause of his death, and explained to him how his anxiety to prevent the closing of the portal by inserting his pole had occasioned his coming in contact with him, towards whom he entertained no evil intentions.

Ismael stretched forth his hand in token of forgiveness, saying: 'Young man, it was my own wilful neglect, my own disobedience to the rules in the "Book of Knowledge," which has brought me to such an end; you are but the tool in the hand of fate, which has too successfully employed you. Fly this place, and, without the "Book of Knowledge" in your possession, enter it no more. The entrance is easy, but the exit difficult.'

'Explain, good Ismael,' said Alnusur, 'by what means I may escape. Instruct me for your own sake, for the air may revive you; you will recover.'

'As you please,' said the resigned Ismael. 'Raise me, then, and when arrived at the top stair press hard the seventh knob on the brass plate; press it thirteen times, and it will then become loose, and fall into your hand; take this my small round staff,

insert it in the place occupied by the brass knob ; it will fit exactly ; press hard upwards ; give the first, the fourth, and the tenth knobs one turn to the right, and the large ebony knob on your left hand two turns to the left ; press hard with the round staff, and the——'
He could say no more ; life was fast ebbing, and he sank exhausted **with the** fatigue of speaking. Alnusur raised the almost lifeless **body,** and ascended the stairs. So long was the operation **of** unscrewing the knobs, and so agitated had he become, fearing the Jew should die, or himself err in his attempt to move the portal, that it was with considerable difficulty he could support the helpless Ismael on the rough and narrow stairs, and expected to see him once more **roll** down into the cavern.

To the joy of Alnusur the ponderous statue gradually yielded to his pressure ; he replaced the brass knob, and, bearing in his arms the **poor** Jew, in safety quitted the treasury. To close the aperture **he** resorted to the means he had witnessed Ismael practise on the preceding day, viz. by pressing the toe of the left foot **of** the statue ; and, to his pleasure, all succeeded. How to recover the Jew was now his sole thought, and lifting him in his arms, once more he carried him into the open air. A refreshing sea-breeze was blowing at the time, from which he entertained hopes his patient would recover. The blood, however, continued to flow copiously, **and the** Jew was totally bereft of speech.

Alnusur fanned him, and opened his vest, that the breeze might refresh him ; but all to no purpose ; the Jew struggled convulsively, rolled frightfully his once shrewd and glistening eyes, now dimmed by the chill hand of death ; essayed to speak, groaned,

and **died.**   Alnusur gazed with horror on the corpse before him;
he called himself his murderer, and cursed his unlucky stars which
had conducted him to the treasure-chamber.   The appearance of
the serpent now rushed on **his** recollection.

‘ Oh fool that I **was !’ said** he, ‘not to have taken warning by
that hideous sight.   **Oh !** would that I had fled from the island for
ever; then should **I have** escaped **the** bitter reflections I now
endure.’

The **twinges of** conscience alone agitated not Alnusur; he
feared lest **he** should be accused as **the** Jew's murderer; flight
therefore suggested to him the only means of avoiding such an
imputation; **yet** flight at every hour from Gharipoori was **not to**
be reckoned upon.   The boat **in** which Ismael had arrived was
the only one to be procured.   To show himself **to the** boatman
and **solicit** a passage to Bombay would **be madness.**   In the first
place, the man would refuse, being hired by the **Jew,** for whom he
was waiting; and secondly, it would only tend to raise a witness
against himself, **in the** event of his being accused as the Jew's
murderer.

To stand where he **was,** hanging over the corpse, undecided
how to proceed, was highly impolitic, and Alnusur turned aside.
As he did so he thought he perceived something glittering suspended to the deceased's neck.   He returned, **and** upon examination discovered the exact counterpart **of** the key **of** the iron box,
which **he** had so scrupulously withheld from the anxious Jew.
Reflecting that now the box might easily become his own, Alnusur
took the key from the neck of the Jew, deeming it wise to prevent
anyone from reaping any advantage by possessing it, as well as

conceiving it prudent **to have two keys,** in **case of** losing or mis-laying one.

On the Jew's person there was **little else of value ; and had** there been, Alnusur would scrupulously have refrained **from touch-ing it.** Possessed of the key, how to effect his escape and avoid all suspicion of having been accessory to the Jew's death now occupied Alnusur's agitated mind. He descended the **hill ;** not a creature impeded **his** progress. He espied from a distance the boatman dozing at the stern of his boat, ignorant of all that had been going on at the cavern, and patiently sleeping **away the time** until his fare should return. Alnusur, guessing the man was not so drowsy **or so** far **distant but** that he could hear his voice, bellowed aloud to him, calling on him 'for the love of Allah to come up to the cavern, for that murder was about to be com-mitted. Help, help, good boatman ! haste, **I** pray thee, or death **will be** the consequence.'

The boatman, thus hailed, raised his head, stared wildly around him, and rushed from the boat, running wildly towards Alnusur, who, speedily descending by another path to the water's edge, leaped into the boat, handled the oars, and pushed **off,** leaving the boatman to manage with the dead Jew as well as he could.

CHAPTER VIII.

THE COPPERSMITH'S STORY (*continued*).

ALNUSUR could not determine whither to steer his boat. Should he proceed to Bombay, he would be called on by the boatmen of the place to account for his being in possession of their fellow-fisherman's boat, and this would be a clue to his apprehension. After much deliberation, therefore, he turned his boat towards the shores of the Maharatta country; and avoiding Panwell, where many boats were visible, he steered towards Salsette, until the river became narrow. He then leaped into the water, and swam ashore, leaving his boat to float where the tide chose to convey it.

By a circuitous path he reached Panwell on foot, appearing as a traveller from the Deccan country. It so happened that no boats were at this moment ready to go to Bombay, the communi-cation at this period between that island and the Maharatta country being very uncertain. After waiting two whole days, however, a boat laden with firewood sailed for Bombay, in which Alnusur obtained a passage.

As they passed the island of Gharipoori in their way the Tindal of the boat was surprised on beholding the landing-place of the island crowded with people, who hailed the boat most loudly, accompanying their **cries by the** exhibition of white **and** red cloths intended for signals, should their voices fail attracting notice. **The** Tindal, being curious to ascertain **the** cause of this unusual **anxiety for** a passage in his boat, steered her into **the** landing-place, leaped into **a** canoe, and joined the crowd **on** the shore. Alnusur, his passenger, well knew the cause **of the outcry, but** of course maintained profound silence.

'Thank Allah !' said an aged Mahommedan to **the** Tindal of the boat ; 'thanks be to Allah you passed this way! Here is a **poor Jew** basely murdered by **this** scoundrel of **a** boatman from Bombay, who, leaving his **boat for the** accursed purpose, she has floated away **with** the tide, and thus fortunately left him behind, and we have secured him. **You** must take him, together with the corpse, to **Bombay,** where **I hope the** villain will **be** hanged without delay.'

The Tindal haggled about the fare he was to receive for the **conveyance of the** prisoner ; and this being agreed upon, he demanded **double** the sum for conveying the corpse of poor **Ismael, which the people of** the island consented **to pay,** glad enough to get rid **of** the body **on** any terms.

Alnusur, who had thought himself quite secure, **and** far from any chance of ever again beholding the corpse **of poor** Ismael, felt now considerably embarrassed **on perceiving** the Tindal bearing it into the boat, and throwing **it down** close to the spot **on** which he was standing. Several of the passengers objected to being thus brought in contact with **a** corpse ; but the Tindal, having agreed with the people of Gharipoori, could not swerve from his word. **Had he** known, indeed, the putrid state of his fare, he would undoubtedly have refused to take it on board. Next came the prisoner, bound with cruel cords around his arms, in which state he had remained since his apprehension.

Alnusur could not but deeply pity the poor man, whom he knew to be entirely innocent of the crime laid to his charge; indeed, he dared scarcely look him in the face, and felt inclined to publicly avow his innocence. He endeavoured, however, to pacify the poor man, who, with tears in his eyes, protested he was ignorant of the murder, and had found the body stretched at the entrance of the cavern.

Alnusur alone believed him; the rest of the passengers either ridiculed or abused him; and all lending a hand at the oars, that they might the more speedily be freed from the offensive smell proceeding from the corpse, sang and joked until the boat reached Bombay, where the prisoner was surrendered to the police, and Ismael's wife apprised of the melancholy event. The good woman bewailed her husband's death sincerely, gave orders for his interment, and shut herself up in her house for three days, seen by no one.

Alnusur was sorely grieved at witnessing the poor boatman conveyed to prison, where he would be doomed to remain until a sort of trial should take place, which was not unfrequently put off for many months, or to such time as suited the convenience of the Portuguese authorities. Alnusur had determined in his own mind, however, to assist the poor prisoner with money, by which he doubted not his acquittal could easily be purchased; he therefore for the present turned his attention to other matters. Understanding the widow of the Jew remained at home immersed in grief, Alnusur, under pretence of soothing her sorrows, ventured to pay her a visit.

After conversing about the mysterious murder **of** her husband, Alnusur enquired whether she intended **to reside** in the same house. She replied that she intended to dispose of all the personal effects of her late husband, and then retire to Surat, where her sister resided. Alnusur observed he should like to be informed when the sale **of** the effects would take place, as he was particularly anxious to purchase some articles of furniture which had some time **ago** pleased **his fancy. The** Jewess appointed a day for the sale, which she intended should be public, and that **all** persons might enter the house to select whatever articles they chose. Alnusur took his leave of the poor widow, promising **to** attend at the sale of the Jew's effects.

It was the **custom** among the people at that period, when disposing of any personal property, **to call in** all their neighbours, and the person most interested in the produce of the **sale** superintended and delivered over each article to the purchasers; taking care, however, not to enter into hasty bargains, but delay as long as possible, in the hope of receiving a more advantageous offer from some other customer. Thus, **on the** day of the sale of Ismael's property, the Jewess was early to be seen arranging each article to be disposed of, and showing the goods **off** to the best advantage.

The house was soon crowded with shopkeepers, brokers, and idlers. The person most interested **in** the sale was Alnusur, who impatiently awaited the production of the iron box, which he doubted not he should be able to purchase for a mere trifle.

After many articles had been cleared off, the Jewess produced the **iron** box, which she regretted not being able to open, her dear husband having concealed the key where she could not come **at it.** ' The value of the box, neighbours,' said she, ' I scarcely know what it may be, but for old iron it will fetch at any rate five rupees.'

' What does it contain ?' cried a voice.

' Only an old book, sir,' replied the widow, ' concerning our religion ; so my husband was wont to tell me.'

Alnusur stepped forward and expressed his willingness to give five rupees for the box.

' Will no one give any more ?' cried the Jewess, according **to** her custom ; ' will no one give more than five rupees ?'

At **this** instant, an influx of visitors coming, either from curiosity or a desire to purchase, caused the widow to delay giving to Alnusur the box, in the hope some one of those just arrived might take a fancy to it, and give more than that small sum. When she perceived the strangers arranged in the centre of the **room,** with outstretched arm bearing the box, she exclaimed, ' Five rupees for this box ! Will no one give me more than five rupees ?'

A voice from the crowd cried, ' Ten rupees I will give !'

Alnusur turned to ascertain who was his opponent: it was, to his dismay, Donga Sette Brahmin, who with difficulty could repress his joy and delight at thus unexpectedly stumbling on his long-lost box.

Alnusur advanced another five rupees ; upon which the Brahmin boldly cried aloud, ' Twenty I will give !' Alnusur **would** not be backward, and being now wealthy, to the amazement of the crowd bid one hundred rupees. The Jewess, delighted beyond measure, and not dreaming anyone would be mad enough to offer more than this last sum, was about **to** hand it over to Alnusur, when the Brahmin instantly doubled the amount. The Jewess was in an ecstasy, and was about to present the box to the Brahmin as she had done to Alnusur, when the latter, **to** every person's astonishment, offered five hundred rupees. The people actually shouted aloud ; the Jewess quite forgot old Ismael, and almost danced for joy.

The report of so much money being offered by a Brahmin and a Mahommedan for an iron box spread all over the town, and the Jew's house was now crowded to excess, everyone striving to get a sight of the two madmen, as they were considered.

The two bidders had now become furious ; they advanced from hundreds to thousands, the Jewess noticing their offers by a scream of joy, which she found impossible to repress. The Brahmin had advanced five thousand rupees, which was quickly increased by Alnusur to six, when Donga Sette begged a parley in private with the young Mahommedan. Alnusur, granting his request, withdrew, desiring the Jewess to await their return. The woman nodded assent, and seemed rejoiced at the prospect of a moment's rest from her fatigues, increased as they were by the anxiety of mind she was labouring under.

Donga Sette, approaching Alnusur, thus addressed him : ' My friend, I perceive you are but too well informed of the contents of the iron box; but of what use the book can be to you, who are ignorant of the language in which it is written, I cannot conceive **Why,** therefore, put me to this expense ? '

Alnusur replied, ' My worthy friend, of what use the box can be to you, without the key to open it, I also am at a loss to imagine; therefore why do you put **me to all this** trouble and unnecessary expense?'

'**Whether** I have the key or not, you cannot possibly know,' replied the Brahmin.

'And whether I can read the language of the book or not, you must be equally ignorant,' replied Alnusur.

'I perceive,' continued Donga **Sette,** 'you **will** not quietly suffer me to bear away the box; let us return therefore **to the** woman, and proceed with **our** offers. He who has the longer purse must succeed.'

Alnusur, assuming **a** placidity of countenance totally at **vari-** ance with his inward feeling of alarm, which the Brahmin's **last** speech had been but too well calculated to inspire him with, replied, '**Be it** so, **worthy** Brahmin!' and moved towards **the** crowded apartment. They were received **with** applause and **loud** shouts, and welcomed by none more cheerfully than the **Jewess,** who, scarcely refraining from laughter, continued the sale by exposing the box, saying, 'Only six thousand rupees bid for **this** valuable box!' A peal of laughter from the crowd followed, and several minutes transpired ere silence could be preserved.

The Brahmin went **as** far as eight thousand five hundred rupees, which Alnusur instantly increased to nine thousand, which the Brahmin hearing, cast a look of fury at his Mahommedan opponent, stamped with his foot, and rushed from the house, **leaving** Alnusur the victorious possessor of the box, which the **truly** enraptured Jewess speedily delivered to him, intimating her intention of following him to his house for the money. Alnusur assenting, he bade her follow him; and, arrived at his lodging, paid her the money, for **which** she **was** exceedingly thankful, and wished him all the happiness his bargain could produce him.

Donga Sette, it has been related, started **on** his journey to Jaggernaut **in** consequence of a dream. Arrived **at** the sacred temple, he scrupulously performed all the sacrifices, and presented all the offerings to the god; all to no purpose—no information did his godship give him respecting his box or anything else; and, vexed and disappointed, the Brahmin prepared **to** return home as expeditiously as possible. He reached Panwell the **day** after that on which Alnusur sailed from thence in the fishing-boat laden with firewood, and in passing the island **of** Gharipoori **the** circumstance of the murder of a Jew, which had recently occurred at the cave, was related to him by the people of the **boat.**

There was something suspicious in this, though nothing which could positively lead to a discovery of his box; nevertheless, the circumstance of a Jew having evidently visited the cavern convinced the Brahmin he had not been led thither either by curiosity or desire to improve himself in Hindoo mythology.

When, therefore, the Brahmin heard of the sale of Ismael's effects he thought he would attend, as possibly the box might be produced amongst other articles; and that, should this be the case, he would find little or no difficulty in securing it. How he was disappointed has already been related. He would willingly have gone on advancing in his offers but for one weighty reason —he knew he had no more money in his possession. When deprived of his box he had but ten thousand rupees in the world, which his living and his journey to Orissa had reduced to the very sum he offered, in the vain hope his opponent would not be able to outbid him. Vexed beyond measure, he gave up the contest, and repaired to his lowly mansion in the woods, where he in secret brooded over his disappointment.

The delighted Alnusur, after the Jewess had left him, quickly opened the iron box, determined to commence his study of the Book of Knowledge without delay. The book, to outward appearance, displayed nothing particular; it had a common red cover, showing evident signs of age, and was tied around with a dirty tape-string, in so many hard and difficult knots as to render the loosening of them no very easy task. Alnusur's impatience considerably augmented his perplexity; and gladly would he have availed himself of the aid of some friendly knife, but feared he should, by so doing, sever some charm which would be injurious to him; he therefore persevered with tooth and nail for nearly an hour, at the expiration of which time he succeeded in opening the last knot, by far the most unyielding of any.

Carefully folding up the string, Alnusur collected all his Sanscrit books, and seated himself in a corner of his chamber in the most studious attitude. Opening the learned volume with reverence, he recited several verses from the Koran, murmuring an inward prayer for success in all his undertakings. The first page, to his surprise, was not written in the Sanscrit, but the common Hindi characters used by the people of Guzrat. Alnusur rejoiced at this, the language being quite familiar to him. When, however, he proceeded to analyse the words contained therein, how was he amazed and alarmed at perceiving a debtor and creditor account regularly balanced! He concluded the avaricious Jew, ever absorbed in calculating his profits, had dared to profane the learned book by his **paltry** money memorandums. **Turning** to the second page, however, **a** similar account met his eye; the third, fourth, and the whole **of the book** contained naught but these debtor and creditor accounts; **and** Alnusur, groaning with vexation, dashed the filthy ledger from him, execrating the **memory** of the Jew, and cursing **the old Jewess and** himself at **the** same time for buying **a box** without first ascertaining its contents. Oh! what a mortification it was, what a bitter reflection was it, **to** think he had given nine thousand rupees for an iron box **and** an old filthy account-book, neither **of** which **could** possibly be of the slightest **use** to him! **The** dejected youth, throwing **off** his turban, **swore never again to wear it until he** should gain the wished-for Book of Knowledge.

A thought **now struck him that** probably the book he so ardently desired might be amongst the Jew's manuscripts and **other** papers. In this làst **hope the** anxious Alnusur, muffling **himself** up in his shawl, and without his turban, ran quickly **to the** Jewess's house, where the sale was proceeding much to the good woman's satisfaction. Perceiving **so** welcome a customer re-enter her house, the Jewess, who was in the act of disposing of some of old Ismael's wardrobe, left her occupation, and desired the **people to** make room for their betters; **at** the same time nodded, smiled, and smirked at the dejected Alnusur, expressing her hopes he **was** come **to purchase more** of her dear Ismael's effects, and enquired what articles he would wish to be produced for sale. Alnusur desired the books and the manuscripts should be put up without delay. **The** Jewess, calling to a little woolly-headed African boy, desired him to bring down from a garret a large basketful of papers for the gentleman to examine. The boy obeying, a mass of dusty account-books were with difficulty hauled down the narrow staircase and brought into the sale-room. The business was now at a stand-still, all persons wondering what Alnusur could be in search of. The young Mahommedan turned over the contents of the basket, and examined every book; but nothing save the confounded debtor and creditor accounts met his eye.

' Have you no other books in your house, good woman ?' he enquired of the obliging Jewess.

' None,' she replied, adding, in a low voice, ' If you will wait until the sale is over you shall be welcome to search every corner; and if you find what you require, make your own terms— I will accept them.'

Alnusur nodded assent, and patiently awaited the conclusion of the sale.

The most valuable of the effects having been disposed of, the lowest rabble now filled the room, and were bidding very trifling sums for the worn-out clothes of poor Ismael. The Jewess, however, was as anxious and keen in the disposal of these rags as she had been with better articles, praising the tattered vests as if they were right new from the tailor's hands. Alnusur, during this tedious process, sat worn out with anxiety and impatience, hoping every old pair of trousers would be the last; but, alas! he was doomed to be disappointed, for when indeed the last of such description of apparel had been disposed of the Jewess produced a huge bundle of worn-out black velvet skull-caps and sashes, which had once been red. To patiently await the disposal of these, one by one, was next to impossible; he, therefore, offered twenty rupees for the lot; **and not being** outbid, they were handed **to** him, and he **hoped** the **sale would now** close. Alnusur, however, quite forgot the old papers and manuscripts, every one of which the Jewess proceeded to sort out for disposal, for the convenience of purchasers. Alnusur bid **ten** rupees for **the** lot, which was instantly delivered to him. **He felt now** quite certain everything had been sold; but, **to** his mortification, the Jewess called aloud, 'Jacob! come hither, Jacob!'

The little African appearing, he was desired to bring **up the** cooking utensils **for the** purchasers **to** examine, and **to** run for the coppersmith, and desire him to bring his scales to weigh the copper pots, that the buyers should know what they were about. Jacob obeyed—the cooking utensils and **the** coppersmith made their appearance. Alnusur, had he the money to spare, for the **purpose of** finishing the sale would not **have** scrupled purchasing the whole lot, as he had done before; **but,** not in the possession **of the key** to wealth, and having scarcely more than one thousand rupees in **the world, he was** constrained to **witness in** silence the tedious process of weighing and selling each copper vessel. **The** day was now far advanced, and Alnusur hoped, should there **yet** be any more articles to **be** disposed **of,** the sale would **be** postponed till the following day. The Jewess, however, again called Jacob. 'Come hither, boy; come and be sold yourself, my active slave. Look at him, gentlemen,' she continued, 'only fourteen **years** of **age,** healthy, active and strong. Cost my poor dear husband two hundred dollars only two years ago; anyone shall have him for two hundred and fifty.' Jacob grinned and showed his white teeth, casting **a** longing look at Alnusur, **of** whose wealth **he had** seen convincing proof. Alnusur, **however, raised** not his eye, conscious of his poverty, and one hundred rupees only **were** bid, by a tall morose-looking Mahommedan at the farther end of the room. Alnusur ventured to add fifty, more to thwart the first bidder than from any desire on **his** part to bear away the boy. Jacob's eyes glistened with delight, and he twitched his mistress's elbow, as if **begging** her to accept the offer. **No** one advancing a rupee more, **Jacob was delivered over to** Alnusur, and the sale at length came **to an end.**

When the people departed Alnusur reminded the Jewess of her promise, to allow him to search the house for old books.

'Search the house, indeed!' she cried. 'I shall allow no such thing, unless you pay me for so doing; so pray go about your business, and let me be paid for my slave, my papers, and my velvet caps.'

Alnusur in vain remonstrated with this sordid woman, whose motive for detaining him under a false promise was now very evident. She had watched his impatience, and purposely length-ened out the sale, in the hope he would, for expedition's sake, become a wholesale purchaser. Having succeeded, as has been related, she scrupled not **to** break her promise; but Alnusur, being extremely vexed and angry, vowed he would not pay her a rupee for his bargains, unless she allowed him to ransack the house as she had promised him. At length, for a douceur of five rupees, the Jewess gave a reluctant consent; and Alnusur, followed by Jacob bearing a light, poked in o every hole and corner of the mansion without finding **a** scrap of paper of any kind. The idea now struck him that probably the book might be deposited, for better security, in the Jew's strong box ; he therefore desired the Jewess to open it for his inspection. The woman produced the key with great reluctance. Alnusur, snatching it from her hand with breathless anxiety, rushed **towards** the iron chest. The Jewess, alarmed by his rude and hasty manner, and imagining he was about to rob her of all the money in her **possession**, screamed violently, calling aloud, ' Murder ! robbery ! **fire** ! Help, neighbours, help !' Alnusur, ere this cry could be attended to, opened the chest, and ascertaining there was no book of any sort or kind within it, banged down the lid, locked it, and threw the key on the floor, desiring the Jewess to dismiss the neighbours, whose footsteps **he** plainly heard approaching. The **Jewess,** possessed of the key, ceased to be alarmed, apologising to her friends for **her** unnecessary summons, and quietness once more reigned **around.** Alnusur, convinced **the** Book of Knowledge was not in the house, walked towards his lodging with Jacob, bearing on his head the bundle of skull-caps, followed by the Jewess, for the purpose of securing her money. Alnusur in vain endeavoured to get off his bargain for the paper and the old caps. The Jewess detailed a long string of losses she would sustain ; and how, had the goods been put up one by one, her profit would have been considerably greater, and that for his accommodation alone she sold them in the lot, and consequently paid she would be. Finding all remonstrance useless, Alnusur paid for his slave-boy and his two lots of useless goods, expressing a hope he should never be so unfortunate as to behold the old hag's face again.

Never was woman so happy as Ismael's widow. In her husband's lifetime she scarcely knew the shape of a rupee **or a** dollar, now she appeared to be rolling in riches apparently inexhaustible. **On the** other hand, never was man so vexed and unhappy as poor Alnusur ; his disappointment, when **he had** made sure **the** Book of Knowledge, **that** grand key to wealth, was in his hand, to find only a dirty ledger, **of** use only **as** waste paper, was too great to bear with patience. He paced his verandah, slapped his forehead, clenched his fist, still heaping curses on the Jew for not informing him **where** to find the book, and abusing his widow for causing **him to waste his money and** his time at her **trumpery** outcry.

'What have I gotten after all?' would he continue to say. 'An iron box worth nothing, and **a slave-boy** who will **eat more** than I shall be able to allow myself. **Fool that I was to** bid **for** him ! However, if I can't maintain him, **he must** be sold again. And what is to become of me ?'

Alnusur continued giving vent to **these far from** comfortable reflections until night advanced with rapid strides. Jacob appeared, bearing a lamp, which placing at a respectful distance, **he** was about **to retire.**

'Come hither, boy,' **cried his** new master. 'Tell **me** truly : when in the service **of the** Jew did **you never see him** deeply engaged in study ?'

'Oh ! yes, master, every **day** : he used to read one book in particular until his eyes were no bigger than peas.'

' **What sort** of a book ; and where did he keep it ?'

' **He kept** it in the iron box master gave nine thousand rupees for.'

'**Psha !**' said Alnusur, **angry at** being thus reminded **of** his bad bargain, '**I** know that ; but tell me, what sort **of a** book **was** it ?'

'**Oh, it was a** small thick book.'

'**How** did it open—like this ?' (Producing **the** account-book.)

'Oh, no ! master, not that way ; like the Koran.'

'What sort of a cover had it ?'

'Oh, a very fine cover, all over gold ; but I only saw the cover once ; for my master, when any one came near him, covered it up with his shawl.'

'Where do you think the book **is** now ?' enquired Alnusur.

'Ah ! I know,' said the boy, looking archly.

'Do you, indeed, good Jacob ? Tell me, **I** command you, then, where is it ?'

'**I** can guess, I know,' replied Jacob, wearing a most sagacious countenance, and exhibiting his pearl-white teeth.

'Tell me then, sirrah,' said Alnusur, 'where is the book ?'

'In master's little iron box, which he gave nine thousand rupees for,' replied the boy, waiting his master's next question.

Alnusur, losing all patience at becoming, as it seemed, the laughing-stock of his very slave, and seizing the identical iron box, was about to level it at the head of poor Jacob, when a knock at the chamber-door arrested his uplifted arm.

Jacob, anxious to escape, opened **the door,** quickly passing a **man** muffled up in a coarse cloth, who enquired for Alnusur. The boy, pointing to his master's apartment, darted out of sight. **Alnusur** demanded who wanted him, and the unexpected visitor boldly entered the room. 'I am come, sir,' said a poor half-Hindoo, half-Portuguese man, 'on the part of my unfortunate brother, whom you promised to assist.'

'By Allah!' exclaimed Alnusur, 'the whole world is conspired against me! Who in the name of wonder are you? and who is your miserable brother?'

'Ah! sir, he is indeed miserable; and I fear his life is in danger.'

'Well, fellow, what is this to me? Let him die, then, and end this wretched life.'

'He has a family, sir, and is loth to die, especially as he is innocent of the crime laid to his charge.'

'Crime! What crime?'

'Murder, sir—the murder of a Jew.'

'Oh!' cried Alnusur, the whole truth now flashing across his mind; 'true, I promised to assist the poor man; but then I had money, now I have none. Did he send thee hither?'

'He did, sir, for his trial is to come on within a few days, and with difficulty did I gain admittance to his prison.'

'Well, my friend, I will visit him and offer him my advice; but as to money, I fear——'

'Ah, sir, say not so. Your advice may be excellent, but without gold my poor brother will surely be hanged.'

'Have you offered any sum to the magistrate?' enquired Alnusur.

'Yes, sir, and am convinced, for a thousand rupees——'

'A thousand rupees! Where is it to come from, my good man? Consider what a sum it is.'

' True, sir ; but then my brother's life, and the lives of five small children—consider them.'   Here the unhappy petitioner shed tears, which, as he fell at Alnusur's feet, coursed down his coal-black cheeks and choked further utterance.

Alnusur, knowing himself to be the cause of **the Jew's** death, was moved by so affecting a scene, and raising the poor man, said, ' I will keep my promise : furnish among you fifty rupees, and to-morrow I will bring your brother the remaining nine hundred and **fifty.'**

The suppliant kissed Alnusur's feet, invoking blessings on him for evermore.

The hour for visiting the prisoner being appointed, the **man** took his departure, uttering thanks and **praises of Alnusur's** generosity, until he found himself in the streets.

Alnusur, when alone, considered his rash promise, by performing which he would reduce himself to actual beggary—nine hundred and fifty rupees being **all** he had in the world.   On the other hand, could he, for the sake of such a sum, see an innocent man hanged **for a** crime himself had unintentionally been guilty of ?

' No !' cried **the** youth, **' I** am young and strong, unincumbered by family or friends ; though I lose my money, I shall not endanger my life, and the rupees shall be given to the boatman.'

With this benevolent intention did Alnusur that night place **his** head upon his pillow; and, notwithstanding his cruel disappointment, slept soundly.

Not so poor Jacob, who had the whole day toiled at the Jewess's sale, without tasting a grain of rice either there or in his new abode; hungry and miserable, he tossed about, anxiously looking for morning, that he might obtain a meal.

On the following day, Alnusur, summoning the obedient slave, gave him some money, desiring him to purchase rice and some onions, which he commanded should be boiled in a particular manner. The delighted Jacob flew to the bazaar, purchased rice and onions, and quickly cooked them to his master's satisfaction, who having eaten as much as he required, gave the remainder to his famished slave.

At the appointed hour, Alnusur, taking the remainder of his small fortune, sallied towards the gaol, where by a fee to the gaoler he obtained access to the cell of the unhappy boatman. The prisoner was pacing his narrow apartment in an agony of mind not to be witnessed without deep commiseration. At the appearance of Alnusur the poor man's eyes glistened with delight as he made his humble obeisance. Alnusur, in the hope he should be able by advice alone to put the poor man in the way of escaping punishment, determined not to produce his cash immediately, and therefore signed to the prisoner to sit down, and desired him to detail to him the true state of the case, and conceal nothing from him. The boatman proceeded to narrate all Alnusur but too well knew already.

' It appears to me,' said Alnusur, 'there is no proof whatever against you. Had you stripped or plundered the corpse, and any of the property been found upon you, then, indeed, your case would have been hopeless.'

' Indeed, sir, I took nothing—that is, nothing of any value.'

' But what did you take?' enquired Alnusur.

' Only an old book, **sir, with** a gold cover, because it looked so pretty.'

' What say you? A book **with a gold cover!** Where **is it?** Was it found upon you? Who has got it? **Tell** me quickly— your life depends upon it.'

Alnusur **was so** agitated that he scarcely knew what he said, or what question he wished to have first answered. The prisoner, as soon as his visitor was **a** little composed, explained that on discovery of the body **of** the Jew he became greatly alarmed, and meditated to bury or conceal it in the cavern; and had actually raised it **for** this purpose, **when** a handsome-looking book fell from some part of the garments; and thinking **it** might be a Koran, which the Mahommedans would value, he **thrust it in his** own sash or kummer-bund, which had not been searched when he had been apprehended. Fortunately, on board the boat from Panwell, which conveyed him prisoner to Bombay, his brother, **who** followed the same profession as himself, happened to be employed. As he was placed near the corpse, avoided by every one, he signed **to** his brother to approach him; and thinking the book, on his arrival in Bombay, might tell against him **if** recognised by the Jew's friends, in a low voice desired him to extract it from his sash, and **take** possession **of it** until his trial should be over.

' And has he got **it now?'** **eagerly** enquired Alnusur.

' He has, sir; and, if you desire it, will surrender it to you with pleasure. He will be here presently, and I will desire him to fetch it.'

Alnusur was inexpressibly delighted; at the same time essayed to conceal his joy, allowing the boatman to remain under the idea that the book was, as he suspected, a valuable copy of the Koran, for which he was most anxious. The prisoner's brother shortly after appeared. He informed them that the magistrate had agreed to receive the sum of one thousand rupees, for which he promised to release the innocent man. The book was then demanded by both Alnusur and the prisoner; and it was with feelings of great joy Alnusur learned it was safe at the house of the prisoner's brother. The man was instantly dispatched for the wished-for book, and quickly returning, delivered it into Alnusur's hands, who joyfully giving the nine hundred and fifty rupees, took leave, and hurried homewards.

Alnusur was never before so rewarded for a good action. Had he deviated from his word and promise to assist the innocent boatman, the book, in all probability, would never have been in his possession. Once more did the happy youth prepare to study the Book of Knowledge. He found that the pedestal upon which the statue stood was guided by twelve different springs, independent of the one which ensured the means of entrance, and that whilst in the act of making use of one of them, by pressing the brass knobs, a second spring was set for another day; so that the stranger would, in the event of gaining an entrance to the cavern, find it next to impossible to ensure an exit, and suffer a lingering death from starvation.

Alnusur studied deeply the moral essays contained in the book, and determined to follow and scrupulously observe its precepts. At present his attention was directed to the proper preservation of the iron box, which the Brahmin knowing him to be possessed of, would spare no pains to deprive him of it. **He** first procured a strong **iron chest,** in the inside of which he caused an iron staple to be fixed ; **to** this he chained the important box containing **the book, and for** additional security fastened **the** larger iron chest by the same method **to the wall at** the head **of** his couch, carrying about his person all the keys, which he guarded with a most scrupulous vigilance.

CHAPTER IX.

THE COPPERSMITH'S STORY (*continued*).

ALNUSUR successfully visited the cavern of wealth, scrupulously attending to the rules and precepts of the Book of Knowledge. Being possessed of immense wealth, he ventured to solicit the hand of his beloved Zaide, who was still unmarried. For this purpose, therefore, did he visit Cambay, and desired an interview with Harak, whose pride had now somewhat subsided, having lost his Deewanship, by having offended the Nuwab. The ex-Deewan, hearing of the sum Alnusur proposed to give him to purchase his consent, at once acceded to the proposal, and Zaide, the lovely Zaide, became Alnusur's bride. The happy pair returned to Bombay, where Alnusur had purchased a sumptuous residence, fit for the reception of his beauteous wife, who expressed her high satisfaction in the most endearing terms.

The happy Alnusur neglected not the rules in the Book of Knowledge; nay, he became the more scrupulously attentive to them, and endeavoured to impress the necessity of observing them on his beloved partner. The beggar was never turned from his gate, the widow never appealed in vain, and the distressed were confident there to receive comfort and assistance. Zaide was to Alnusur as the sun to the earth ; his love for her daily increased, and he felt that without her life would be a burthen to him, even though master of immense treasure. Zaide loved Alnusur with equal ardour, and happiness reigned throughout their dwelling.

Donga Sette Brahmin, although deprived of the means of doing as much good as his benevolent disposition dictated, nevertheless continued to bestow his mite on the distressed, to comfort the afflicted, and educate the little children in his neighbourhood. His wife would, however, continue to sigh after the Book of Knowledge, through which, she had been informed by her spouse, riches could be attained, although the exact method had been withheld from her knowledge ; she knew also that Alnusur was in possession of the volume, and frequently threw out hints to the worthy Brahmin of the possibility of his being able to purloin it from him. Donga Sette spurned the idea. 'No !' he would say, 'were I to succeed by artifice or violence success would not attend me. Should it be the pleasure of the mighty Brahma to possess me of the book, cheerfully will I receive it, and become his humble instrument for disseminating knowledge and relieving the destitute.'

His wife, perceiving the Brahmin immovable, discontinued urging him on the subject.

As wealth is often the parent of pride, it will not be wondered at that Zaide, intoxicated with the homage she received, assumed so haughty a deportment as to disgust all her own and her husband's friends. Confident in her Alnusur's riches, she grew tired of adhering so closely to the rules of morality preached to her by her anxious husband, and by degrees neglected them one by one. Her example, unfortunately, was followed by Alnusur, who, perceiving his success at the cavern continued, attached daily less importance to the golden rules in his Book of Knowledge. The inconsiderate **couple, it is true,** coldly doled out their charity to those who petitioned **for** it, but sought not out, as at first, the destitute and afflicted, and even **at length were wearied by** the sight **of** the beggar at their **door.**

Feasting and dancing, music and mirth, occupied their attention. Zaide's ambition was display; to exhibit her jewels and diamonds, and outvie other women, and throw open her splendidly illuminated apartments night after night, was now her study—on this did her happiness depend. The least failure or trifling disappointments irritated and vexed her so that she became, from **loss of** temper, absolutely insufferable. Alnusur, loving Zaide as **he** did, caught the infection; he became haughty and tyrannical, **improvident and** intemperate; even the laws of the holy Prophet **were expunged from his** memory, and he indulged so freely in wine, that **for** days he would wallow in **a** state of beastly intoxication. The Gosayn and the Fakir were now unceremoniously driven from their gates, and Zaide, in her rage, absolutely abused them.

A great festival was at hand. Zaide, from ostentatious motives, demanded ten thousand rupees to fling into the streets from her splendid litter as she proceeded to the Ead-gar;[1] and **Alnusur,** scarcely recovered from the effects of a recent debauch, bluntly refused her request, and darted from the presence

[1] Mausoleum where the Kutba is read.

of his enraged wife. From this **moment a want** of confidence in man and wife arose, and happiness, even in their construction of the word, fled from Alnusur's mansion. Still he loved Zaide, and she had not the smallest reason to doubt the fact. To her he was constant : no strange beauty bewildered his senses, and he felt without Zaide life would be far from desirable.

One day, returning from his ride, Alnusur, as he passed the outer wall of his house, which, as he sat on his horse, afforded him a commanding view of his courtyard, to his surprise perceived his wife holding converse with a Fakir, or religious mendicant. He fancied she smiled. Burning with jealous fury, he alighted, rushed to the entrance-gate, and drawing his dagger, speedily approached the beggar with an uplifted arm. **Zaide** screamed aloud, but the Fakir stood immovable, watching the motions of the infuriated Alnusur with a collected firmness which saved his life ; for when his assailant thought the deadly instrument would penetrate the Fakir's heart, to his surprise, owing to the beggar's slipping on one side, the dagger, aimed with a hellish fury, struck against the wall of the house and was shivered to atoms.

'Oh, Alnusur, what wouldst thou have done?' cried the alarmed Zaide. '**A** holy man to be thus assailed ! **Thou art** surely mad.'

Alnusur, indeed, rejoiced at **the poor** man's escape ; and turning to command the Fakir's **departure,** to his astonishment perceived he had fled.

'Zaide,' he cried, 'till now I thought you faithful.'

'And what,' she cried, 'has caused you now to think otherwise ?'

'Oh, woman, woman !' he replied, 'wert not thou the first to drive away the beggars. And how is it, then, I see you now in cheerful converse with the man I would have sacrificed to my fury ?'

'Oh, Alnusur, do you thus basely suspect me ? Then hence all happiness—let us part for ever.'

'Oh, no ! no, beloved Zaide, forgive me : I have acted wrong, very wrong ; let us live for one another ; forgive me, dearest Zaide.'

'Alnusur, hear me. I have not in thought even been untrue to you : think, then, what I feel at your unjust suspicions. The holy man whose life you would have taken is the friend of my father. From pious motives does he wander to collect alms for the erection of a mosque at Cambay. We talked of former times, of days gone by. If I were pleased, have I been guilty of a crime ?'

'Oh, no ! no, Zaide, my beloved : I will seek out the holy man—I will even build the mosque to pacify him and obtain his forgiveness. Grant me your pardon, and I shall be at ease.'

Zaide held out her hand, saying, 'Be it so, but beware how a second time you entertain such dire suspicions.'

Time passed as before. Alnusur in vain sought out the offended Fakir, and he imagined he had departed. One morning, however, as he was preparing to take his ride, the Fakir walked past the house, crying, 'Woe, woe to the house of Alnusur !' Zaide, who was at an upper apartment, screamed with terror ; and Alnusur, leaving his horse, pursued the beggar, praying him to return and receive alms. The Fakir waved his hand contemptuously and passed on. The following and each succeeding day did the Fakir stalk past the **outer gate, crying,** 'Woe, woe to **the** house of Alnusur!'

Zaide became greatly alarmed, and Alnusur's spirits failed him. **He** was visited by horrid dreams : **he fancied** his Zaide a lifeless corpse—murdered by his own hand! At such **a** time he **would start** up and seize the arm of his sleeping wife, who in vain demanded the cause for such disturbance. This dream more than once haunted his imagination, but he concealed its dire import from his beloved Zaide, and strove to disregard it ; but in vain. Something dreadful, he felt convinced, **was hanging** over his head, but what he could not possibly conceive.

Zaide received **from** Cambay the melancholy **news of her** father's death. This, perhaps, was the only calamity, and in this idea Alnusur endeavoured to compose himself. **Zaide** kept to her apartments, indulging in bitter grief. The Fakir failed not daily to foretell woe to the house of Alnusur, and the dreams still haunted the couch of that dejected man.

About one month after the receipt of the melancholy news from Cambay, Zaide requested permission to visit an aunt, lately arrived **at** Thanah, **or** Salsette. Alnusur, thinking a change would alleviate his wife's distress, assented, promising to **come** for her himself **after** ten days' time. Should he not be punctual, he bade her not be under any alarm, for that he should certainly delay no longer than three days beyond that period. In thus saying **he** had his reasons, which will presently be explained. Zaide, therefore, without any suite, attended only by a female slave, proceeded **to Salsette, leaving** Alnusur alone in his spacious mansion.

Alnusur knew that after thirteen days he might visit the cavern, and it was his intention to call there on his way to Salsette, whither he preferred going by water, and to select a handsome sum of money to present to the aunt of his beloved Zaide. He knew nothing would please his wife so well, and he therefore prepared accordingly. Just as he was setting out from his mansion the Fakir crossed his path, uttering, ' Woe, woe to the house of Alnusur ! '

Accustomed to this ominous croaking, Alnusur allowed it not to depress his spirits ; and thinking only of the pleasure of again meeting his dear Zaide, passed rapidly to the water's edge, where a boat being in readiness, he quickly embarked and was rowed in safety to the island of Gharipoori. Previous to leaving his house he had carefully made an extract from the Book of Knowledge, that no difficulty might occur in attempting an exit from the cavern. Confident, therefore, of his usual success, he pressed the toe of the colossal statue, which receded at the touch. Descending the stairs an unpleasant smell saluted him, which he concluded arose from the pent-up vapours of the place ; but to his surprise and horror he perceived at the foot of the stairs a corpse. If he was shocked at this appearance, how was he horrified and distracted by discovering, on a farther examination, it was the corpse of his beloved Zaide ! Woe was indeed come upon the miserable Alnusur; he tore his hair and beat his breast, his screams resounded through the vaulted cavern, he threw himself on the body of his beloved, and wept in agony. The truth burst upon him : she must have watched him in his visits to the cavern, and dared to tempt an entrance by herself. He was indeed correct. Zaide, it will be remembered, on a particular occasion demanded from him ten thousand rupees, which he refusing, though not on the plea of inability, she determined to ascertain from whence his wealth proceeded. She did so, and planned a visit to the hoard in secret.

Having obtained permission to go to Salsette, an opportunity she conceived now offered to put her plans into execution. The second day after her arrival at her aunt's she expressed her intention of visiting a peer, or religious place, in the neighbouring islands; adding that probably she should from thence return to Bombay, and bring back her husband to Thanah. Her aunt dared not to oppose her intention, and alone did the imprudent Zaide, rowed by a single fisherman, reach Gharipoori. She desired him to return whence he came, trusting she should easily procure another conveyance when ready to quit the island.

She had disguised herself in male attire, covering her person with an immense shawl, one which Alnusur had but lately presented her with. She entered the cavern. Alas! little did she imagine it would prove her grave. She feasted on the piles of riches, and delight danced in her eye. When she had selected as much as she could carry and conceal under her shawl the ill-starred Zaide prepared to quit the repository of wealth. Closed was the portal, and all her attempts to force it ineffectual. The wretched woman laid her down in an agony indescribable. Soon did hunger commence its dire attacks, a dreadful thirst parched her lips, and madness almost seized her brain. For one day she bore patiently all the horrors of starvation, living on the hope that Alnusur might visit the cavern and extricate her from the jaws of death.　Alas! he **came not; another day, and no** helping **hand to** succour the dying Zaide.　**At** length nature unsupported **sank;** and Zaide, actually famished, lay down and died.

The distracted Alnusur, having spent many hours in weeping **and giving vent to the most** poignant grief, began to consider **what** steps **he should** take to bury his wife's **corpse.**　To leave it there was **an** idea **he** entertained **not for a moment.**　**At last he determined to remove it from the cavern, and bury it** in some **one** of the dark **cells above.**　**He** with difficulty raised it to the head **of the** stairs, and opening the portal, dragged **the** body after him.　**He** next went **in** search of some implement **with which** a grave might be **prepared.**　In a field below **the hill he** fortunately found an iron implement **of** husbandry; this he quickly **seized and returned to the cavern, where, having** with difficulty **found a** soft spot, **he** dug the grave **of** his once beauteous Zaide; **and as** he closed over her remains the last earth felt as if he had **shut from** himself all hope of happiness for ever.　He returned to **Bombay.　Arrived at his own** house, **he** shut himself up in his apartments, and was seen by no one.　It was reported his wife **had** eloped with a Mahommedan of rank, and Alnusur, when he did make his appearance, was pointed and laughed at by all the city.　Disgusted **and** dejected, the miserable Alnusur came to a determination to do one good act. and then in seclusion pass the remainder of his days.

It was evening.　Donga **Sette** Brahmin had dismissed his little urchins, and was enjoying the exhilarating breeze in his verandah, when a stranger, muffled up in a coarse cloth, appeared **before him,** begging an audience.　The Brahmin signed him to enter, and desired him **to be** seated. 'Brahmin,' said a **low** hollow voice, 'you once possessed a treasure.'

Donga Sette stared in mute astonishment, but nodded assent.

'You,' continued the stranger, 'used your riches properly: you fed the hungry, you instructed the ignorant.'

'**I did** all in my power,' replied the worthy Brahmin.

'You did. A villain robbed you of this key to wealth. Know you who it **was?**'

'The Jew Ismael, I suspect,' said the Brahmin.

'For him I basely robbed you of your keys at the Jatra, **and** possessed myself of the iron box. Ignorant of the contents, I gave it to the Jew.'

'Heaven be praised!' **said the** Brahmin. '**Is it** the rich and powerful Alnusur who speaks?'

'It is indeed Alnusur,' replied the stranger, 'the once rich, **once** happy Alnusur, but now the most miserable of all mankind.' **He** here related **every** particular to the Brahmin, concluding by presenting him with the iron box, and both its keys, saying, 'Take it, worthy Brahmin ; **you** alone know how to use the treasure when in your possession, **and** yours it shall be ; **for me,** all the wealth of the world is now of no use. I deserve the misery I am suffering, for I neglected the rules of the **Book** of Knowledge. As a Fakir, as a religious mendicant, will I wander through Hindústan, and resign the world and all its allurements ; for Zaide is dead, and I, alas ! am the cause of her death ; for had I obeyed the precepts of the book, and cherished, instead of expelling and aiming at the lives of beggars, woe would not have come on the house of Alnusur.'

Donga Sette endeavoured to dissuade **Alnusur** from his intention of becoming a Fakir, but to no purpose : he left the iron box and keys at the Brahmin's feet, and making a salaam, left the house.

The Brahmin, once more possessed of his Book of Knowledge, continued to live beloved and respected by all who knew him, assisting the poor, relieving the distressed, teaching the ignorant, and practising every moral virtue.

The Nuwab made no remark on this story of the Coppersmith, but arose, intimating his attention of being present next day to hear another tale; and in consequence Moye-ed-din summoned all the remaining persons to his palace, when the lot fell upon Kuzl-bashee, the Dyer, who on the following day appeared and commenced his narrative as follows.

CHAPTER X.

THE DYER'S STORY.

In the Hegira 1070,[1] the mighty Aurungzebe reigned at Delhi; and notwithstanding the war with his brother Suja, which was carried on at the extremity of the empire, the indefatigable Emperor suffered not his attention to be diverted from the civil affairs of the state. Accustomed to business from his youth, he suffered nothing of the minutest kind to escape his observation. He was extremely particular in framing rules for the administration of justice ; and that he might be assured his orders were obeyed, and his regulations enforced, often condescended at night to wander, in company with his Vizier, through the city, both being closely disguised. By these means circumstances not unfrequently came to his notice which otherwise he would have been entirely ignorant of.

One moonlight night, as the Emperor and his Vizier were passing through an obscure lane in the city, they were met by three beggars in a most miserable condition, one of whom was evidently lame. The mendicants failed not to beg alms; and the Emperor, considering the lonely situation of the place, thought it prudent to present them with a few rupees, upon which, all falling

[1] A.D. 1660.

to the earth, one of them exclaimed, ' Oh, generous strangers, suffer us each to prostrate ourselves to the ground thirty times for your generosity.'

The Emperor, anxious to return, would willingly have dispensed with so tedious a demonstration of their gratitude; but the beggars declaring, if they were not permitted thus to thank their donors, they must be under the necessity of returning the money, the Emperor thus addressed them:

' It is inconvenient for me this night, and in such a place, to receive your humble and tedious prostrations; but suffer us to accompany you to your lodgings, that we may know where to find you, and I promise faithfully to send for you early on the morrow, and then receive your thanks in any manner you may deem expedient; and, moreover, promise to double the sum now offered to you.'

The mendicants, acquiescing in the arrangement, insisted on the Emperor receiving back the money he had put into their hands, whatever might be his intention on the following day, as it was their invariable custom not to retain a pice[1] given them as charity, unless the donor suffered them to prostrate themselves thirty times before him.

Aurungzebe was therefore compelled to take back his money, and follow the beggars to an obscure part of the city, where a miserable shed, he was informed, was the only habitation they enjoyed.

The Emperor having taken leave of these singular beings, conversed with his Vizier on their extraordinary conduct, an expla-

[1] Small copper coin.

nation of which he was most anxious to hear. **He** therefore directed his Vizier to cause the beggars to be summoned to his palace the next day, but not to inform them who it was that demanded their attendance. The Vizier, bowing to the earth, swore to execute his orders, and when arrived at the palace took leave **of** his royal master for the night.

Early on the following day the beggars, who had **purposely** remained within their shed, beheld a messenger approach ; and that he should not fail to understand to whom he ought to apply, stood at the front of their miserable dwelling. **The messenger** delivered to them his orders, and they proposed **to follow him·** When brought before the Emperor how great was the astonishment of the mendicants at beholding **in** him their charitable friend of the preceding night ! Aurungzebe beheld their surprise, and thus addressed them :

' Persians — for I see you are of that country—I have summoned you according to my promise, to double the sum I offered you last **night, on** condition that you faithfully inform me the reasons which compel **you to** prostrate yourselves thirty times at the feet of your charitable **friends.** I perceive one of you to be lame **and** the other to have lost an eye, and congratulate the third on his apparent perfect state of body.'

The beggars all made **a salaam, but the third did so** with his left hand, which failed not **to attract** the notice **of the** Emperor, **who** demanded the reason. 'Our **friend,'** said the lame man, ' can do no otherwise ; he has lost his right hand.' The maimed man, **in** corroboration **of** his brother's statement, thrust from under his long sleeve **a withered stump, which he again quickly** concealed from view.

' **In the** name of wonder,' said the Emperor, ' how happens **it that you are** all in this very miserable condition ?'

The beggars were silent, not willing, apparently, to give **the** wished-for explanation; **but** Aurungzebe **insisting** on being fully informed on the subject, the lame man replied, ' Most mighty Emperor, if the adventures of three miserable beggars can interest your royal heart, we are ready to relate them to **you.'**

Aurungzebe declaring he was most anxious **to** learn by what accident they were thus reduced, the lame man thus commenced his **history :—**

THE STORY **OF THE FIRST BEGGAR.**

I am a Persian, a native **of Yezd,** and my name is **Yasmin.   My father was a** corn merchant, and **a** man **of considerable** wealth, but, like many other **men of Yezd, was a Sufi,**[1] in which persuasion I was brought up.   **Yezd** being celebrated for the number of learned

---

[1] 'The Arabic **word Sufi** means wise, pious.   **It may** be derived from the word Saaf, pure, clean.   **Some** think this class were so called from the word Soof, which means wool, **the** followers being invariably clothed in coarse woollen garments.   It appears, **from several writings** of Mahommedan authors, that a **class called** Sufis were **co-existent with** their religion, but are now considered as among **the most** dangerous of its enemies.   The **Sufi contemns the** forms **of the true faith,** and entertains **very free** opinions regarding its **dogmas. These,** with their claim to a distinct **communion with** the Deity, have subjected **them to the accusation of** entirely disbelieving what **they outwardly profess to respect, and,** consequently, they are considered infidels.   **The teachers** offer **their disciples** of this sect their own absurd **and varied** doctrines, instead of **the forms** and **usages of** the Mahommedan religion.   They are required to consider their teacher superior to all other mortals, in short, expected to adore **him.'**—*Malcolm's Hist. Persia,* vol. **ii.**

Sufis it contained, I soon became, through the introduction of my religious teacher, Syud Mahommed Ali, acquainted with several of the most learned of the sect. Owing to my father's flourishing circumstances, I had abundance of leisure time to make myself **a** perfect Sufi, and firmly believe a more zealous one than myself was not to be found in Yezd. I therefore strove, **by** diligence and application to the most difficult studies, to become celebrated as one of the most learned of the Itâhedeah[1] sect, which was that to which my father and Syud Mahommed Ali belonged. Poetry is the very essence of Sufiism, and to that I bestowed unwearied attention. Syud Mahommed Ali daily impressed on my mind the glory I should attain by procuring proselytes to the sect, and **I** set to work with the most unremitting perseverance to convert young men of my own age, **and** lead them into the path of Sufiism.

This anxiety on the part of the Syud to gain proselytes was, I believe, more to increase the number of his adorers than from any true religious feeling for the welfare of their souls. Devoted, however, as I was to the service of my enlightened teacher, and at that time firmly believing the Syud was actuated alone by religious motives, I strove to imitate him in every particular, looking up to him as a divinity. I became acquainted with two youths, whom, from their staunch adherence to the ordinances **of**

---

[1] 'There are two principal sects of Sufis, viz. the Hulooleah and the Itâhedeah. The former is the 'Inspired,' who believe God has descended or entered into them ; the latter, that God is as **one** with every enlightened **being** ; in short, considering themselves, from their union with the divinity, to **be God.** One of their spiritual leaders, who **professed to have** arrived at the last stage of Sufiism, proclaimed that he was indeed God.'—*Malcolm's Hist. Persia*, vol. **ii.**

Islaam, I determined to convert, anticipating the warm approbation of my preceptor, and hoping by this act to arrive at the second stage of Sufiism,[1] when I should no longer be required to follow my teacher, and be allowed to dispense with all exterior forms of devotion, and obtain credit for spiritual worship. This release from the leading-strings of Syud Mahommed Ali would be to me, whose gods were vanity and pride, most truly acceptable.

To sacrifice, therefore, a hundred Mahommedans, to maintain my own independence and superiority, was an act so necessary to my happiness, that I hesitated not laying close siege to my two friends, Yusoof and Mohabet Ali, the sons of respectable merchants of Yezd, and the same which now stand before your Majesty. These, my unhappy companions, will in their turn relate how indefatigable I was to effect their conversion, or, in other words, their ruin.

Being by nature gifted with a handsome appearance and great volubility of speech, I gradually worked upon their minds, representing the advantages of Sufiism, both in this and the next world, launching out into the praises of every stage of it, and setting forth the vast superiority we possessed in learning over every other mortals on earth—a fact which our worst enemies could not deny. The youths listened, and listening fell into the snare. I

---

[1] 'There are four stages through which a man must pass ere he can attain perfection and beatitude. The first is humanity, which means obedience to the holy law, and a strict observance of all the rules, customs, and doctrines of the established religion. The second stage is the road or path, and he who arrives at this leaves that state wherein he was admitted to admire and follow a teacher, and enters into the pale of Sufiism, and is allowed to abandon all religious forms, changing practical for spiritual worship. The third stage is knowledge, and he who arrives at this is considered inspired. The fourth is ruth, which means an union with the Divinity.'—*Malcolm's Hist. Persia.*

brought them before Syud Mahommed Ali, **whose eyes** bore witness to the delight he experienced.

Thus did Yusoof and Mohabet Ali become Sufis, and deserted the true faith ; they had **yet,** however, to learn **the** consequences of their apostacy : their fathers and friends renounced **them for** ever, and the youths became wanderers, whom I felt myself compelled to support and humour in every possible manner, fearing they might otherwise desert **us.** If they were treated with neglect and contempt by their own friends, the attention and respect they received from the Sufis sufficiently compensated them **for** their loss, at least so I thought ; and by my advice and governnance soon succeeded in persuading them to banish the recollection of their friends' displeasure from their minds.

The time now came when I was considered **to be** worthy admission into the second stage of Sufiism, **and** with pleasure hailed the day that saw me independent of Syud Mahommed Ali, **under** whose guidance I had remained from my infancy. I now harangued the sect in public, and gave full scope to my powers **of** language, so that I was looked upon as a prodigy, approaching perfection **by** more rapid strides than **any of** my predecessors. My father **was** particularly delighted **at** my promotion, having himself but lately arrived at the state of knowledge. Although it was extremely gratifying to me to observe the progress **of** Yusoof and Mohabet Ali, it was not so pleasant to provide for them : for, holy and pure as we considered ourselves, it was utterly impossible **to** live without eating. My father having lost one of his clerks, who died suddenly, was, through my intercession, persuaded to appoint Yusoof to the vacant situation. The youth was rejoiced beyond measure at the provision I had procured for him, whilst Mohabet Ali was particularly downcast at perceiving he must for awhile continue a dependent on my bounty.

I had now reached the zenith of my ambition, in the second stage of Sufiism ; and as many years must pass away ere I could aspire to the third stage of knowledge, I determined to make the most of my present acquirements. My acknowledged superiority in learning and eloquence, I conceived, justified me in assuming a haughty demeanour toward my own sect, and a profound contempt towards those of the opposite persuasion, so that I felt sensible I was beloved by none. 'What does it signify,' I would say to myself, 'whether I am beloved or despised? I am wealthy and in the path : I am nearly at the head of all who have been admitted into the second stage, and my eloquence and acquirements are acknowledged by everyone. The friendship of man can neither add to my happiness or ensure my promotion.'

As I was walking one day in one of the principal streets, a poor beggar asked alms of me. With a look of anger mingled with contempt I retreated from him, holding my clothes close to my body, lest I should become contaminated by his touch. 'Mark me, Sufi,' cried the beggar : 'if thus thou shunnest him who asks for aid in the name of God, the time is not far distant when that God, whom you consider to be ever with thee, will desert thee, and bring thee to my deplorable state. Nevertheless, may Allah protect thee ! '

The words of the old mendicant made a deep impression upon my mind for a moment ; but meeting a party of my sect soon after who flattered and praised my learning, wealth, and power, I no longer burthened my mind with the remembrance of the beggar, or his awful prognostications, and treated in the same manner every miserable petitioner for aid who presumed to approach me. My extravagance kept pace with my pride and insolence ; and although the allowance made me by my father, together with a share in the profits of his merchandise, was more than enough, with economy and prudence, to have enabled me to purchase the indulgence of every luxury, yet a mind like mine was difficult to be kept in check by any regular limited income, and I entertained serious thoughts of robbing my own father, and was only deterred by the recollection that by so doing I should, in truth, be only robbing myself, as I had become a partner in his concerns.

I proposed, at a meeting of the sect, to proceed to Afghanistan, for the purpose of enquiring into the condition and progress of the Sufis in that country ; and to enable me to secure converts, and maintain our consequence, insisted upon sallying forth in the most sumptuous manner, intending, in reality, to convert the money I might be furnished with entirely to my own use and amusement. A large subscription was collected, and everything was ready for my departure, when an event happened which entirely put an end to my projects. This event was the death of my father. He had received an account of a great failure in his mercantile speculations, which, with my consent, had been entered into. My father could not stand the shock of this intelligence ; he took to his bed, from which, alas ! he arose no more. In his dying hour he thus addressed me :

'Yasmin, my son, I am about to leave you for ever. Persevere in the faith, neglect not the ordinances of Sufiism, and you will yet succeed in all your undertakings. I have now little wealth to leave you. Here are the keys of my strong-chest; its contents, with several bonds and notes, are yours by my will, but this house is your cousin's. On his arrival be kind to him. Strengthen each other in the true religion, and may you prosper.' Thus died my father, leaving me, who expected on his decease to become possessed of unbounded wealth, heir to almost nothing.

On examining the contents of the chest, a bag, containing one thousand toomauns, with several bonds, were all that met my eye. I could not, would not believe that this was the only sum the house contained. 'There is some trick,' cried I; 'and my cousin, who is to have the house, is doubtless correctly informed where the money is buried.' As soon as the remains of my father were interred I set to work to search for treasure; a hundred labourers were dispersed all over the house, with orders to dig and penetrate walls, although they might be six feet thick. I myself assisted, until, unused to such fatigue, I was compelled to desist, carrying, however, lighted torches into every nook and corner of the building. I was interrupted in my search by hearing the cries of 'Fire, fire!' from persons above and in the street.

I attempted to rush from the place where I was, to gain access to the strong-box, hoping to be able to secure the little money it contained; but the number of the workmen, together with the volumes of smoke which filled the narrow staircase, rendered a hasty retreat impossible. At last I approached the small treasure closet, and was in the act of stepping on the floor of the room which led to it, when it gave way, and a burst of fire dreadful to behold rendered my progress impracticable. Still hankering after the toomauns, I maintained my ground until several voices begging me to withdraw aroused me, and I quickly retreated into the street, which I had scarcely gained when the whole edifice, with a tremendous crash, fell to the earth, amidst **the** screams of the affrighted populace.

No one afforded the least assistance ; nor, had they been **so** inclined, I saw not how it could have been of any service, for I had no doubt but that the fire was owing to myself, in carelessly thrusting my torch into every corner of the mansion ; and **the** sudden falling in of the building was doubtless to be attributed to the zeal of my workmen, who had undermined its foundations. In situations like mine a show even of inclination **to** lend assistance is gratifying ; but, alas ! how could I expect aid from persons I had contemned, from the rabble I had despised ? **It** was provoking to behold the apathy of the mob ; but it was insufferable to see the Guebres[1] falling **down** and worshipping with delight the very flames which caused **my ruin ;** and, as if the sight of these wretches was not sufficient to add to the sting of adversity which now goaded my heart, on turning round I beheld the old beggar who had predicted my downfall. **He thrust** forward his dirty-bearded chin, saying, with a look of malignant joy, ' I told **you so, Sufi ;** the time is **come** sooner than I had imagined. God preserve thee, Sufi ! '

He then turned on his heel, leaving me to view the progress of **the** desolation before me. Why I stood there I know not. I suppose I imagined when the **fire should have** consumed the building, the strong-box and the bag **of** toomauns were to rise

[1] Fire-worshippers.

from its ashes. The poorer classes now flocked around the burning wood, striving to secure something from the conflagration.

'Of what use is that piece of half-burned wood to you?' said I to a ragged old man, who was walking away with a blackened rafter on his shoulders.

'Whatever is saved from a burning house must be reckoned gain,' said the old Mahommedan; 'and surely, Sufi, you must in the course of your learning have heard or read this proverb.'

Angry at the fellow's insolence, I cried, 'That gain, as you call it, is mine, sirrah ! Throw down the wood.'

'Take it !' said he, throwing it with violence on my toes, which caused me to bellow with pain.

'What have you gained, Sufi?' said another forlorn fellow, who was raking amongst the dying embers.

A laugh from behind me made me turn my head, when the abominable old beggar once more met my eye. Enraged at thus seeing myself the sport of the very rubbish of the city, I gave the insolent old fellow a box on the ear, and bade him begone. Instead of resenting, the provoking old man only laughed louder and louder, and at last screamed with delight, walking slowly away, tapping his lean belly and pointing to his mouth, as much as to say, 'You will come to this, and I rejoice at it.'

CHAPTER XI.

THE DYER'S STORY (*continued*).

THE only persons who condoled **with me were my** two prose-lytes, who might perhaps more justly have **been** denominated satellites, though not of a glorious but a fallen **star.** Well aware the sympathy of these youths proceeded from interested motives, I received their sighs and expressions **of** regret with a peevishness which I hoped would have rid me of their company, but in this I was mistaken. They followed me wherever **I** went; if I stopped, **they did** so likewise; if I walked quick, they kept pace with me. I was about to dismiss them in anger, when prudence whispered, ' It is policy for a ruined man to be friends even with beggars.'

We therefore walked **about** the streets, where I had **the** mortification of perceiving, by the leer of the fakeers and beggars, how rapidly the report **of my** ruin had **run** through the **city. Some** of the latter when passing me would, in imitation of myself in the **days** of my prosperity, hold their tattered garments close to their miserable bodies, pretending to fear contamination from my touch. All this I was compelled to suffer in silence; an angry word would otherwise have drawn a swarm of insolent ragamuffins around me, like eagles about a carcass in the deserts of Arabia. Oh, heavens ! how my cheeks burned with wounded pride ! At that moment, could I have seen any way towards my former state, I verily believe I should have hesitated at no crime by the commission of which success could have been ensured.

We approached the dwelling of Syud Mahommed Ali. ' Here, my friends,' I exclaimed, addressing my companions ; ' here, at least, is a refuge for the destitute.'

We entered. The holy man was sitting with his books before him, intent on deep study. It was a considerable time ere he deigned to raise his eyes, and then shook his head as a sign he wished not to be disturbed. We retired, and waited an hour in his verandah, and then again ventured to approach the learned Syud. Determined to arrest his attention, I cried aloud, ' Oh, Syud, I am a beggar.'

The venerable teacher, from whom I expected so much commiseration and relief, answered me in the words of the Prophet, saying, ' Oh, Yasmin, poverty is my glory !'[1]

Poverty might be a glory to the Syud, but it was far different with me and my companions.

Syud Mahommed Ali, immediately he had finished this charitable reply, bent his eyes again on his book ; nor could we, I

---

[1] A poor man once went to Mahommed, who was sitting in an assembly of learned men, and cried, ' Oh, Prophet, I am poor !' Mahommed replied, ' Poverty is my glory !' Presently afterwards another man came, saying, ' Oh, Prophet, I am poor.' Mahommed replied, ' Poverty makes men blush in both worlds. You are surprised, my friends,' said he, turning to his companions, ' at my giving such contradictory answers to these two beggars ; but the fact is, the first is a pious man, who for religion's sake has left the world, but the other is a man whom the world has deserted.'

verily believe, had each of **us** shed scalding tears of agony, have induced him to bestow another look upon us.

'Let us be gone,' said Yusoof; 'the Syud is perhaps engaged in some difficult pursuit, which it would be indecorous in us to disturb; probably at another time we may find him disengaged.'

I shook my head, doubting the probability, and **when** in the street was convinced how erroneous was my friends' supposition, by hearing the door **of** the Syud's house slam-to with **a** violence which clearly evinced his disposition.

'There, my friends,' said I, 'what think you now?'

'Alas!' replied Mohabet **Ali, 'I** think **that** sound **is the** thunder of despair; for if the Syud thus despises us, what can **we** expect from the world?'

'My dear friends,' said I, 'there **may** yet **be some** hope for **us.** Leave me awhile, and go to the ruined tomb without the **city** walls, and there await my coming.'

My companions did not much relish the idea of even a momentary separation; but when I urged the necessity of the case and represented the certainty of a complete failure in my attempts to procure money, unless I were suffered to make the trial in private, they wisely departed, and I confess I wished **the separation** to be eternal.

My intention **was to** proceed to several merchants whom I knew to be debtors **to my** father, entertaining hopes that all would **not** be so base as to deny their just debts; and my object in getting rid of my companions was, that they might be kept in ignorance as to the extent of my success. I first went to a grain-dealer. '**You are** aware,' said I, 'there is a trifling sum due to me from you on account of the wheat you purchased from my father about six months ago ; I am come therefore to demand it.'

The dealer said not a word, but held out his hand.   Not comprehending his meaning, I repeated the cause of my visit, upon which he said, still keeping his hand outstretched, 'Bond, note, account—produce, produce.'

'Oh !' I replied, 'the recent unfortunate conflagration has destroyed all instruments of that description ; but I am convinced you must remember the purchase of the corn I allude to.'

The dealer on this burst out into a loud fit of laughter, too insufferable for me to bear; and not daring to trust to my impatient and irritable disposition, I walked hastily away.   I met another debtor in the street, whom I reminded of his small sum due to me.

'Don't molest me, fellow,' cried he, 'or I will have you imprisoned.'   So saying he walked hastily by me, muttering the words, 'Insolent rascal !   Wuld al haram !'[1] and other appellations most galling to me to hear.

Thus was I treated by all my father's debtors in Yezd.   Some laughed at, some abused me, and others pulled down large and ponderous account-books, pretending to search for the items therein; and after detaining me nearly a full hour, coolly shut up the unerring folios, saying, 'See nothing of the kind in my books. Go about your business.'

Thus was disappointment heaped upon disappointment, and insult upon insult, and above sat poverty staring me in the face. ' Is it possible,' said I to myself, 'that I, who was so lately courted

---

[1] 'Base-born.'

by the wise and the wealthy, should so suddenly be thrown on a
level with the ignorant and the wretched?' I now repented
having dispensed with the company of my two inseparables; for
it would, I imagined, be a difficult matter to convince them I had
returned poor as themselves.

I was just turning down a narrow street leading to **one of the**
gates of the city, for the purpose of joining my friends in distress,
when the impertinent old beggar stood before me. He signed me
to approach; and having **by** this time received many a severe
lesson to beware how I deported myself even before the dregs **of**
the people, I obeyed his signal. He called me, he said, not to
irritate or jeer me on my reverses, but to advise me to quit Yezd
immediately.

'Quit Yezd!' exclaimed I. 'Wherefore should I **fly?**'

'Your cousin is arrived from Schiraz, said he, 'to take possession of his house, and the officers of justice are searching for you,
to answer for your having wilfully set fire to and demolished the
property.'

'Oh, heaven!' I exclaimed, 'am I never to be at rest? I did
not purposely demolish the house.'

'That may be,' said the beggar; 'but you are thus accused, and
that is more than half-way to conviction, especially **as** you are a
Sufi; and the Governor, you know—'

'I know indeed,' cried I. 'Thanks, my friend. Would I could
reward you for your information!'

'Talk not of rewards,' replied he; 'remember; look here!'
Saying which he tucked up the ends of his coat, gliding past

me in the same manner as I had done to him on our first meeting. 'Nevertheless,' said he, 'God protect thee, Sufi.'

I hastened to my companions, who, in the ruined tomb, were awaiting my coming.

'**Well** !' cried Yusoof, and 'Well !' exclaimed Mohabet Ali. 'What success, Yasmin ? '

' Expect not success from Yasmin,' said **I.** ' The whole city are Syud Mahommed Alis ; all have treated me with contempt and scorn, and I am **warned** to quit Yezd immediately.'

' **To quit Yezd !' cried they.**

' Ay, indeed, my friends. **My** cousin is arrived, and, enraged at finding no house to inherit, seeks to wreak his vengeance upon **me.** I am therefore determined to avoid the pending danger by immediate flight. Say, will you, my friends, accompany me, or **again** brave the insults of the Yezdys? '

' We will follow you,' cried both in one breath. ' We will live **and** die together !'

' Not so, my friends,' cried I ; ' we will singly roam the world, and, after a lapse of ten years, let us agree to meet once more in **Yezd. One of** us, at least, may, **by some** accident, become wealthy, and he shall provide for and maintain his less fortunate companions.'

' Agreed,' cried Yusoof and Mohabet Ali. ' Let us separate immediately, for we feel satisfied success will never conjointly **attend us ;** and, situated as we are, there is no time to be lost.'

We agreed, however, to walk on together until Yezd should disappear, and then to part. We arrived at a place where three roads met ; and, having divided the slender contents of our purses, swore, if living, to meet again in Yezd, after ten years should have passed away; and as we now shared each other's property, so should we agree to go halves in the wealth **either** of us might chance to accumulate. Swearing to maintain the doctrines of Sufiism until we again met, we embraced and took a long, long farewell.

Alone in the wide world, I almost repented our proceeding: for the youths, whose company I was wont to consider irksome to me, I now sincerely sighed for. 'They are true friends,' said **I to** myself; '**and** should either become rich, will not fail to assist the wretched Yasmin.' 'But,' said Conscience, 'will Yasmin **aid** them?' 'Oh! fortune, fortune, pour on me one golden shower of thy kindness, and if I aid not Yusoof and Mohabet Ali may **I** suffer a reverse, if possible, more severe than my present.' Thus I thought when no gleam of hope existed of my being the wealthiest of the three; how I regarded my **vow,** when fortune did favour me, your majesty shall presently learn.

· I found I had taken the direct road to Ispahan. 'In that vast and populous city,' cried I, 'it is hard, indeed, **if** a man with my talents cannot find employment.' Nevertheless, I sighed at leaving Yezd, my **own** dear Yezd. 'Surely,' thought I, 'it would have been better had **I** stayed and braved the anger of my cousin and the vengeance **of** the Governor; for, had I been imprisoned, Yusoof and Mohabet Ali would have **been** my companions; and wisely hath the poet said, " Pae dur zunjeer peesh-i-dostan, Beh ki ba begānāgān dur Bostan." '[1]

<hr>

[1] 'It is preferable to be in chains before friends, than to roam at large in a garden with strangers.'

At a small village I obtained a verandah to lie down in, and procured a little refreshment, which I partook of in solitude ; no one spoke to or noticed me. How different to my former life ! where, when the repast was concluded, I was the first to commence a learned argument or recite the stanzas of a much admired poet. Here I was surrounded by boors, who knew not Alif from Bè, and who scarcely comprehended my high-flown language.

The night was truly wretched. A mat was my bed, pillow I had none ; and the keen air, penetrating through and through me, effectually banished sleep from my hard couch; whilst the ruddy inhabitants of the house were snoring around me in every direction. In the morning, as I was preparing to depart, a horseman came at full speed through the village He appeared to be a man of consequence, although not an attendant was to be seen. I was convinced the rider's horse had become unmanageable, and that great danger awaited both horse and man, unless the speed of the former were checked ere they approached the river, which was broad and deep. It was, however, impossible for me to attempt seizing the bridle of an ungovernable brute who was proceeding with the rapidity of lightning ; I therefore called out as loud as I could, when the rider passed me, ' The river, the river ! turn your horse, if possible.'

The horseman heard me, but was helpless. Aware of the coming danger, therefore, he threw himself off, and fell to the ground with a dreadful shock. I hastened to his assistance, and found he had not received such serious injury as I had reason to apprehend. I hastily procured water and bathed his bleeding temples ; and perceiving his arm to be broken, carefully tied it in a sling, and attempted to lead the unhappy man (who was advanced in years) towards the village ; but, alas ! he could not arise from the earth. The aid of the inhabitants being necessary, I prevailed on two stout fellows to assist me in removing the injured horseman. We at last brought the wounded man into the village, and placed him on a rude bed, provided by the head man of the place, and soon after had the pleasure of hearing him speak and express his thanks for our trouble. I begged him to remain quiet and undisturbed, and that farther assistance should soon be procured.

I now began to reflect whether, in the days of my glory, I should have thus interested myself to save from destruction a fellow-being. Alas ! I fear not. Had I seen him galloping through the village, with the knowledge that he would certainly be engulphed in a yawning abyss, my proud lips would not have opened to have warned him of his pending fate, or aided him had he escaped the coming horrors ; but now,—oh, poverty ! what lessons dost thou teach us !—I could scarcely believe it was Yasmin, the proud Sufi, who hung over the couch of the wounded horseman. I had scarcely finished my reflections ere the sound of voices called me to the door. 'Where is the Governor ?' cried several men (whose appearance and the distressed condition of their horses convinced me they had ridden a considerable distance in search of their lost master). 'Safe,' cried I ; 'your master is safe, but not uninjured.'

One of the men dismounting, I conducted him towards the sick man, who, I learned, was the Governor of Tebriz, proceeding on business to Ispahan, whither it was deemed expedient immediately to convey him, there being no skilful surgeon in the village to set the fractured limb. The Governor of Tebriz desiring **the** person who had been instrumental to his safety should forthwith be introduced to him, I entered his apartment and made my obeisance ; but I fear rather awkwardly, my proud head having had but little practice that **way.** He expressed his gratitude and thanks in the warmest manner, and enquired into my circumstances. I was too proud to confess my poverty, and yet too cautious to allow him to suppose **I** stood not in need of assistance. I represented myself as the son of a merchant, who had experienced sad reverses; and that seeing little or **no** prospect **of** success in the mercantile line, which was ever my aversion, I had determined to proceed to Ispahan, hoping there to obtain a situation more genial **to my** habits and disposition. The Governor, convinced from my address that I had received a good education, offered me a situation under his secretary, who had preceded him **to** the imperial **court.** Accepting the offered place, he bade **me** consider myself **one** of his suite, and gave orders that I should be furnished with a horse, to **accompany** him to Ispahan. 'I would offer you my own,' said the old man, smiling, 'but for two reasons—one is, that I fear you have already seen a specimen of his temper ; and the next, the probability the brute is dashed to pieces, as the bank of the river, I understand, is extremely high and steep.'

We marched by easy stages to Ispahan, and on our arrival I was introduced to the secretary, whose appearance was far from being prepossessing ; he was a tall, thin, debauched-looking fellow, with a hatchet-face and staring eyes, and his whole countenance buried **in hair.** The secretary, however, whatever might have been his feelings towards me, received me with true Persian politeness, which nevertheless was regarded by me as anything but a favourable omen, politeness being the constant cloak of the Persian when he meditates an injury. I certainly had given no cause for offence, except that of having accepted the situation of his assistant ; but I soon understood nothing could have annoyed him more, as the place was one he had long intended to procure for his **own** nephew. This being the case, I was well aware all attempts to please and give satisfaction would prove futile ; diligence would **be** denominated officiousness, whilst idleness or inactivity would not fail being urged as a plea for my dismissal.

The Governor was accustomed to write a great deal himself, but his recent accident now prevented him, and I was accordingly sent for to write from his dictation. **It** appeared he was preparing a report on the condition of the people over whom he ruled, which **he** was anxious should be presented to his majesty before his **return** to Tebriz.

The Governor, on the departure of the doctor who had set his fractured arm, desired to see the result of my labours : he read with attention every word, and commended my style and my beautiful handwriting. Ismael—so was the secretary named—I perceived was burning with envy at the visible progress I was making in the good graces of the Governor, and strove hard to secure my absence at the very hour he knew the Governor would send for me. Finding all his contrivance ineffectual, he one day ordered me to go to **the** Treasury, to get several receipts signed.

Of course I could not refuse, and **in** consequence Ismael was summoned to the Governor's presence in my stead, and wrote a portion of the report. On the following day the Governor called for our production, and reading over the work of Ismael, **expressed** himself much dissatisfied with it, saying, ' Had the fellow used my own words, that was all I required of him ; but **he** has put together such long-winded sentences as will puzzle not only Abbas, but any king that ever reigned. Where were you, Yasmin?'

' **Please your Excellency,' I** replied, ' Ismael deputed me to go **to the** Treasury.'

' Humph! would **he** had been pleased to have gone himself! We must write all his stuff over again. **Throw** aside his sheet, and re-write **it** in better language.'

' I fear that will greatly displease Ismael,' said **I.**

' 'Tis my report, not his,' said the Governor, rather sharply ; upon which I durst make no further objection, but sat down to my **task.** Accident again gave the manuscript into the secretary's **hands** whilst I happened to be present. He turned over the leaves **to search for** his own handwriting ; **but** what **a** diabolical look did **he give me** on finding all his labours had been expunged—not a vestige to be seen ! Of course this heinous crime was attributed solely to me, and I dreaded **the** consequences, and not without reason. My salary was liberal, and my situation, but for Ismael, might have been agreeable ; and indeed nothing happened during our stay at court to **cause me** trouble, for Ismael continued as polite as ever, and even invited me to a grand dinner he gave to some of the principal officers of the court.

At this feast the conversation turned upon religion, although **not** one of the asses, in my opinion, knew anything about the sub-ject. ' **Ah !**' thought I, ' how I could astonish you all, if I durst!' But to declare my Sufiism among the Sheahs of Ispahan would have been madness; and as to the other persuasions, I knew little of them ; consequently I maintained a profound silence. One of the company, however, nearly compelled me to give loose to my tongue by calling aloud, 'Ismael, how go on the Kāfirs[1] of Yezd ; are they as numerous as ever?'

'Indeed I know not,' replied Ismael, 'but **one of the** richest and most infamous has died lately.'

'And is damned of course,' said the first speaker.

'Of course,' answered Ismael, as if he had been present at the judgment of my poor father, to whom they doubtless alluded. Although I durst not speak, yet my feelings were such as to induce me to quit the company as soon **as** I possibly could. This I considered, on reflection, to have been highly imprudent, and might cause strong suspicions to arise in the breasts of Ismael and his guests. I fancied on the following day many of the company whom I met at court eyed me in a peculiar way, and consequently felt extremely uncomfortable. The urbanity and goodnature of the Governor, however, banished in a measure my fears, and the time passed pleasantly.

The departure of the Governor being fixed, the report was sent in to the King, with a letter penned entirely by myself, and approved of by the Governor, who was loaded by his majesty with compliments and presents. There being no more business to transact, we prepared to depart. Ismael examined the royal gifts in the presence of myself and the Governor. Amongst the presents was an emerald ring of great value : this, with others, was ordered

[1] Infidels.

to be carefully packed in a box, and to follow with a guard on the day after the Governor and his suite sallied forth.

Ismael having the arrangement of the line of march, deputed me to follow with the treasure, and giving into my hands the jewel-box, appointed Sirdar Khan and twenty men as an escort. I had rather not have been so employed, but durst not decline the honour. The Governor, attended by Ismael, set forth, and I followed on the succeeding day. We made three days' march of it, and on the fourth reached Tebriz, where I lost no time in presenting my casket to the Governor. Ismael, opening it, spread out the contents, over which he seemed deeply employed. The Governor demanded what he was searching for. 'Your excellency may remember,' said he, 'the emerald ring which we admired.'

'Truly do I,' said the governor; 'is it not there?'

'I hope it is,' said Ismael; 'but, by the Prophet! I cannot find it. Yasmin, where is the ring?'

'Nay,' said I, 'the box is just in the state you delivered it to me, and I call Sirdar Khan to witness I have not presumed to open it.' Sirdar Khan advanced, saying, 'I certainly have not seen Yasmin open the casket; but as he constantly kept the same under his care, and as I of course could not be ever at his elbow——'

'What would you insinuate?' said I, alarmed beyond measure.

'I mean to insinuate nothing,' replied he; 'but I mean to say very plainly that the Governor will be obliged to you to produce his ring.' This was too much, and my hand was uplifted to chastise the insolent officer, when the secretary interposed, saying,

' Respect to the presence **of** his Excellency should at least prevent the commission of violence.'

'Am I,' said I, 'tamely to submit to **be called a thief?'**

The Governor now spoke, saying, ' Young **man, I** must own appearances are against **you**; but as you s y **you are** innocent, you can have no objection to undergo a search.'

'Certainly not,' said **I**, loosing **my** coat and taking off **my** turban.   In the former nothing was found; **but** the secretary, **on** searching the lining of my turban, found, **or** pretended he had found, the emerald ring, which he artfully contrived **to let fall at** the feet of the Governor.   The sound covered **me** with shame and confusion.

' By mine eyes !' I exclaimed, **' an** enemy hath done this, **my lord.**   I am innocent of this robbery, nor knew **of** the ring being concealed in my turban ; and my readiness to submit to the search, I trust, has convinced you I speak the truth.'

The secretary maintained profound silence, and Sirdar Khan **most** prudently followed his example.

The Governor thus addressed me :

' Whatever **may be my** private opinion, young man, **matters** not, as long as all around me are fully convinced of your **guilt.   In** my situation, therefore, it **will be** impossible to keep you longer near my person ; therefore, henceforth presume **not to** appear **in** the city.'

' **In** the city !' I exclaimed ; **' am I** to be actually banished the place ?   **Is it** not enough for **me** to lose **my** situation, without being banished like a felon ?'

' Nay, this is **as** you choose ; I only advise, not command.'

'Why, your Excellency?'

'Come hither,' said the Governor, 'and I will whisper my reasons.'

I approached; and stooping down to him, he softly whispered, 'You are a Sufi.'

I had not a word to say, but adjusting my turban and coat, hastily left the palace.

I had doubtless fallen a victim to the jealousy of the secretary Ismael, whose agent was no doubt Sirdar Khan, who, I suspect, introduced the ring into my turban whilst I slept at our second halting-place, on our march to Tebriz; and that the artful Ismael, although apparently most particularly careful in packing up the jewels had contrived to conceal the ring for the abominable scheme in which he so admirably succeeded. How the Governor found out I was a Sufi I know not to this day, but fear my retiring from Ismael's party at Ispahan had been noticed, and probably discussed between that shrewd man and his true-believing guests. 'But then,' thought I, 'this would have been a sufficiently substantial plea for my dismissal from the person of the Governor; but doubtless Ismael, not being quite certain of the fact, determined to have two strings to his bow, justly concluding, if one failed, the other would effectually shoot forth the poisoned shaft of his deadly hatred.'

There was no help, and I submitted to my hard fate, and still hoped for better success in future.

I listened to the advice of the Governor and quitted the city. It was evening, and the country around was beautifully picturesque; a gentle breeze played over the waving corn, and Nature seemed enjoying her own **sweets—all** was harmony **and** composure. Yasmin alone was miserable and disturbed, and this forlorn condition must be attributed to his religion **and to his** learning. The former I will not, the latter I cannot forget.

At this moment a peasant approached me, and seeing me busily employed in arranging my dress, enquired whether I had **been** plundered. 'Ay,' I replied, 'most cruelly plundered, **by a** dog of a Sheah.'

The countryman took **to** his heels as if he had been bitten, anxious **to** get away from a person who, by his speech, he conjectured must either **be a Suni or** a Sufi. I travelled **onwards,** not knowing whither I went, until night overtook me; **and then,** fatigued, sank to sleep under the branches of a majestic tree. **In** the morning I met several peasants, who informed me their village was not far distant, and that, although I might procure lodging, **yet** it would be difficult to obtain any food, large quantities having been purchased for Ilm Ali Khan, the Sufi, who, with a numerous suite, was passing that way from Schiraz.

'If that is the case,' said I, 'there **is** no need of alarm.'

Thanking my informers, I proceeded onwards. **As I entered** the village I perceived a number of horsemen, apparently just arrived: **these I** rightly conjectured belonged to the celebrated Sufi, whose name I had often heard of, but to whose person **I was** a stranger.

'Is the holy **man** arrived?' I enquired. **To** my joy I was answered in the affirmative. I soon got introduced to Ilm Ali Khan, and convinced him I was indeed a Sufi who had arrived **at** the second stage, and toiling, notwithstanding my **misfortunes,** towards the third stage of Sufiism.

Ilm Ali Khan was **a** powerful, strong-built man, with broad **shoulders,** and a fist which would have stunned a bullock ; a large round face, thick bushy beard, and staring, prominent eyes, which would **have** induced anyone mindful of his safety to be careful how he made such a man his enemy. My proud spirit, though it would not submit **to** be humbled before every **rich** man, hesitated not in bowing before one my superior in my religion. I therefore prostrated myself before him, and soon perceived he **took a vast** liking to me.

I learned he was proceeding to Bussorah, where he intended taking **ship** for India, in order to convert the Sunis of that country **to Sufiism.** With permission I joined his suite, and partook of **the** Sufi's own repast. All the Sufis in the towns and villages through which we passed flocked to Ilm Ali Khan, on whom they forced presents of sheep, rice, money, and shawls. This was just the situation suited to my disposition. I could imagine nothing on earth so delightful as to travel about having no care for provisions, and receiving the homage and adoration of the sect wherever I showed my face. 'Surely,' thought I, 'by accompanying this learned Sufi, who after all knows not much more than myself, I may, by displaying my acquirements, chalk out for myself the situation **of** successor to **him, and** then in my turn levy contributions on the bigoted Sufis of the country.'

All this was vastly comfortable to dream about, but how was I to get rid of Ilm Ali Khan, and attach to my person his followers, **so as to convince the people I was** indeed the authorised suc-

cessor. ' I will,' thought I, ' take the first opportunity of displaying my eloquence and learning; perhaps I may draw off the crowd from Ilm **Ali** Khan, and see them flock around Yasmin Yezdy.' This opportunity came not till we reached Bussorah, where Ilm Ali gave a great feast. After the ceremony of eating and drinking had been gone through each began to display **his** knowledge. Ilm Ali launched out as well as he could on the advantages **of** Sufiism, but made, in my opinion, a very lame address; and, impatient to exhibit my vast acquirements, **I** arose ere **he** had well concluded, and in an elegant speech of two hours riveted the attention of my audience, whose repeated cries of ' Wah, Wah !' were most gratifying to my pride.

When I had concluded, many of the company crowded around me, kissing the hem of my garment. **So** delighted was I at the effect my eloquence had produced, that I scarcely noticed Ilm Ali Khan, who sat neglected by his hitherto devoted worshippers. The following day at sunrise the vessel which was to convey Ilm Ali and his suite from Persia was ordered to be in readiness to weigh anchor; and the company, in order to allow the pious Sufi sufficient time to rest, retired at an early hour.

Ilm Ali and myself alone remained in the banqueting-room, neither of **us** speaking **a** word. It was a fine moonlight night; and my patron expressing a wish to enjoy the prevailing serenity of the scene, invited me to walk awhile and enjoy in private some holy conversation. Ever ready to obey and please the man whose place I presumed to sigh after, I quickly attended him. He was most friendly, affable, and courteous. Our conversation turned upon future rewards and punishments, and Ilm Ali seemed pleased with my opinions on the subject. When we had walked some way distant from any human habitation my patron enquired my opinion concerning good and evil, and if I thought there existed any of the latter in the world.

' Undoubtedly not,' said I ; 'everything proceeds from God, and must, therefore, be good.'

' Then take that,' said Ilm Ali, plunging his dagger into my side, and running quickly away. I fell weltering in my blood, and now a second time repented my boasted display of learning, which, no doubt, had excited the jealousy and anger of Ilm Ali Khan in a far greater degree than my writing had worked upon Ismael, the secretary of the Tebriz governor.

I began to think my prospects of realising wealth bore a very melancholy appearance ; and to keep body and soul together seemed as much as I could expect. Shunned at one time by the enemies of Sufiism, and then stabbed at another by one of its most staunch advocates, I almost determined to give up all idea of success, and laid me down to die, without attempting to staunch the wound, the blood from which flowed copiously. 'Alas! poor Yusoof and Mohabet Ali,' said I ; 'if ye have not succeeded better than I have, I fear we shall, if we do meet, meet in rags and poverty.'

Some Arabs, driving a herd of horses laden with dates, discovering me soon after sunrise, humanely placed me on one of the animals and conducted me into the town. Surgeons there were none ; I therefore placed myself at the mercy of the Arabs, who healed me in the same manner they had been accustomed to doctor their horses, and I slowly recovered. I became partial to the Arabs, and strove to gain their good opinion. I succeeded, and when recovered made myself of considerable use to them, **by** writing their accounts, for they were rude merchants of the desert. I followed these men for nearly three years, still a beggar, and no opening whatever appearing **by** which **I** could **even** hope to **be** otherwise.

As the Arabs were marching near Ispahan I seriously thought of leaving them, and trying my fortune in that **great city. The** more I thought on the subject the stronger became my determination; and one night, without **apprising the Arabs** of my intention, I silently left **their** camp, and soon found myself **in the city of** Ispahan. The very first person I met was one of the company at the dinner **given by** Ismael, the **secretary of** the **Governor of** Tebriz. He looked hard at me, and well he might. **I** was **dirty,** thin, and even ragged; looking, in short, exactly like the Arabs **whose** company I had just quitted. **I walked** on, anxious to quit **this** person, for he was an officer of some consequence; he followed me, however, and coming up **to** me, said, 'Surely **I** remember that countenance.'

I answered him in Arabic, and it had the desired effect. **He** begged pardon and retired, looking not unfrequently behind him. I lost no time in proceeding to a barber's shop, for the purpose of having my beard dressed, which was quickly done, but not so quickly paid for, having no money about me. The barber stared prodigiously, and I looked amazingly awkward. ' Be not alarmed, friend,' said I, ' you shall be paid to-morrow.'

' To-morrow !' said he, ' with your leave I will be paid **to-day,** and immediately, or you quit not my house; and, moreover, by

Allah, **I will show** you to every one of my customers, and relate to them the shabby treatment I have met with.'

' My good man,' said I, ' you may show me to whoever **you** please; no one will, I should imagine, pay you for the sight of a man whose appearance bears no marked peculiarity.'

' **Wah,** wah! here **is** fine language from a beggar! By Allah, my fine fellow, if I can't get any money by letting folks see you, when they hear **you** speak I think I may expect some profit.'

' Perhaps so,' said I, ' when they do hear me; but suppose I don't choose to open my lips?'

' Suppose **I** get you well bastinadoed, **my good,** worthy customer; **I** think that will make you open your lips.'

' **I** don't know that it would. **I am** not certain that it would; **but still, where will** be your profit? **Trust** me, honest barber, I **will** undoubtedly pay you for your trouble.'

' Who are you?' said the barber.

' **I** am the son of misfortune. I was wealthy—am now poor; **but** unless the star of my destiny **is** for ever shrouded in the cloud of malignity—unless men and angels have conspired against me, the day may come when I shall burst forth in all my former splendour; I will then——'

' Then,' interrupted the barber, ' you will, I suppose, pay me **for** trimming your beard. Harkee, sirrah: I cannot afford to wait for your stars, and your clouds, and your angels, and devils, either coming or going ; pay me directly, or it will be the worse for you.'

' **Barber,'** I cried, ' I see you have a tender heart.'

' **The** devil you do ! You must see very deep then, for I have not yet evinced much tenderness.'

'That I know,' said **I**; 'your education has naturally tended to sully a heart fraught with every virtue.'

'No, no, my friend,' said the barber, '**this** won't do. I am not such a fool as you are anxious to make me out; and give **me** leave to say, **your** education, though it may have filled your mouth with vain words, has not had the same effect upon your purse.'

I could not deny this retort, but determined on trying whether he were a fool **or not**. I therefore said, 'Friend, **I see** you **are a** clever, honest, upright man; I have the money in my purse, **but on** this day **certain** circumstances **prevent** me from paying **you**. I am a magician—nay, be not alarmed—stand still, and look earnestly on the wall before you, and there **will** appear some writing, the attention **to** which will make you **a rich man.**' Saying which, I turned him to the wall, with his back towards me, saying, '**Turn** not until I command you.' The **barber** stood patiently, whilst I sneaked out of the shop, leaving him to make what he could out of the wall thereof. It **was my** intention, however, to call and **pay** him as soon as possible.

On this day the only lucky accident I ever met with happened to me. **Two** Persians were fighting in the street; much blood was spilled, **and** with difficulty the combatants **were** separated; a crowd followed them, however, leaving me standing **aloof.** On the ground where the action had been so strongly maintained I perceived a small bag; **it** was laden with toomauns.[1] 'Here begins my fortune,' said I. '**In** this city I distinguished myself under the Governor of Tebriz, **and** here it is, doubtless, destined I am to remain.'

---

[1] Gold coin current in the country.

The first use I made of my treasure was to pay the poor barber. On seeing me he began a volley of abuse, which soon ceased on beholding a piece of money between my fingers. 'I am come to pay you,' said I, 'according to my promise, and to give you some advice. Never boast again of not being a fool. All men are fools, though they imagine themselves vastly clever.' I here recited some stanzas, much to the wonder of the pacified barber.

'By my faith,' said he, 'you would be no small acquisition to Gazub, the king's poet.'

'Is he in want of an assistant?' I enquired.

'He is,' replied the barber. 'Would you like to try your hand at poetry?'

'I would not scruple becoming his assistant,' said I, 'provided it be worth my while.'

'What will you give me if I procure you the situation?' enquired the shaver.

'A fourth of my first month's salary,' said I.

'Sit down, then,' said he, 'and pen a specimen of extempore poetry, and suffer me to take it to-morrow to Gazub, who, if he approve, will probably hire you.'

I obeyed, taking care to enquire what religion Gazub professed.

'Why,' said the barber, in an undertone, 'he professes to be a Sheah ; but there are some who strongly suspect he is a rascally Sufi, to whom be perdition.'

Upon hearing this I penned some lines, which, from their

peculiarity, could not fail of letting Gazub know that the author was a true Sufi, and thus I anticipated a lucrative situation in the city of Ispahan. Having given the lines into the barber's hands, I departed, promising to call again **on** the following day.

CHAPTER XII.

THE DYER'S STORY *(continued)*.

I VISITED the barber next day, and learned with pleasure the poet
had expressed a strong desire to see me.   I therefore hastened to
the dwelling of Gazub; and seeing a little misshapen hump-backed
creature in the verandah, enquired for Gazub, the poet.

'I am he,' said the little hunchback, to my no small surprise
and astonishment.

I made a salaam, and mentioned the barber, into whose hands
I had given my verses. The little poet begged me to enter his
house and be seated, when we conversed for some time.   It
required little penetration to discover that Gazub was indeed a
Sufi ; and, I fancy, he as quickly fully understood I was of the
same persuasion. Gazub, though misshapen and deformed, was
by no means advanced in years ; he appeared to be about the age
of forty. He bore a most intelligent countenance, as much as
could be seen of it, for his whole face was so enveloped in hair of
a coarse carroty colour, that two sparkling eyes and the tip of a
well-formed nose were alone visibly distinct. On his head he
wore a purple velvet skull-cap, cocked a little on one side, which
added greatly to the little fellow's self-sufficient appearance. His

coat was of dark chintz, wadded throughout with fine cotton-wool, and a pair **of once handsome keemcab** [1] trousers covered his ill-formed legs, whilst **in a** broad leathern **girdle stuck a** ponderous booghdah,[2] the hilt of which was studded with precious stones.

After some time spent in conversation, I ventured to ask if **my** services would be acceptable, as **I** understood he was in want **of** an assistant.

'Why,' said he, 'there is an allowance for a deputy, which **I** have hitherto enjoyed myself; but owing to some misunderstanding with the treasurer, he has **contrived to** procure an order **for its** discontinuance, unless an assistant is actually employed. **So you** may as well receive the salary as **let it lie in the** treasury; and as I shall frequently require you, it will be advisable you should lodge under my roof.'

I consented with pleasure, and **he** demanded my name.

I replied, ' My name is **Yasmin.**'

' **Is that all ?** ' said he.

' All,' replied I.

The little fellow took up his kulm, and scrawled **on** a scrap of paper the word ' Sufi.'

I nodded assent.

' Well, well,' said he, ' it is no use adding that word; indeed, the seldomer you use **it in** Ispahan the better. You shall **be ap-**pointed, rely on it.'

A few days more saw me regularly installed as deputy king's poet. **My first** task was to **compose a** poetic address to his

---

[1] A gold brocade.
[2] A large Persian dagger ; literally a butcher's knife.

majesty on the first of the ensuing month, a custom invariably adhered to by Gazub. I took very great pains and trouble with this my first production, and, without vanity, declare they were worthy the perusal of a monarch. The only mortifying circumstance was, they were presented as the production of Gazub's instead of Yasmin's brains. My master, on returning from court, informed me that the king read them, but made no remarks ; whereas, I soon after learned that his majesty had highly complimented Gazub on the very elegant poetry he had that day been presented with.

I said nothing, however, hoping one day to succeed to Gazub's situation, which was a most lucrative one ; for, besides a very handsome salary, he frequently received from the king magnificent presents, and was employed by hundreds of persons to write petitions and letters for them, in all of which I had my share of labour, though not of profit.

Opposite the house of Gazub was a large building, very ancient, and of curious construction, but apparently uninhabited. I one day enquired of the poet concerning this singular edifice.

' It belongs,' said he, ' to a wealthy merchant, who is unable to procure a tenant, the house being supposed to be haunted, on account of a horrid murder said to have once been perpetrated therein. But I hear,' said he, ' that the merchant's daughter is about to occupy the mansion, during her father's journey to Bussorah on mercantile affairs, and they say she is a lovely creature, a perfect houri.'

I had at this time been about a year with the poet, whose temper I had dexterously managed, so as to become a great favourite with him, and but for the merchant's daughter and the haunted house, might have enjoyed my situation to this day, and most probably have become king's poet.

The merchant's daughter arrived, and unfortunately occupied the room the windows of which overlooked the apartment wherein I sat to compose my verses and copy letters. The lady through her blind would occasionally look at me, and oh, heavens! how did I linger at my window to catch a glimpse of her beautiful countenance! One day I fancied she smiled; I placed my hand on my heart, and she vanished.

We continued gazing at each other for a month: I could think of nothing else but the fair lady in the haunted house; my poetry, in consequence, breathed the most enraptured strains of love; and having with great labour composed what I must ever conceive to be a set of the best lines to be met with all over Persia, felt most anxious to get them conveyed to the fair lady whose image had so entirely taken possession of my mind. Just at this time Gazub came to my apartment, saying 'he had been ordered by a person of rank to prepare a set of amatory verses, and that aware of my talents in that way, he had come to desire I would assist him.'

I promised obedience, and sat down to my task; but my thoughts and eyes would only wander towards the window of the opposite house, and evening came without a line being penned for my little master. Unwilling to disoblige him, I gave him a copy of my own verses, intended for the fair inhabitant of the haunted house, with which he seemed much pleased. I do not recollect the verses at present; they commenced, however, thus:

'Say, lovely houri, wilt thou deign to view,' &c.,

and the whole seemed throughout to breathe flattery and love, so that the lady could not fail becoming acquainted with the passion of the writer.

The only difficulty I now laboured under was how to present my poetry; and should this be accomplished, I entertained considerable doubts as to the lady's ability to read it; however, as I well knew the Persian ladies in general could both read and write, I determined to convey my lines into her hands if possible. One evening, about a week after I had prepared and copied my verses, I saw my friend the barber proceeding towards the haunted house, carrying on his arm a basket containing perfumes; I hastily descended to the street, and slipping my paper into his basket, and a few toomauns into his hand, said, ' Present this to the lady, and I will double your reward.' He nodded assent, and I departed, congratulating myself on my success.

Oh the following day I proceeded to the barber's shop, where my friend was employed on the beard of a customer. He placed his finger on his lips, and I silently seated myself in one corner of the room, anxiously awaiting the departure of the person whose presence imposed such restraint upon my tongue; when, however, the important ceremony of snipping and curling ceased, the man retired, and I impatiently asked the barber if he had delivered my letter.

' I have,' said he, ' and think you will succeed. The lady read your poetry, and blushed; but,' continued the barber, ' to obtain her favour you must aid her in getting rid of a troublesome rival.'

' A rival!' cried I. ' I will stab him to the heart.

' No, no,' said the barber, 'that is not necessary : a good beating will alone be required.'

' Well,' cried I, ' who is the man that dares step between me and happiness?'

' **Who it** is,' said the barber, ' is of no consequence. **You** may one day **know,** but I am not authorised to inform you at present ; only to learn whether you will aid in punishing him for his presumption.'

' Ay,' said I, ' by Allah ! I will cane him myself, if necessary.'

' Nay,' replied the shaver, ' demean not yourself so far. **Pro**cure three stout fellows and an **ass, and have them** ready to-morrow night at twelve, when you, **in his stead,** may depend on being received.'

' Is the lady rich?' I enquired.

' **Her** father is very wealthy, and he that weds his daughter **may** hold his head as high as any Khan in the country.'

' Enough, my friend,' said I. ' Here is more gold for you, and with **it** provide the fellows who are to treat my rival with the rattan.'

The barber received the money, and I, delighted beyond measure, returned home. ' Now,' said I to myself, when shut up in my own apartment, 'now, Yasmin, is thy fortune made ! I question if my two friends will be as lucky as myself; all this may be attributed to **my** poetry, my abilities, my Sufiism. Shall I, when in power and possessed of wealth, take my bride to Yezd, and **share my** fortune with too ragged **fellows** like Yusoof and Mohabet **Ali?** No, no ! truly **I have had toil** enough, and wil solely reap **the benefit. Besides,** what would my wife think if she saw me in company with a couple of half-starved beggars? No, no, it won't do! I will remain in Ispahan, dear city, wherein I was destined to flourish.' Yes, my friends, such was my intention— to desert ye, to whom I swore everlasting friendship, and with whom I promised to share the gifts of fortune.

The hour approached, and, dressed out in gay attire, I proceeded to the mansion of my beloved. The barber was awaiting my arrival, and at a preconcerted signal the outer door was slowly opened by a eunuch, who signed us to silence. Three lusty fellows were attending the barber, who also being admitted, begged to know where the ass was to be fastened. After some few words between the barber and the eunuch it was settled the animal should be led into the first courtyard of the mansion, and, as there was much grass, be suffered to graze until he was wanted. The eunuch led us into the interior of the building, smiling and bowing to me most obsequiously.

Halting at a room the door of which was closed, he opened it, and bade me enter, saying he would return to me as soon as my rival should be delivered into his hands. I waited for some time, and at last heard the effects of my hirelings' canes on the back of my unhappy rival, and at every agonising shriek which issued from the poor victim I inwardly chuckled with delight. The cries became more feeble, and a slamming of doors and loud laughing now reached my ears. The eunuch soon after appeared, and placing his finger on his thick blubber-lips, led me into a splendid apartment, illuminated by silver lamps suspended from the ceiling, at the upper end of which sat a lady veiled.

The eunuch led me up to the enchanting angel, at whose feet

I instantly fell, and was beginning a rhapsody of admiration, when from a side-door issued the very men who had been hired by myself to chastise my rival, headed by a tall, well-made man, who cried, 'Seize the Kafir,' and serve him as you did the other scoundrel.' The lady burst into a loud fit of laughter, and the barber and eunuch stood grinning with delight. The **men** approached me, and I resisted, when their leader himself seized my arm. I struck him on the face, when men, barber, and eunuch fell upon me, securing my arms with a strong rope. **'Give him** the bastinado,' said the mysterious instigator of the violence. 'Lay it on thick,' said he. 'And fasten this **around** his neck,' said the lady, tossing **on** the floor **my** elegant verses, from which I had anticipated a very different result. 'And hark'ee,' cried the man whom I had struck, 'place him on the ass with the other fellow, and when morning dawns lead them through the city.'

Mortified and humbled, my arms secured, and my mind distracted, what could I do? Alas, alas! how unexpected a termination of my love affair! I was led down narrow staircases into a dark dungeon, where the bastinado was cruelly applied to the soles of my feet, and it was **now** my turn to yell, scream, and beg for mercy. When my tormentors had finished their cruel work I was left to myself, and the door of my dungeon secured. I fancied I heard the groans of **the poor** man, who, like me, had fallen in the snare, and was writhing under the torments to which I hesitated not in being accessory. In the morning my prison-door was opened, and in came the treacherous barber, whom I began bitterly to reproach.

'**All** men **are** fools,' said he, 'though they think **themselves** vastly clever; but you are the greatest fool I ever met with. What induced you to strike the prince?'

'The prince!' cried I. 'How could I know it was him?'

'Whether you knew it or not,' said the barber, 'it was madness to use your fist when surrounded by so many men, and you have suffered for your folly. Blame not me,' said the barber. 'I was employed by the prince long ere you applied to me.'

'But then,' said I, 'why not have informed me of this?'

'Because, fool that thou art, he himself received your poetry, and commanded me to act as I have done.'

'Heavens!' said I, 'was it not you yourself to whom I gave my verses?'

'No, truly; it was the prince disguised as me. But with your wisdom one would have imagined you would have been more cautious than to act as you did. I am sorry you have been bastinadoed, as I had begged no violence might be practised on you; and it was agreed that a ride upon the ass, with your still more foolish rival, whom you were so ready to punish, would be a sufficient warning for you in future.'

'Who, then, is to be my companion in disgrace?' I enquired.

'You will see. Here comes the eunuch; and your steed is ready; and the lady standing at her window to see three asses together.'

Here the fellow grinned, and turned on one side to admit the eunuch, who raised me up in his arms, my feet bleeding and lacerated. Arrived in the courtyard, what was my surprise at beholding, mounted on an ass, with his face towards the tail, my master, Gazub!

His arms like mine were tied behind him, **and** his feet, which had not suffered, fastened under the animal's belly. I saw the surprise with which he beheld me about to become his companion, and never before did two poets look so foolish. Around the neck of Gazub were suspended my verses, pasted on a long slip of wood, and the original was quickly affixed to my neck ; **and in** order to distress us the more, I was placed with my face almost touching my companion's ; and thus were we led from the courtyard of the building, the lady above us laughing immoderately, and singing **a** few lines of my **poetry—**

'Say, lovely houri!' &c.

A crowd was soon collected in the streets, although the hour **was** early ; and amidst the hootings and hissings **of the** mob, **we** arrived at the poet's house.

The barber, who acted as surgeon, attended me and bound up my wounded feet, and dressed the **sores on** the hump-back of my master.

'**In the name of mercy,**' **said I,** 'cure my wounds.'

'I will,' replied the barber, 'if I **can ; but one of your feet is** indeed in a bad state, **and I** fear you **will** lose the use **of it for** ever.'

This was a melancholy **piece** of intelligence, which I with **diffi-**culty resigned myself to.

'Pray,' enquired I, 'what is the meaning of my verses being all **got** together in the haunted house? And who in the name **of wonder is** the she-devil that inhabits it?'

'Listen,' said the barber. 'The lady is in truth the daughter of a merchant ; and the prince, having accidentally beheld her, determined to secure her as his mistress. He applied to Gazub for some amatory verses by way of an introduction, and being a prince and not a poet, was admitted privately, disguised as myself, having previously largely bribed the eunuch who guards the lady. As he was one evening sitting with his beloved, the eunuch entered, bringing a paper which, he said, had been given him by the poet over the way—by Gazub himself. The prince begged, for amusement sake, the contents might be read aloud ; when what was her astonishment and diversion on perusing the **very first line**—

' Say, lovely houri ! ' &c.,

the very counterpart **of the prince's own** verses, through which **he had** obtained admission into the mansion! The prince confessed **he had** employed **a poet, as he was unable to** set forth his passion **or** describe the **beauty as** forcibly as **such beauty** deserved. **The lady laughed aloud, so diverted was she** at the assurance **of the** poet, especially when she was informed what **a** deformed, misshapen animal **he was.** The prince and the lady, at that time, **determined** to play Gazub **a trick, and** punish him for his assurance ; **but, not** then being able **to hit upon a** scheme, postponed **all plans until they** should meet again. A few nights after this **laughable** occurrence, the prince, disguised, as he invariably was **when** he visited his mistress, **was** stopped by yourself, **who** desired him **to** present the lady of the haunted house with **a** folded letter. He nodded assent, and you, ass that you were, imagined you had secured a friend through whom you might succeed. On reaching his mistress he produced the paper, saying, " More verses for the lovely houri ! "

She, to convince him no correspondence **was carrying on with her consent,** opened the billet, and casting her **eye** over the first line, **burst** out into an immoderate fit of laughter, for sure enough " Say, lovely houri !" &c., **once more met her eye.**

' " By Allah ! this is too ridiculous," said the prince, when he comprehended the cause of the lady's mirth ; ' we must hit on some plot by which these two impudent poets may be punished for their presumption." '

' Nothing, however, could **be** arranged without a consultation with me. **The** prince, therefore, **on** quitting his mistress, came directly to my house, where **he as** usual threw off his disguise. He mentioned the circumstances which had **occurred,** commanding me, should the poet, that is, yourself (for, **from** his description, I guessed it was my sagacious magician) come to enquire into the re-**sult** of his experiment, by no means to undeceive him, but flatter him with hopes of success, and induce him to consent to the chastisement of Gazub, that one poet might belabour another, and that the lady and himself might be gratified with seeing you undergo the torments you would be so ready to award your rival.

' At the same **time** he desired me, should you possess soul enough to be above taking so mean an advantage of **your** rival, **to** report the same to him, when another plan should be conceived. As, however, you so readily assented **to** the proposed cruel treat-ment **of** Gazub, the prince determined to have no mercy on yourself, and arranged you should **be** well bastinadoed, whilst Gazub should only have the cane applied **to** his deformed shoulders.

' When **the** time approached, however, I succeeded in turning

the prince from his determination of the **bastinado, saying** that
the disgrace of being mounted on an ass, with your verses suspended **from** your neck, would be sufficient punishment. Your
own imprudence and **rash** conduct, however, in striking the prince,
has drawn upon you his **anger** and severe displeasure, the effects
of which you will feel **as** long as you live.'

The barber here **finished** his narration and elucidation of the
strange **events which took place during the week.** I could only
blame **my own** imprudence **and excessive vanity,** which has
through **life been my ruin.**

Gazub visited me, and his first words were, '**Confound** your
verses !'

'**And** confound your folly !' replied **I,** 'to suppose you could
succeed with the lady by sending her them. It serves you right,
for stealing my compositions and attempting to pass them off as
your own. To this Gazub **had** nothing to **say ; and** it is fortunate
for me he was unacquainted with the readiness I had expressed
to aid in his chastisement, or he would not have allowed me to
remain another moment under his **roof.** ' Can we obtain no
redress,' enquired **I,** 'for our cruel treatment ?'

' Oh, brother !' **said he,** '**you** little know the power of the
Prince Humza. **We must be** quiet ; and I **confess to** you my
disgrace is such that **I** intend quitting my situation, and I apprehend you will scarcely have impudence enough to hobble before
his majesty, who **will** doubtless have heard of your folly. Besides,
when I retire, the situation is promised to another, more learned
than **either of us,** who will of **course** provide an assistant from
among his own **friends.'**

'More learned, indeed!' said I, my vanity prompting me to argue the point. 'I should like to see the man who would pretend to cope with me.'

'I am glad you have so high an opinion of your own talents,' said Gazub; 'but were you as wise as Lokhman, or as able a poet as Hafiz, the king would never admit into his presence a fellow whose withered stump would betray the appearance more of a felon than a poet.'

There was sense in this observation, and my golden dreams once more vanished. Gazub allowed me to remain until my wounds were healed; but, as the barber had foretold, I lost the use of my right leg, the foot of which, as your majesty may see, is a withered member. I left Ispahan for ever, and by the help of camel-drivers arrived at Bussorah, where I had the mortification of hearing of the return of Ilm Ali Khan from India, with double the number of followers than when I had seen him.

I felt my life so miserable in Persia, that I determined to quit it until the term of ten years should be expired, when I was to meet my two friends in Yezd. I sailed for India, where I have been a complete vagabond and lame beggar, with difficulty contriving to keep life and soul together. I was seriously meditating suicide, when in this city I beheld, to my surprise and joy, Yusoof begging alms. The unhappy man had, I perceived, lost one eye, and suffered so much from weakness in the other as to be unable to procure an honest livelihood. His astonishment was equal to mine, and we retired, to relate the accidents and adventures that had befallen us.

About a month afterwards, Mohabet Ali suddenly crossed our

path ; the poor fellow embraced us with tears in his eyes, so great was his joy at thus unexpectedly beholding us. We were not long together ere we discovered he had lost his right hand. By what accident he was deprived of it he will himself inform your majesty. I have no more to say, but to confess the justice of my punishment for my vanity, arrogance, and meditated ingratitude towards these my true friends.

The Emperor, turning to the other two beggars, desired they would also relate their adventures. Yusoof, the man with only one eye, commenced the tale contained in the following chapter.

CHAPTER XIII.

THE DYER'S STORY (*continued*). ·

When I parted from my friends Yasmin and Mohabet Ali **I felt** as if all attempts at obtaining riches without their aid must **prove** abortive, and my present condition shows how well-founded were my apprehensions. The first place I **visited** was Schiraz, where I hoped to obtain employment under the Governor's collectors. I tried in vain, by sundry well-written petitions, to bring myself to the notice of the Deewan or Vizier, then again to the secretary, to the treasurer, and to all the junior scribes about court. This I soon found was only a waste of paper **and** time, without the least prospect of benefit, so I at last determined to apply to the secretary in person, although fully aware of the great difficulty in gaining access to him, knowing how little claim I had to his patronage.

I verily believe I might have waited until this moment at his door without seeing him. Rudely hustled by the guards and fortunate persons who enjoyed free ingress to his mansion, losing all patience, and convinced of my presumption in daring to expect that any of the proud men in power would provide for me, I departed from the court, and enlisted as a common soldier. In this capacity I had no idle time; **for,** what with guarding the treasury all day, and cleaning my horse in the evening, preparatory **to the next** day's duty, I was nearly sick of my military occupation, and was meditating desertion, although I had bound myself to serve two years, when the Buckshee, the paymaster of the troops, **came to** deliver our monthly stipend. Requiring some **one to** make memorandums and take accounts, **his own** clerk being accidentally absent, **he** enquired if there were anyone amongst us who could **write.** I stepped forward, offering my services, which were accepted.

So active was I in **my new** capacity, that the Buckshee offered to appoint me to the situation of clerk under him, which I joyfully acceded to. Following him into the districts, I assumed the airs **and** consequence of a fine gentleman, treating the poor soldiers **with** neglect and contempt ; so that I became no great favourite amongst them, especially as I made it my practice to clip their **pay and** pocket the money myself. The Buckshee himself hesitated not to adopt this mode of enriching himself; and by having **a** good understanding with the officers and muster-master, whose list contained the proper number of men, but whose ranks told a very different tale, **we all, from first to** last, made a tolerable harvest.

The clerk whose place **I had** taken *pro tempore* returned ; but the Buckshee, finding I was by far the shrewder fellow of the two, dispensed with his attendance, desiring him to remain in his office **at** head-quarters until his return. I imagine I must have given a triumphant grin as the crest fallen **clerk** passed me, for he intuitively put his hand on the hilt of his dagger, stopping immediately opposite to me. **He** said nothing, however, but **walked away.**

There was, nevertheless, a diabolical expression of countenance on the man, which created in my bosom the most uncomfortable sensations, which his subsequent mysterious whisperings with the half-paid soldiers by no means tended to alleviate.

I foresaw a storm was gathering; nevertheless the Buckshee proceeded with his wonted audacity and imprudence to cut, clip, **and** pocket as many toomauns as he possibly could. 'We shall all be ruined,' said I to myself; 'this infuriated clerk **will** doubtless inform the Governor of our shameful system of fraud **and** peculation, in which I have entered **too** deeply to escape implication.' Besides, I was well aware it **was the** invariable practice of the head **of** the department to lay **all blame on his unhappy** deputies; so that in all probability my eyes **would** be put out, or I should be subject to some dreadful punishment. The next time, therefore, I had an opportunity of fingering the cash I concealed as many toomauns around **my** body as **I well** could, and then decamped, leaving my master to answer both for his **sins** and **my own.**

I proceeded to a small town, where I **procured** a dye which stained my beard a light-brown colour, parted with **my** turban, and wore an Arab **cap,** so that it would have **been a** difficult matter to have recognised me. From Schiraz **I** somehow or other contrived to get to Bussorah; but not fancying myself quite far enough out of the reach of the Schiraz governor, travelled on to Bagdad, where, soon after my arrival, I fell sick, and was con-**veyed** by an Arab to his stables, where **I was** placed amongst the horses. When **I** recovered what was my consternation at finding that my generous host, or his followers, having ridden me of my ill-gotten toomauns, had departed, leaving me again a beggar!

This was a pretty specimen of Arab hospitality, and I determined to take warning by it in future. To obtain a livelihood I served a merchant by filling all day bags of dates, which he daily dispatched into the interior. In Bagdad I could find no situation where my pen could advantageously be employed; and my labour was so heavy and constant, that I was entirely confined to the merchant's storehouses, without having a moment to spare to wander through the city. I thought myself, however, so very lucky in escaping the Schiraz governor, that I complained neither of my labour nor confinement.

My master one day fell sick, and in my anxiety to summon medical aid, no one being at that moment at hand, I ran about the city enquiring for a doctor. A shabby-looking fellow undertaking to conduct me to the abode of a clever physician, I followed him through narrow lanes and bye-streets, until we came to a lonely dwelling encompassed by a courtyard, the wall of which was built of coarse black granite, having a low door of solid iron. 'Call aloud,' said my conductor, 'and some one will surely answer you.'

Saying this he departed. I called aloud, and soon heard the rattling of chains and bolts, and the iron door grated on its massy hinges. But how can I describe the being that opened it? So hideous a little dwarf, I verily believe, no man ever set eyes upon. He was about three feet in height, with a head suited to the largest giant; his hair hung about his shoulders in the wildest and most disorderly manner, whilst his beard appeared neatly trimmed and dressed. Two eyes he had, but one would have imagined they had belonged to some other person, and been only borrowed by their present possessor—they were extremely bright and small, though every other feature of his face was large, **in** proportion to the gigantic head in which they were situated.

One of the arms of this monster was shrivelled and withered, but the other, his right one, strong and muscular; his nose was flat, and his mouth reached from ear to ear, which, on opening, displayed a set of large but regular teeth, whose whiteness formed a striking contrast to the sable exterior of this disgusting monster.

' Well,' thought I, ' with all my misfortunes, I am not reduced to the necessity of residing with this hideous object. **I** informed him of the sickness of the merchant, desiring him, if the doctor resided within those walls, to summon him immediately. The dwarf bowed, and went into the house, from whence he soon returned, followed by a venerable old man, with a white silvery beard, reaching nearly to his middle; his fair countenance indicated mildness and benevolence, and I was quite struck with his noble and dignified mien.

The doctor kindly embraced me, bidding me lead the way towards the sick man's abode. I did so, and rushed into his apartment with joy, to announce the doctor's approach. Around the sick man's couch stood his mother, his wife, and lovely daughter, with whom I had frequently conversed, and on whom I gazed with more than ordinary interest. Umbah (so was the girl named) looked sternly at me as I entered the room, and motioned me to retire, her father being asleep. I informed the doctor of the sick man's slumbers, when he assured me that that was the very time he wished to behold the patient; upon which, without consulting

Umbah **or the** other attendants **in the** chamber **of** sickness, **I** opened **the** door, and seizing the hand of the doctor, led him **into the room.**

No sooner had the mourning relatives beheld my venerable physician then one and all uttered violent screams, covering their faces **with** their hands, loading me with abuse, and desiring us both **to be gone. The sick man,** disturbed by the shrieks of his family, awoke, and sitting upright in his bed, beheld the doctor, when he also screamed, **groaned, and** fell backwards, **to** all appearance dead. Umbah **flew out of the** room, and the doctor whispered me, saying, **'We had better be** gone.' **I took the hint,** and gaining the street, **my** companion in a **low** tone said, 'Take my advice : go not **near the** merchant's house again ; **you will** repent if you do !'

Now all this seemed **to me** most unaccountably strange. **What had I done?** what offence could **I** have given? My master was sick, and **I** called **a** doctor—and a more mild, civil, prepossessing **man I never** before beheld ; **but though** I seemed **so** vastly pleased **with** the learned Hakeem, it appeared **no one** else was of the same opinion. His very appearance, which had so charmed me, disgusted everyone else. **I thus** walked on, **as I** imagined, by the side **of the doctor ; but** lifting up my eyes to make some **few** enquiries into the recent affair, **to** my astonishment he was gone, and I was alone **in the** middle of Bagdad, **not knowing where to go or what to do.** 'Perhaps,' thought I, still ruminating on the **recent** unaccountable behaviour of the merchant's family, 'perhaps **they have** had some quarrel **with** this physician, and the very sight of him drives them distracted ; yet this cannot surely be the case, **or** the doctor would not have accompanied me where he must have known his appearance alone would be attended with such direful consequences.'

The whole was inexplicable, and I determined, on visiting the doctor, to enquire from him the probable cause of the agitation to which I had been witness, and in some measure the cause. I passed a long and sleepless night under a shed, and in the morning proceeded to the doctor's sombre abode. **The** whole place was surrounded by tall and graceful cypress trees, which shed a solemn gloom around the habitation truly awful **to behold;** and it was not until **I** had seriously debated with myself that **I** ventured to approach the iron door. **At** length, picking **up a** stone, I knocked with it, and called aloud. **The dwarf** once more appeared, bowing and grinning. I informed him I wished **to** speak with his master on particular business; he signed me to enter, and I obeyed.

The dwarf slammed the gate with a violence the noise of which frightened from her nest a raven of a prodigious size from one of the lofty cypress trees; and as she flew slowly over my head uttered three distinct and, as I thought, ominous screams. The dwarf, heedless of either the bird or myself, hurried and shuffled on **with his** little bandy legs into the house, motioning me to stand still. **I** began heartily to repent my rashness, and essayed to open the iron gate, but it resisted my utmost efforts, and remained firm as a rock.

The dwarf returned, beckoning me to follow him; tremblingly I obeyed, and just as my foot was on the threshold the ill-omened **raven** flapped its sable wings immediately over my head, repeating her screams. **I** therefore hesitated, saying to the dwarf, ' If you please, **I will call** again to-morrow; I had **rather not enter** just now.' **A** vile parrot, which **hung in** a cage over my head, in **a** large hall, paved with black marble, cried 'Come in, come in!' and seemed by its brain-rending laugh, which followed **these** words, to rejoice in my dilemma. The whole house now suddenly became perfumed **so exquisitely that** my senses became bewildered, and I entered.

My arrival at this singular mansion seemed to give universal delight to **the inhabitants of** this strange abode. The dwarf rubbed his hands and grinned; the parrot screamed more shrilly than before; and a great black cat came close to me, rubbing her sleek and glossy sides against my leg, mewing and whisking about a tremendous long tail. **A** monkey also capered and seemed ambitious of outdoing the dwarf in his grimaces; but what struck **me as most** unaccountable was, that parrot, cat, and monkey had **each lost** an eye. Having crossed the marble hall, I came to a flight of stone stairs. The dwarf placed his foot upon the first step, when up scampered cat and monkey, trying which should get first. Not so quickly did I ascend the stairs, and once turned back, half-determined to refuse proceeding any farther; but the dwarf scowling and looking displeased, I once more slowly ascended. Arrived at the top, the dwarf, monkey, and cat stopped at a black door studded with iron knobs; the cat was in ecstasies, **and** the monkey jumped on the dwarf's head, where he squeaked and showed evident signs of impatience. The dwarf **gave** three distinct knocks on the black door with his heavy fist, which slowly opened apparently of its own accord. The dwarf, seizing my hand, led me over the threshold, whilst the cat and monkey contented themselves by peering with their single eyes into the half-darkened chamber. The physician was seated on a huge block of wood; and seeing me, arose and embraced **me,** which salute I coldly returned.

'What may be your commands with me?' cried the white-bearded doctor. I briefly told him the curiosity which the conduct of the merchant's family had excited in me, and that I had come to him for an explanation. 'Young man,' said he, 'the merchant's family are ignorant people; but their reasons for the reception they gave me you had better, if you dare, demand from them. But I perceive you **are** a young man of education, and might, if you pleased, turn your acquirements to advantage.'

'How?' cried I.

'Enter my service. Every convenience shall be afforded you, and your salary shall be handsome.'

'What service is expected from me?' I enquired.

'A service,' he answered, 'which will profit you greatly. My professions are various. I am a physician and alchemist, and your labours will be the attention to the compounding of medicines, grinding colours, arranging shells, stuffing animals, **and** scraping skeletons' bones.'

I shuddered at the composure with which the mysterious man mentioned the services I was expected to perform. I was silent, and the old fellow proceeded.

'You will gradually become acquainted with the mysteries of **my** profession, and, I foresee, will rise to great eminence.'

'**But,**' said I, 'if in my professional character I, like you, terrify my patients to death, I am at a loss to understand what profit I am to reap.'

'The fact is,' said he, 'you are impatiently curious; but you must know I am only called in by particular persons when at the last stage. No one will apply to me except the finger of death be on them. Now, the merchant was by no means in such imminent danger, and your mistake in bringing me to him will now reduce him to a lingering and miserable death.'

I was still more and more astonished, but remained silent.

'Will you enter my service?' said the doctor.

I hesitated, for it was very clear the people of the city avoided this learned doctor, who doubtless was a magician and a man of bad character. He repeated his question, saying my salary should be five toomauns per diem; and if ever he failed to pay them every morning, I might be at liberty to quit his service.

'At liberty!' said I, 'yes, whether you pay me or not, I conceive I should not be compelled to remain in a service which I disliked.'

'There you mistake; you must let yourself for five years, or not at all.'

'Then,' said I, 'my mind is soon made up. I beg permission to depart, and shall not approach your gate again.'

'Oh, foolish man!' said he. 'But, as you are determined to go, I must treat you as a visitor.' Saying which he took up a vessel containing rose-water, which he sprinkled over my face in the most courteous manner, and then embracing me, opened the chamber-door, saying : 'Farewell! but I fancy you will soon find mine is the only gate that will henceforth be open to you, and when you come I shall be glad to see you.'

This was strange, unaccountably strange, after my positive assurances of never intending **to** approach **his** house again. I looked the alchemist in the **face, but he** maintained the same dignified look, and called out aloud ' Budnuzer !' Up came the frightful dwarf, accompanied by the cat and monkey. The doctor ordered him to open the iron door of the courtyard and allow his visitor to depart, saying, ' Be at hand, however ; he will soon return.'

I turned round to demand an explanation, when **the door** of the apartment **was shut-to, and the doctor** disappeared. I followed the dwarf down the stairs, the cat mewing piteously, **the** monkey crying like a child, and the parrot in the hall shrieking **in** a most lamentable manner. Budnuzer, the dwarf, was, **I** imagine, dumb, or he would most probably have joined in the general mourning my departure occasioned. Arrived at the courtyard, I felt much relieved, and when the dwarf, with a melancholy face, opened the iron door **I** was in an ecstasy, and ran for a considerable distance, so delighted was I at escaping the horrors of the gloomy mansion. ' The doctor,' said I, ' may be very learned, but, **by** Allah ! I will disappoint him this time, and show him he can sometimes err in his prognostications, **for I** am determined never **to** go near the lane leading **to his** gate again. No, no ; I am safe, and mean to continue so.'

The first person I met was an Arab labourer, who no sooner set eyes upon me than down he fell insensible, groaning most piteously. ' Heavens !' I cried, ' what can be the meaning of this extraordinary conduct ?' I attempted to raise the poor fellow, but **he only** groaned and yelled the more, so I left him to his fate.

When some distance from him I turned **round, and** beheld the man running so fast as never, I believe, an Arab had run before.

'Well,' said I, 'it seems strange that my appearance should have this extraordinary effect; however, I will go to a barber's and have my beard dressed; perhaps I have need of his scissors.' I looked into a house **to** enquire where I could find a barber. **No sooner** did the people therein set eyes upon me than, like the labourer in **the road, down** they fell flat on their faces, roaring and screaming **for** mercy. I quickly retreated, feeling extremely uneasy at finding myself an object of horror to all the inhabitants of Bagdad. By chance I passed a barber's shop; it was full **of** customers waiting to be attended to. I entered; every head was turned towards me, and every mouth uttered a frightful yell; whilst some dropped down in a state of insensibility, and others **hurried out** of the shop, uttering **dismal** groans and muttering **over prayers and** portions of the Koran.

Determined to ascertain the cause **of** this terror which my appearance inspired, I seized the barber's mirror, and on viewing my face therein I was soon able to account for the mystery—my face being spotted all over with patches of blood, of so horrid a nature that I must have appeared like a creature from the other world. I had no doubt **but this** was to be attributed to the doctor's sweet-smelling rose-water, which, **as I** imagined, he had **so** courteously sprinkled over **me.** I **flew** to the water which stood in one corner of the shop **and** attempted to rub off the **stain; but, alas!** it was indelible. I most cordially cursed the **doctor,** being now under the necessity, notwithstanding my determination on **the** contrary, of once more knocking at his iron gate, to desire he would remove the bloody spots on my face ; and, as he foretold, I soon returned.

Dire necessity compelled **me** once more to approach his horrid abode; I was shunned, abhorred, loathed; how could I, then, obtain a livelihood? 'Oh, misery!' cried **I, '**the alchemist has indeed secured me; I must become his slave.' With a heavy heart I knocked at the iron gate, which was instantly opened by the dwarf, who appeared as if expecting my return.

'Lead me to your master,' cried I.

He bowed, and I followed him into the hall, **the parrot once** more crying, 'Come **in, come in!' and** laughing most immoderately ; the cat and monkey also testified their delight by a thousand antics and grimaces. Once more **I** was at the study-door of the accursed doctor. He received me politely, saying, 'I told you we should soon see you again—that mine was the only gate open to you in the world.'

'Remove these accursed stains,' cried I, pointing to my face, 'and I shall then be enabled to obtain a livelihood.'

'Impossible,' said the doctor; 'I must first have your services for five years. Be prudent ; agree to remain with me, and after that period, if you obey me in every particular, you may bid adieu to service for ever and become independent. Reject my offers, and go abroad once more as you now are ; but remember, my gate will not again be opened unto you.'

'**Oh! cruel** fate that has led me hither!' cried I. 'Curse the villain **who** pointed out this hellish place to me! What must I do ?'

'Obey, serve, and honour me,' said the doctor; 'and as you

diligently get through each year of servitude two of the ten spots on your face will vanish; I cannot, if I would, **wipe them away** by any **other** means.'

'**Will** you promise,' **cried I,** 'that **after five years** I shall become rich, and be suffered to depart without stain?'

'It depends on **yourself,**' said the doctor; 'if you obey me, **are not** headstrong **or** imprudent, you shall retire wealthy, and **perfect in** appearance.' ·

I consented **to** remain, and promised to obey. At this moment the monkey and the cat set up a scream of delight, and hurried down stairs, I suppose, to inform **the parrot of** the good news, for **I soon** after **heard** his thrilling shriek throughout the house. Budnuzer, the dwarf, entered the study, and the doctor drew forth **a** parchment, on which he wrote our agreement, **he** binding himself to pay me five toomauns per diem, and provide food and **lodging** for five years, after which he should have no farther claim upon me, provided I did not disobey his instructions and orders; **in** which case, though he might allow me to depart, I was to refund all the toomauns I might have received, or keep them, binding myself to stay **for ten** years more in his service, in which · case I should be allowed to keep my money. I,. **on** my part, bound myself to serve **and** obey, and signed my name, the dwarf being witness. **From** the deed **I** learned my master's name was Tabnag; and, **oh!** curse the **day** which first brought me near Tabnag and Budnuzer.

CHAPTER XIV.

THE DYER'S STORY (*continued*).

BEING now regularly in the service **of Tabnag, I** was anxious to examine his gloomy abode, and so expressed myself to my master. He willingly undertook to conduct me about **the** premises. **The** first room into which we entered was a laboratory, containing surgical instruments, stuffed birds, and skeletons; **in the second** room, on the first floor, was **a** valuable collection of shells, with several curious swords, daggers, and matchlocks; **but** what struck me more forcibly, amongst the collection, was an enormous bow, made of one buffalo's horn.

'Could you string it, think you?' said the doctor.

' I fear not,' said I.

' Try,' replied he. ' **I** fancy you are strong, and that **is one** reason why I was anxious to secure your services.'

The bow being taken down, **I** set to work with all my might, desirous of exhibiting my muscular powers, but nevertheless failed **in** my attempt. Tabnag assured me of all the assistants he ever **had** none had displayed so much strength as myself, adding, **' And I am glad** to see it, as you will need it, I assure you.' I was somewhat alarmed at this speech, and enquired if it were impossible to string the bow. 'There is only one person,' said he, 'who is able to string it, and that is Budnuzer. You shall see him.' Saying which, he took from his girdle a whistle, which applying to his mouth, he produced a noise, answered from below, not by the dwarf, but by the parrot, and soon after Budnuzer stood before us.

Tabnag pointed to the bow; and the dwarf, placing his foot upon it, with his strong and powerful arm strung it at one pull.

We passed on through many other rooms on this floor, some empty, and others containing medicines, bottles, and tools of all descriptions. The windows were all securely barred, but the shutters appeared to have felt the iron hand of time. We now descended the stairs and entered the hall, where the parrot welcomed us with his usual exclamation of 'Come in, come in !' and when the doctor informed me that the hall was paved with marble from a quarry near Mount Chasagiri[1] the parrot cried, 'Dur een che shuck?'[2]

'Your bird,' said I, 'seems able to converse.'

'No, indeed,' said Tabnag; 'all he can say is, "Come in," and "What doubt is there of this?" I purchased him of a fakir from Hindustan, who was very unwilling to part with him.'

Tabnag now opened a door to the right of the hall, which I had not before observed, which was strange, for close by it was another door—both painted black. The room into which we entered was spacious, and in the centre was placed a tremendous wheel, with leathern straps, which passed through into the adjoining apartment. Close to the great wheel was a smaller, placed

---

[1] Caucasus. [2] 'What doubt is there of this?'

horizontally, with cogs and springs, such as is used in many places to draw up water with from the wells. This I concluded was worked by an ox, although a very singularly constructed yoke lay on the floor.

'You will know more of this room shortly,' said the doctor; 'and I **have** now shown you as much as I intend—and seek **to** know no more.'

'Are we not to look into the adjoining room?' enquired I.

'Young man,' replied Tabnag, in **the** most solemn manner, 'mark me—never presume to venture near the door of that **room**; the consequences of disobedience may be fatal to you. Be ready to-morrow at sunrise, when we will commence our labours. Budnuzer, conduct the young man to his apartment.'

Saying which, he left me in charge **of the dwarf,** who conducted me to a low damp cellar, where was a miserable bed, beside which stood an iron treasure-chest, which was open. The dwarf fastened the same, and put the key into my hands, by which I understood the box was intended for a place of deposit for my wages. I was allowed to walk around the spacious courtyard in the evening, and was joined by the doctor, who was pleasant and facetious enough, indulging in severe remarks on the ignorance of mankind in general, and contemning all forms of religion. To fathom this man was impossible, nor could I discover whether he was Suni, Sheeah, Turk, or infidel; he was undoubtedly a clever and experienced man, but certainly leagued with the evil one.

I joined my master at meals, **and we** were waited on by Budnuzer, who afterwards fed himself, the cat, monkey, and parrot.

' Pray,' said I, ' what could make these animals so delighted at seeing me enter the house ? '

' Why,' said Tabnag, ' they have had little or no food since my last assistant left me ; and seeing another approach, they very sagaciously imagined their food would be continued to be given them as before.'

' But why,' said I, ' did not you feed them until you had procured another assistant ? '

' I ate but little myself,' said the doctor ; ' I could not. But ask no questions.'

' I must,' said I, ' ask one more question : how happens it that all your animals have but one eye ? '

' Because,' said he, ' they all were imprudent, and dared to disobey me.'

This was a very unsatisfactory answer, but I was constrained to be silent. I passed a quiet night, and was awakened by Budnuzer in the morning, and signed by him to enter the hall, where Tabnag was awaiting my coming. The dwarf conducted me into the room with the wheels, whilst the doctor entered the sacred and forbidden apartment. What was my dismay at finding the horizontal wheel, which I had imagined was constructed for an ox, intended for myself! And the curious yoke was actually fastened on my neck by the ready dwarf ere I had well recovered from my surprise ; my eyes were then blindfolded, I suppose to prevent dizziness, whilst each hand was placed on a bar, where they were tightly strapped ; and here I stood like the patient ox, awaiting the signal to move on. The signal soon came in the shape of a smart crack on my shoulders from the dwarf's whip, which I had not before observed him to carry. **The labour** was dreadful, and my knees tottered under me.

I continued at this truly bullock-work for half **an** hour, when a shrill whistle from the forbidden chamber, which I vainly imagined **was** the signal for cessation, brought the whip of the dwarf once more about my shoulders, and the **shrill** voice of old Tabnag, crying out, ' Quick, quick !' I was obliged to strain every nerve to please both master **and** driver. **At last** a loud and continued whistle I found was the signal to discontinue **my** labour, for the dwarf, pulling me back, released me. I fell to **the** ground exhausted, and covered with perspiration. Presently **in** rushed the doctor, half-naked, and fell by my side, perspiring at every pore, panting and puffing, and calling for water, which the dwarf brought him forthwith.

I was of opinion that I had suffered greatly, but the internal **agony of** old Tabnag baffles all description, whilst the dwarf appeared the only composed person in the house, for the mewing **of** the cat and the shrieks of the parrot and monkey were now become disagreeably audible. After some time the doctor arose, and was led out of the room by Budnuzer, leaving me to recover my fatigues as well **as I could.** I had experienced quite enough of the nature of my duties **to** make me anxious to quit so abominable a service, where the work of a beast was expected from me, in order to aid my master **in** some diabolical proceeding. What **could I** do? The demon doctor had fixed his accursed stamp on my face, and rendered me a loathed object, a monster **on** whom none for a moment dared rest their eyes.

With this most effectual preventive to escape, the doctor

kindly allowed me egress from his infernal den whenever I was inclined. I determined to remonstrate with him before another day's labour commenced. The dwarf returned to me, and leading me from the room, fastened the door. I had great curiosity to know all that had been going on in the contiguous apartment; but as the dwarf was dumb, and I had been warned not to attempt gratifying my curiosity on the subject, I silently followed Budnuzer to my cellar, where, tired and hot, I laid down to sleep.

In the evening the dwarf called me, and I accompanied him to the study of my master, where I found him wearing the same serene and placid countenance as when I first beheld him. Before him were dishes of rice and sweetmeats, with sherbet and cool water, of which he politely invited me to partake.

'No,' said I; 'one who has been treated like a brute cannot now sit down as a human being to eat rice and pilau.'

The doctor made no reply, but ate his fill, and then went to sleep. Being very hungry, however, I followed the dwarf out of the room with the dishes, intending to snatch a handful or two of rice; but, lo! the cat and the monkey, ever watchful, jumped on the dwarf's shoulders, and soon, between them, cleared the dishes, with the exception of some sweetmeats, which Budnuzer reserved for the parrot.

'Well,' thought I, 'to-morrow I will be more prudent, and eat while I have it in my power.'

The following day was productive of nearly the same misery to me. I was put to the hand-wheel, and as I turned it something in the adjoining chamber went round with a whizzing noise, accompanied by the sound of hammers and clinking of metal.

Being greatly fatigued, I began to relax in my exertions; but the dwarf, who stood by me, immediately applied his hellish whip to my unfortunate shoulders. Irritated beyond measure, I left the wheel, and was approaching the dwarf to chastise him; but lifting up his arm, he levelled such a blow on my stomach as made me reel **to** the other end of the room, where I fell. All this time the operations, whatever they were, were at a stand, and in consequence in rushed Tabnag to enquire the cause. I explained to him how the dwarf had presumed to serve me.

'Presumed!' said Tabnag. 'Why, 'tis his duty to **keep the** wheel going till he hears my whistle. If you are lazy **of course** you must be whipped; and I advise you **not to** attempt striking him—you are no match for him in strength. Come, to the wheel once more! I have not yet finished.'

I assured him I was half-dead with hunger, and had not strength to turn the wheel any more that day.

'That is your own fault,' said he; 'I offered you food. If you did not choose to accept it, I don't see why my business should stand still in consequence.' So saying, he nodded to the dwarf, who with his whip soon brought me from my corner again to the accursed wheel, where, after another hour's hard **work, I was** gratified by hearing the whistle from the next room. This being the signal for cessation, the doctor came smiling into the room and shook me by the hand, hoping, he said, to see me at dinner. **I** this day partook of his meal, and an excellent one it was.

Thus passed day after day. I was sometimes put to one wheel, then to another; but every time I was yoked to the heavy one the doctor, at the conclusion of my labour, evinced symptoms of terror similar to those I witnessed on the first day. My salary, according to agreement, was regularly paid me, **and my** food was **excellent.** I had remained with **the doctor** one year, during which **time** I had worked hard for my toomauns, and apparently gave great satisfaction. **Two of** the spots on my face disappeared, **as** the doctor had assured me, **so** that I hoped, when my term **should** expire, **to become** quite **free from the** horrid stains. I shall not dwell upon the **toil I** endured for **four years** and a half, but proceed to relate events which then took place.

The doctor was summoned to the sick-bed of an Arab captain **of a merchant** vessel, who had come from Bussorah to **visit his family,** resident in Bagdad. The dwarf **was** occupied on the **terrace** of the house drying certain herbs **for** the doctor's use, **and I** was left alone and unemployed. **I felt a strong** inclination **to** peep into the forbidden apartment, and more than once found myself at the door ; prudence, however, whispering in my ear, I turned away, considering, as my term of servitude was so near at an end, I would not run the **risk of incurring** the displeasure of the alchemist, although **it would, I** imagined, be next **to** impossible he should find **me out.** The doctor returned one day, informing me the Arab **captain** was quite recovered. ' Yes,' said he, ' Maghroobia ' **(so** was his patient named) **' will ever** bless the **day he sent for me.'**

About one month after this event, **as I** was assisting the dwarf **in** his labours on the terrace, **I heard** the town-crier proclaiming **the** sudden disappearance of a girl named Zenna, the daughter of **Maghroobia, a** captain of a merchant-vessel. Immense rewards were offered **to** anyone who could give information which would lead to her discovery. I was **surprised,** but mentioned not the circumstance to my master, who doubtless **had** heard the crier as well as myself.

Several days after I was again by chance left at liberty in the house, and fancied **I heard a voice,** sobbing and weeping bitterly, proceed from the forbidden apartment; it was unquestionably the voice of a female. 'Heavens!' thought I, 'it must be the daughter of the Arab captain. Oh!' said I, 'were I certain this were the case, I would, when my term expires, give the distressed father information **on** the subject, and thus gain an immense reward, which, added to my savings, would possess **me of a** handsome sum of money **to** take with me **to** Yezd, where **I** anticipate the pleasure of sharing it with my two friends, **Yazmin and Mohabet** Ali, should they both be still in want.'

No one was near, and I determined to hazard a peep into the mysterious chamber. Not a sound was to be heard in the house; the parrot, whose cage hung opposite the fatal door, was even sleeping, and the cat and monkey were reposing below. Cautiously did I, on my toes, creep towards the door. The female wept, and fain would I have called to her but for the parrot, who invariably, on hearing anyone talk, would scream violently, and thus bring down the dwarf. I tried the door; it was fastened. I placed my eye at the keyhole, when a flash of fire seemed to go through my brain, and my right eye was for ever destroyed, whilst my left felt painful and weak, and **it was** with difficulty I could bear the light. No sooner had this misery befallen me than the parrot gave a lengthened scream, and threw himself violently from one side of the cage to the other.

'What a fool I am!' cried I.

'What doubt is there of that?' said the parrot, whilst the dwarf came hobbling down the stairs.

I endeavoured to turn my back towards him, that he might not perceive my blindness, but to no purpose; he seemed to have divined what had taken place, for I found myself drawn by a strong cord and fastened to one of the pillars of the hall, so cruelly tight that the circulation of my blood was impeded; my eyes, particularly my left, ached violently, and I found I could see less and less every minute. I, however, saw the doctor enter, and beheld his chagrin at seeing me tied in the manner I describe.

'Fool!' said he, 'did I not caution you against attempting to gratify your curiosity? You have got your reward. This day you go hence a beggar, and a blind one. Budnuzer,' said he, 'release the poor wretch, and turn him away for ever.'

In vain I begged for a few toomauns; not one would the ill-natured Tabnag give me; my labour and toil for nearly five years was all clean forgotten by this one act of disobedience, although dearly had I been punished for it. Thus did I leave the mansion of Tabnag, not indeed quite blind, but nearly so; one eye, however, my right, had become dark and useless, and two of the red spots on my face to this day remain, but are, fortunately, on my chin, so that my beard, which I strive to make grow thick, completely covers them. I trust your Majesty will excuse my not showing them, having the greatest horror of having them exposed to view. I begged my way to Bussorah, and from thence by ship to Mocha, where, I should have said, the infernal doctor advised me to go, for what purpose I knew **not,** but soon comprehended **his** motive.

Arrived at Mocha, my left eye **gradually** recovered, and **I** could see to walk about. As I was **one** day begging in the street a stout fellow laid hold of me, and demanded his daughter.

'Heavens!' cried I, 'what mean you? Who are **you?** I have no female in my possession.'

'I am,' said he, 'Maghroobia, **and come to demand my** daughter Zenna, whom the good Tabnag has assured me **is under** your protection, and that you have absconded from him **on her** account.'

'Oh! sir,' cried I, 'call him **not** good; **he is, I believe, the devil** himself; and, not content with having caused me to suffer **toil and** labour and blindness, has now deceived you, doubtless imagining you would sacrifice me to your fury. Thank heaven, **you are a** wise man, and have not proceeded so rashly. Your **daughter, sir,** is in the mansion **of** the doctor, at least so I have reason to fear; and it was my wish to be certain of the fact which has cost me my right eye, and ruined the vision of the other.'

'Oh, Allah!' **cried the** captain, 'can this be possible? Is the doctor indeed such **a man?** Now do I repent having called him in during my illness.'

'Go,' said I; 'lose not **a moment** in returning **to** Bagdad to demand your child; you will **find** her in the second room on the **right** hand of the marble hall; but **for** heaven's sake be cautious, **or** your life may be forfeited.'

'I will apply to the Governor,' **said** the captain, 'and have his house razed. Will you accompany me?'

'Excuse me,' said I; 'worlds should not tempt me to approach those detested walls again. Farewell! and may you succeed, noble captain.'

Maghroobia was by no means surprised at my declining to accompany him, when he heard all my past sufferings. Some time after his departure I got into the service of a merchant, for whom I was employed in preparing coffee for exportation. My service requiring me on an estate about four miles distant from Mocha, I was one day proceeding thither on an Arab horse, when I missed my way, and got amongst wild and inaccessible places. At last, finding my horse could not proceed over the rocky and uneven ground, I fastened him to the stump of a tree, and ascended a hill, where I endeavoured to discover my lost path.

A venerable old man suddenly appeared, and I made him a salaam and enquired my road. He gave me the necessary information, and invited me to his cave close by, where, he said, he had resided for years retired from the world. I rather hesitated to trust myself a second time with the venerable-looking men of that country, but at last followed him to his retreat, where he produced milk, coarse bread, and dates. The heat of the day had caused my poor eye much pain, and I frequently put my hand before it.

'My friend,' said my host, 'you seem in much pain. How happens it that you have lost the use of your right eye, and appear to suffer much pain in your left?'

'Oh, sir,' cried I, 'I am the victim of a villain at Bagdad, who calls himself a doctor.'

The hermit started, crying, 'God forbid! have you served Tabnag?'

'Oh!' said I, '**then thou** knowest him?'

'I do' he replied; '**he cured me** when **all other** physicians had given me over; but I paid dearly for my recovery: my daughter was carried off, my wife died suddenly, and my ships **(for I** was a merchant) sunk, and I became a wanderer. When first I insisted on the attendance of Tabnag my friends were horror-struck, and fain would have turned me **from** my purpose, saying he could cure, but would cause me sorrow for the remainder of my days. I heeded not their superstition, as I then deemed it. **He** came and cured my body, but wounded my peace of mind for ever. **It** is now about five years since I fell in with a man like yourself, blind in one eye **and** suffering pain from the weakened state of the other; and he related to me his sufferings whilst under the roof of Tabnag; and you, like him, I imagine, dared to peep into the forbidden apartment.'

'I did,' said I, and proceeded to relate everything that had happened **to me.**

'You are unfortunate,' said he; 'but in my inner cell is **a** poor wretch who, I fear, is dying, and one who has also served not only Tabnag, but Satan himself.'

The hermit conducted me into a small cave, where on a pallet lay an emaciated being, apparently dying. I approached, and on examining his countenance what was my astonishment on recognising the very man who had first pointed out to me the doctor's infernal abode!

Informing the hermit of the circumstance, he said this was **very** likely, 'For as long as he could supply Tabnag with victims he lived; but all his attempts failing at the time of your emancipation, he is now about to suffer for his rash intimacy with the alchemist. His incoherence of speech and his dreadful agony of mind allow me to gather from him the following particulars :—He, it appears, was entrapped into the mansion of the doctor, and being poor and destitute, accepted his service ; and, unfortunately for him, did not peep into the forbidden apartment.'

' Would I had been as unfortunate !' said I.

' Not so, my son,' said the hermit; 'you have reason to rejoice at rather than lament your disobedience. Listen to me. After the expiration of his term of servitude, the doctor, as he said, to reward him for his forbearance and strict obedience to his orders in not prying into his secrets, offered to conduct him into the mysterious chamber.

' Eagerly did he follow his master, when scarcely had he passed the threshold before a gigantic figure, with huge sable wings, touched him on the shoulder, crying, " Mine, mine, mine for ever !" and instantly disappeared. The poor fellow sank to the earth, overcome with terror, and on recovering begged an explanation from the alchemist, who coolly informed him he was now the servant of Satan, but that provided he could procure for him a strong and able assistant every five years, or whenever he should require one, he should live wealthy and happy, and for this purpose he was allowed to be at large in the city ; but if he failed, then would come his dreadful hour, and Satan would come and claim him.

' He succeeded in providing two assistants, whose curiosity lost them their eyes, but saved their souls. After you, the unhappy man, having been unable to provide an assistant, fled, vainly imagining he could elude the grasp of Satan ; but in this wild **and dreary place** his enemy has overtaken him, and I dread the hour **of** his dissolution. He **has** also informed **me that** he verily believes the nature of his duty at the wheels in the alchemist's **house was to draw up** in one the devil, laden with gold and silver, **and** in the other **to put in** motion some machinery for the purpose of coining money.

'From your account I imagine that Tabnag, failing to obtain another assistant, **has endeavoured** to appease **the devil by pro-**curing a virgin, **and this may** account **for his secreting the** merchant's daughter.'

'**But,**' said **I,** 'can **you account for the horror I** inspired **by showing** my spotted face in the city?'

'**Yes,' said** the hermit. 'This is one **of** the old fellow's tricks —**a** young man, a patient **of his, having, it is** said, come from the other **world** so marked, thus stalked through the streets, **to** the alarm and terror of the inhabitants. When **you** appeared, there-fore, doubtless they imagined the same spectre had again visited them.'

If this was **all** correct I had reason to rejoice at my getting off with the loss of an eye only. 'What think you,' said I, 'has now become of old Tabnag, since he has failed to procure another assistant?'

'I cannot say,' replied the hermit, 'unless Satan has spared **him,** in consequence **of** his offering the merchant's daughter, **though I** question if he has been suffered to possess his immense **wealth.'**

Whilst **we** were talking the sick man groaned and writhed in

agony, crying, with a feeble voice, ' He is coming ! he is coming !'
Alarmed, we rushed out of the cavern, not daring to venture near
it again for an hour. The hermit at length summoned courage to
peep into the inner cell, and returned to me, saying the place was
filled with black smoke, so that nothing could be distinguished.
After a short time he again repaired to the cell, followed by myself. The cave was free from smoke, but the victim was gone—not
a trace of him was to be seen.

CHAPTER XV.

THE DYER'S STORY (*continued*).

THE good hermit condoled with me in my misfortunes ; and after breathing a **prayer** for the unhappy man **we had so** lately **seen,** conducted **me** towards the high road.   **Having found my way, and** transacted my business in tolerable time, I returned to my master, who was satisfied with my explanation.   **Many a time** did I long **to** know what success Maghroobia, the Arab captain, met with **in** his attempts to discover **his** daughter **beneath** the roof of the accursed alchemist, and was often more than half-inclined to quit **my service** and proceed to Bagdad, merely to gratify my curiosity —so little had the severe lesson I had received cured me of this disease, **for so** I may well call it.

Tired of Mocha and coffee, I quitted it, and proceeded in **an** Arab dhow **laden** with horses to Bombay.   I offered my **services** as a horse-keeper, which the owner of the animals accepted. Arrived in Bombay, our horses were soon got on shore, **and** some few purchased on the first day.   The merchant, my master, was delighted at the success likely to attend his speculation, especially **as** he was expecting another lot to follow immediately.   Owing to bad weather at sea, however, they did not arrive until nearly three months after us.

I was dispatched to superintend the landing of the horses, and
went on board one of the vessels to consult with the captain concerning the time and best method of slinging the horses, so as to
prevent accidents. My surprise was beyond description on recognising, in the person of the captain, Maghroobia, the father of the
lost Zenna. He did not at first remember me; but when I mentioned circumstances of interest to him he seized my hand, and
expressed his joy at meeting me. I eagerly enquired if he had
succeeded in recovering his lost child.

' Alas! no,' said he; 'the accursed villain has deprived me of
her for ever. On my return to Bagdad from Mocha I applied to
the Governor, who commanded a troop of armed men to surround
the alchemist's house. The iron door of the courtyard was wide
open, at which I was not a little surprised. We entered the
interior of the building. The first sight we beheld was a parrot
dead in its cage; and on the stairs lay a monkey and a cat, also
both dead. I opened the first door on the right hand of the
marble hall, but such a volume of black smoke issued therefrom
that the house was filled in an instant, and all search was useless;
we could neither see nor breathe, being blinded and suffocated by
the smoke, the smell of which was abominable.

I applied once more to the Governor, who ordered the house
to be razed; but as no one could be prevailed upon to set to
work on its demolition several large guns and mortars were
placed before the gate, and a brisk fire soon commenced. Our
shot, however, had not the slightest effect; notwithstanding all
the care and skill of the gunners, every ball went many yards over
the house; and at last a number of people came running up to

us, begging us to cease, for that our shot were falling into the city, and had killed several of the inhabitants. **We** were all struck dumb with amazement, and immediately discontinued firing. The Governor was no less astonished than ourselves, and ordered that the building should be blown up with gunpowder· For this purpose expert miners were employed, and a train laid which would have been sufficient to have blown up the strongest fortress. All ended, however, in an insignificant "phiz," with a little harmless smoke ; and thus were we compelled to abandon the attempt, and the building stands as firm as ever.'

When I informed the captain that **it was the abode of** Iblis, whom I had myself unconsciously served, his surprise vanished, saying, 'If this is the case, it is no wonder we could not shake **the** foundations ; it requires very strong powder and very powerful **cannon ere** we fight with the devil.'

Scarcely had he uttered these words when **a** shivering came over his whole frame ; he fell on the deck of the vessel, groaned, rolled his eyes in a frantic manner, and in five minutes was a corpse. What an awful sight ! My friend, who, but a few moments before, was a healthy living being, was now an inanimate lump of clay : the vengeance of Tabnag had overtaken him.

' Oh, wretched **man,' said** I, ' ever to have employed that deceiver for thy physician !'

Having given orders for the burial of the unfortunate Maghroobia, I landed my horses, some twenty or thirty of which were selected to be sent into the interior of Hyderabad and Nagpore, and **I** was deputed **to go in** charge **of** them, with orders to pay whatever money I should **receive** into the hands of Mahommed

Ali Khan, an Arab merchant at Hyderabad.   I was to be accompanied by thirty horsekeepers, some Arabs, and some natives of Bombay, so that there was no fear of my acting unfairly; and the price of each horse being previously decided, with strict orders not to abate a single rupee, it would have been impossible, had I been so inclined, to have played the cheat.

All being ready, I proceeded to Hyderabad, through Poonah, Seroor, and Aurungabad.   One day, as we were encamped within a day's march of Hyderabad, a man came up to me, saying his master was riding a sorry beast, and was anxious to purchase an Arab horse from me, if I could recommend him one.

‘ Where is your master?’ I enquired.

‘ His tent is pitched near the tope of trees at a small distance, and he will await your coming.’

‘ Is he rich?’ said I.

‘ Very,’ was the answer I received.

‘ Very well,’ said I ; ‘a horse shall be at his tent presently.’

So saying, I went to my lot of horses and selected one of the very best and highest price ; indeed, he was a noble beast, fit for a monarch to ride upon. ‘ As I am at liberty,’ thought I, ‘ to receive more money than the fixed price if I can get it, why, I will even demand from this rich man a thousand rupees over and above, and will pocket the difference myself.’ With this intention I led the horse to the knot of trees, and stood with him opposite the tent-door of the wealthy stranger. The servant who had summoned me said his master was anxious to try the horse, if I had no objection.

‘ Certainly not,’ replied I ; ‘the ground is good about here, and I beg he will gallop him and try all his paces. He is quiet and free from vice.'

' Can he go fast ?' **said** a voice from within the tent.

' Indeed, sir,' I replied, ' he is equal in swiftness **to the** Prophet's Borak.'

I had scarcely uttered the words when my customer, with his head muffled up **in a** shawl, leaped into the saddle, and when firmly fixed, with the bridle in his hand, he threw off the shawl, turning his face full upon me, what was my agony at recognising the accursed alchemist of Bagdad, who, I had sincerely hoped, was too deeply engaged with the devil ever again to cross my path ! He struck his spurs into my horse's sides and galloped away over hill and dale, and I have never seen or heard of him since, and may Allah forbid that I should ! What was I now to **do?** I seized his unhappy servant, who was **a** low-caste man of **the** country, and probably an innocent one ; but, in my anger, I demanded from him the money for my horse. I might as well have expected him to have raised a gale **of** wind as the money, and felt pity for the poor trembler before me.

' Indeed,' said he, ' I know not who the man is that **I** have served, but you can take his horse in exchange.'

I looked at the animal the doctor had left me, and surely so miserable a wretch never trod the earth. He was one of the most inferior sort of Bengal horses, with **a** high nose, sharp, narrow forehead, staring, vicious-looking eyes, ill-shaped ears, square head, thin neck, narrow chest, lank belly, cat-hams, goose-rump, and legs full **of** splints and spavins. Here was an exchange for my handsome Arab ! What could I **do?** how appear before the horsekeepers? Would they believe my story? Surely they would not credit my assertions, and I must suffer on my return to Bombay.

I took with me the poor servant, and still poorer horse, and related to the horsekeepers my misfortune. They said nothing, but cast peculiar looks at one another, which convinced me I was not believed. The Bengal horse was, however, conveyed to Hyderabad, where I had not long remained ere I was taken into custody by Mahommed Ali Khan, who had learned the loss of the Arab horse from the horsekeepers. In vain I swore, declared, and protested I had been imposed upon and robbed of the animal, and in vain did the alchemist's servant corroborate my assertions. I was imprisoned and badly fed for nearly a year, when, finding it useless to detain me any longer, I was released, and turned away once more a beggar, in which state I have ever since remained, and wandered about until I arrived at this vast city, where I was one day surprised by beholding Yasmin, the author of all my sufferings, limping through the bazaar. It was with grief I learned he had been as unsuccessful as myself, and we both anxiously looked forward to the expiration of the ten years, indulging in the hope of finding in Yezd our friend, Mohabet Ali, rich and powerful. How were our expectations blighted, by meeting with him in this city about a month after my arrival, a beggar like ourselves, maimed and wretched! How and by what means he became so he will himself inform your Majesty.

Aurungzebe remarked that this was one of the most singular stories he had ever heard, and enquired of Yusoof whether he had heard any account from the people at Hyderabad concerning the alchemist.

' I made many enquiries, your Majesty,' said Yusoof, 'but all I could **learn was** that he had frequently been seen in that city, but never remained long in it; **was** always mounted on a different horse, and spoke to no one. People from Aurungabad also gave the same account, and I have no doubt it was correct: he **was** flying from himself, or perhaps vainly attempting to elude the devil; but he is giving himself a vast deal of unnecessary trouble, for I imagine the devil is pretty sure of him **at any time.'**

The Emperor **here** intimated his desire to hear the story of Mohabet Ali, the third Sufi, who, advancing, commenced the following account of himself.

CHAPTER XVI.

THE DYER'S STORY *(continued)*.

WHEN the time of separation arrived, and I found myself alone in the wide world, I began most heartily to repent forsaking the true religion to become a Sufi. I determined to make an attempt at becoming reconciled with my father, and for this purpose penned a letter to him from Tehran, which was the first place of consequence I arrived at. Anxiously did I wait his reply, but waited in vain, so little did he now regard me. In Persia I found no friendship, no employment; I therefore determined on trying my luck in happy India. Alas! it was to me far from happy. I have been miserable ever since I set my foot in it.

The vessel in which I departed from Persia encountered a very heavy gale, which threatened destruction to all on board. A violent altercation arose between the captain and his officer, for he had but one, about the propriety of cutting away the masts. I ventured to give my opinion, which happening to coincide with that given by the officer, the captain threatened to throw me overboard if I presumed to speak another word on that or any other subject connected with the affairs of the ship. This effectually silenced me, and I withdrew. As it happened, we weathered the gale without the necessity of cutting away the masts, and **after a** tedious passage arrived safe at Calcutta.   **The** cargo was consigned to Saduk Beg, a Persian **merchant of that** city, and, as it chanced, a friend of my father's.

I introduced myself to him, and was received **in the** most cordial manner, by which it was evident he was a stranger to my apostasy, and, situated as I then was, I tried every means in my **power** to allow him to continue in his ignorance.   I informed him I was travelling for pleasure, and had no idea, when I first set out, of visiting Calcutta, or should certainly have provided myself with letters from my father, whom I **represented as** well **and** in excellent spirits.   'I am desirous,' said I, 'to draw upon my father for a sum of money, and hope you will have **no** objection to cash my draft.'

'Certainly not,' said the polite Saduk **Beg. 'How much do you** require?'

Sure of being discovered sooner or later, I thought it prudent to draw **for a** good round sum at once, **so** I named one thousand rupees.   The **merchant observed** it was a large sum, but had no doubt my father, as he consented to my travelling, was prepared for the expenses incident thereto.

'Of course,' said I, with well-affected indifference.

The draft being soon made out, the money was given into my hands.   With this sum I determined **to** set up as a Persian of consequence, which character I calculated could safely be maintained until Saduk Beg should hear from my father.   As long as the rupees lasted I took lodgings amongst the Mahommedans of the city, lived miserably at home, but cut quite a dash when I went out.   I hired a palanquin, in which I paraded the streets in the daytime, and in the evening sauntered about in fine clothes, dangling a splendid gilt axe between the finger and thumb of my right hand, and wearing a handsome khunjur[1] in my girdle.

I was frequently invited to the parties of Saduk Beg, and by these means introduced into the best society of the place.   My rupees, alas ! began to dwindle away, and I was under the necessity of reducing my establishment ; my palanquin was laid aside, and only one servant, instead of four, now attended me.

At last the time began to approach when an answer might be expected from Yezd ; and one did indeed come, although not in answer to Saduk Beg's, with my enclosed draft.   Not in the least aware of this event, I visited Saduk Beg, who, in a careless manner, enquired when I had left Yezd.   I informed him.

' And you left your father quite well ? '

' Yes.'

' And since that time you have been in Persia—in Tehran, I think you said ? '

' Yes,' I replied.

' It is strange, then,' said Saduk Beg, ' you should not have heard of his death.'

' His death !' exclaimed I.   ' Is it possible ?   Not one of my relations would write to me ; I have quarrelled with them all.'

' Indeed !' observed Saduk Beg.   ' It must have been a sad quarrel, that they should refuse even to inform you of your father's death.'

' Yes,' said I, ' it was a sad business.   I was ready to make it up, but they determined to continue at variance with me.'

---

[1] A dagger.

' Young man,' said Saduk, ' this will not do.   I know full **well**
the cause of your unfortunate business, **as you** term it ; and I can
tell you another piece of unwelcome news, which **is,** that you will
this day **go to prison,** unless you pay me my **money,** of which you
have defrauded **me** by your artful tales.   Your cousin has succeeded to your father's property, and has apprised me of all that
has taken place.   Now it is not likely he will honour your draft,
which, when you penned, you must have been aware, had **your**
father been living, would have been unattended **to ;** I therefore
arrest you for the money.'

I had **not a** word to say, but was taken before the judicial
authorities of the city, and **an** enquiry instituted.   **By** a miracle **I**
escaped, my detention not being countenanced, on the presumption
only **of** my **bill** being returned dishonoured.   Saduk Beg now
repented his imprudent haste to arrest me, rightly conjecturing that
ere my bill could arrive I should be far enough off.   He gave me
a look, however, which I shall never forget ; **and** turning on his
heel, left me in the street, and I have never seen him since.

As soon as possible I hired a palanquin and departed from
Calcutta, determined **to** go to Chittagong.   Why I fixed on that
place I know not, unless it was the greatest distance I knew of.
Having paid my bearers half their wages in advance, I had barely
sufficient money to provide myself with food on the road, **and** as
we approached Chittagong my poverty was so evident, that the
bearers, halting near **a** thick jungle, demanded the remainder of
their wages, which I of course was unable to pay them.   The
enraged men, turning me out of **my** comfortable palanquin, set
upon me, stripped and beat me cruelly, and muttering abuses,

left me to my fate.   Here ended the character of fine gentleman, and here, thought I, must terminate my existence.   Alone in a strange country, where no one understood my language, what could I do?   A band of armed men approaching, I made up to them, begging for food.

As it happened, one of the men, being a Mahommedan, understood Persian, and enquired into my unfortunate condition. I told him I was a traveller, robbed and plundered, and cruelly beaten and deserted.   'Come along with us,' said the Mussulman, 'and you shall be provided for.'

I accordingly accompanied these men on a long journey, and found myself ascending the mountains which lie to the north-east of Chittagong, inhabited, as I soon learned, by a strange race of men, called the Kookies, many of whom followed the band which I had joined.   They exhibited, indeed, a most singular appearance, having flat noses, small eyes, and broad round faces, short in stature, and very black.   I had not at this time any opportunity to enquire farther concerning these people, but trusted to my friend the Mahommedan for more information on the subject.

It required little penetration to discover that the band which I had joined were robbers; nor did the discovery cause me much uneasiness; for, situated as I was, what could I do but take by force what I was certain no one would make me a present of? 'Yes,' said I, 'I have commenced by deserting my religion, continued by becoming swindler, and will now end by turning robber.'

I was conducted to the summit of a mountain, where one of the band, apparently the leader, stamping with his foot upon a

smooth square piece of rock, it slowly moved, and opening discovered a flight of stone steps, which we all prepared to descend.
Arrived at the bottom, a spacious cavern, hewn from the very
bosom of the mountain, appeared to view. Men to the amount
of twenty followed me into this den of thieves, and shortly after
arrived about a dozen more. Food was called for, and soon
spread before us, and nothing could be more acceptable to me
than it was. My friend the Mahommedan informed me that the
chieftain, having taken compassion upon me, offered to allow me
to become one of his gang if I chose; if not, I was at liberty
to depart. I accepted the offer, but was cautioned to beware
how I ever meditated either treachery or desertion. I frankly
confessed that urgent business demanded my appearance in
Yezd, after seven years, so that I could bind myself for no longer
period.

The chieftain, before whom I was now conducted, agreed to
the terms, promising a fair division of property on my quitting
them. He informed me that the most perfect harmony existed
between each member of the band, and the utmost faith and
reliance was reposed in each other; he showed me the treasury,
which was on one side of the cavern; it was not unlike a large
copper, closed at the top, but at the bottom was a narrow hole,
just sufficiently wide to admit a man's arm; and as it was expected
no money would be extracted thence but for the benefit of the
gang, there was no lock or fastening of any kind. 'There is the
way in to the treasury,' said the chieftain; 'beware how you make
use of its contents.' I had heard of honour amongst thieves, but
never dreamed of its being carried to such an extent as this. I

promised, nay, swore, never to extract the smallest coin but for the general good of the community, and was then created a robber of the Kookie mountains.

I began to consider that, as the treasury was well filled, I should come in, after seven years, for a very handsome share, and therefore wisely determined to be strictly honest, conceiving it to be the best policy. The Mahommedan bandit at my request informed me that the Kookies and the Mugs are the offspring of the same progenitor, who had two sons by different mothers—the Mugs are the offspring of the elder, and the Kookies of the younger son. The Kookies are all hunters and warriors, and are divided into tribes, all independent of each other, though all acknowledge, more or less, the authority of three different Rajahs, who are hereditary.

The only difference in the Rajahs is the singular mode of dressing their hair, which they bring forward to tie in a bunch, so as to overshade the forehead, while the rest of the Kookies have theirs hanging over their shoulders. The Kookies are armed with bows and arrows, spears, clubs, and large knives, and he is considered the most accomplished warrior who is the most expert thief.

The leader of the present gang of freebooters, he informed me, was a Kookie named Halcha, who was too proud to acknowledge the authority of either of the three Rajahs, and had set up a petty empire of his own, openly avowing determined hostility towards them and their subjects. Many had been the attempts to seize Halcha, but his cunning and excessive bravery, together with the warm support of his gallant gang, had hitherto rendered them futile, and he was still able to excite awe whenever he chose to appear. Robbery was the aim of the banditti, who seldom or ever spilt blood if they could possibly avoid it.

I remained five years with this gang, and was considered a brave man. I became, however, heartily sick of my employment, yet could not bring myself to resign before my time and retire empty-handed. At this period four Mahommedans were enlisted in the service, with whom I became extremely intimate. One day, my new acquaintances having been employed on some perilous undertaking, returned home unsuccessful. The captain of the gang expressed his dissatisfaction in rather harsh terms, which seemed to threaten a serious dispute—my friends being as anxious to defend as the captain to condemn their conduct.

The surly chieftain, however, was the first to retire, muttering as he went he would take care in future to leave cowards at home. My friends were mightily nettled at this unmerited accusation of cowardice, and sat for some time after the captain had withdrawn busied in giving vent to their displeasure in low and hollow murmurings. I was silent for a considerable time, contenting myself with tracing the diabolical expression of anger and rage depicted on each of my companions' countenances, feeling certain the rolling eye and the quivering lip indicated some determined plan of revenge.

Anxious to discover their intentions, instead of attempting to quell the rising storm, I said, 'Of course, my friends, you will not put up with this insult?'

'No!' cried Peerbuksh, the senior of the men, 'I swear——'

'Hush!' cried his friends, 'we are not alone.'

Peerbuksh seemed to be aware of his imprudence, for he bit his quivering lip and maintained a profound silence.

'I have a plan,' said I, in a low tone, 'by which ample revenge may be taken and ourselves benefited.'

'How?' cried one.

'Name it,' said another.

'Are we alone?'

'No one is near; but what cause have you for dissatisfaction?

'I pant for my freedom,' said I. 'I detest the gang and its commander. Why should we waste our lives in this cavern, accumulating by plunder what will never be fairly divided, notwithstanding the fair promises of these Kookie infidels?'

'What!' cried Peerbuksh, 'are we to go away as poor as we came? Are the many days we have passed here to go for nothing? Better had we each taken opium and slept away our days in the jungles.'

'My friends,' said I, 'you have heard but part of my plan. Cowards are to be left at home, remember. Is this fair, is it honourable thus unjustly to stigmatise brave fellows? What is the object? Why, clearly, when the time of division of the spoil arrives, to furnish a plea for depriving you of your just share.'

'Can this be possible?' cried all of them.

'Nothing more so,' cried I. 'Will not those who have exposed themselves to peril abroad declare against an equal division of their plunder with a few lazy cowards (as they will call you) who have slept away their time at home?'

My friends seemed convinced my suspicions were well-founded, and hastily demanded my plan. I pointed to the treasure, representing how easy it would be to appropriate its contents to our own purposes.

'Yes,' said one, 'but you forget we shall have no opportunity of conveying it away.'

'At present,' I observed, 'there seems **none**; but you **must** endeavour, by humility and contrition, to assuage the anger **of the** chieftain, and——'

'Humility and contrition!' exclaimed Peerbuksh. 'I would rather die like a dog than cringe to the Kookie scoundrel.'

'Pardon me,' said I; 'this is unwise. It is the only method by which we can succeed. Open violence, **you must be aware,** is absurd; and your affected humility **will** be but for a short duration.'

'Well, well, go on,' said Peerbuksh; 'let us hear.'

'I propose, then,' said I, 'to go to the chieftain and intimate to him how deeply you grieve at his unjust accusation, and beg him once more to allow you all to accompany **him** in his excursions. Having once yielded, you will all, by turns, have egress as before. You know it is the custom for two of the gang always to remain at home; when it falls to the lot of either of us to remain, then let us take the opportunity offered by that gaping hole **at the** foot of the treasury; and whatever we extract from it, let it be given to some one or two of us whose turn it may be to go aboveground, where, at an appointed spot, we can bury it; and when enough has been accumulated then let us fly.'

'Excellent!' cried my companions, 'so be it. Let us swear to be true to each other, and success must attend us.'

All swearing to be faithful, I proceeded to the captain, to

whom I represented the dejection of my friends, declaring they were brave and faithful fellows, who panted for an opportunity to wipe away the stain he had cast upon their characters. The captain, who was by this time cool, and had leisure to reflect on the impolicy of denying himself the services of three stout able men, desired me to return to them with the assurances of his forgiveness, and to desire the four Mahommedans to be ready to take their accustomed tour of duty. I did so, and observed Peerbuksh knit his brow and bite his lip hard on hearing the word 'forgiveness.'

Nothing now remained to be done but speedily to commence putting our schemes into execution. I chanced to be out on the following day, accompanied by my four friends, and we were thus enabled to fix upon a particular spot under a teak-tree, where the money from the treasury could safely be secreted. Having thus determined this important point, we anxiously awaited the time when we should be enabled to enrich its root with our golden harvest.

The band separating, we proceeded, unobserved, to dig a wide and deep hole under the tree; so that long ere our turn came to remain at home our treasury was completed. The first of us who remained at home in the absence of the gang was Peerbuksh; but his companion unfortunately was a Kookie, so that we were sadly afraid he would not be able to dip into the treasury. On our return, however, the countenance of our worthy ally plainly evinced success, and he soon took an opportunity of informing us he had helped himself but sparingly, for fear of discovery. The money he had concealed about his person; and as he should himself go abroad on the following day, proposed placing the money under the friendly teak-tree **with** his **own** hands.

Peerbuksh conjectured correctly. **He followed** the gang, leaving me in the cavern, having for my companion a fierce-looking Kookie, who, however, busied himself in preparing the rice for the band, whilst **I**, no less active, drew largely **on** the treasury. Nothing could succeed better than my scheme. **At** last two of my friends were left at home, and their joint drafts on the treasury were so enormous, that **I** entertained serious apprehensions **of a** discovery; but fortunately all was well—not the least suspicion attached itself towards us. Avarice being now my ruling passion, **I** began to consider how I could appropriate to my **own** use **all** the money collected by myself and **my** companions. 'Yes,' said **I**, 'I will take it all, and leave my Suni friends to their fate.'

My turn to remain at home again coming round, **I** meditated taking a good haul at the money, intending to adopt measures for my flight. Peerbuksh was my companion; and scarcely had the band ascended the stone stairs when he approached me **in a** mysterious manner, saying, 'Friend, I have thought of a scheme by which you and **I** may be richer than we dreamed of.'

'Ay, indeed!' said I. 'What may it be?'

'Let us share the money buried under the tree, and leave **our** three friends to their fate.'

'Abominable!' cried I. 'You disgust me. Was there ever anything so dishonourable? I will denounce you to your companions. **How** could so disgraceful an idea ever enter your head? However, thank Allah, you have developed your true character in due time, **so** that we may guard against **your** treacherous machinations.   My friends shall be informed of your intentions, rely upon it.'

Peerbuksh, who had evidently anticipated a joyous acquiescence in the scheme, was now covered with shame at his disappointment, and fell at my feet, begging me not to mention the circumstance to his friends.   Reluctantly I promised—not without reading him a severe lecture on his unprincipled disposition. ' The time is near,' said I, ' when it will be policy for us to decamp; therefore let us this day take due advantage of our present situation: scruple not to load yourself with as much as you can possibly carry, and I will do the same.'

Saying which, I bared my right arm, and thrust it into the hole, when, instead of the grateful touch of gold and silver, I found my wrist grasped in a trap, whose sharp teeth caused me to roar with agony.   I attempted to extract my hand, hoping to draw with it the trap, from whose merciless grasp I was naturally desirous to be freed; but alas! the trap was chained in the hole, and all my attempts to escape rendered fruitless.   Peerbuksh ran about the cavern in an agony of alarm for himself, anticipating the return of the robbers.   ' I will fly,' said he.   ' Farewell, my friend! You had better have followed my advice and made sure of what we have already under the tree, as now I intend seizing it all myself.   Farewell !'   Saying which he rushed up the steps towards the trapdoor, which, to his mortification, he found resisted all his attempts to raise it, being fastened above.

The wretch, who would have thus deserted his friend in distress was now compelled to descend, and at my earnest solicitation attempted to free me from my misery. The more I laboured and dragged at the trap the more poignant was the anguish I endured; nor could our united efforts enlarge the hole, so that there was no **remedy** but **to** await patiently our approaching horrors. Death appeared inevitable; and I lay down, still grasped by the trap, groaning and bitterly repenting having broken the confidence reposed **in** me. Here was a termination of my golden dreams! I was, indeed, justly rewarded for my meditated treachery **to**wards my friends. Peerbuksh, as if I were not suffering enough already, commenced upbraiding me, denouncing me as the author of all the woe awaiting him. 'You,' said he, '**planned** this business; but for you we might have escaped—poor, **I grant ye,** but not covered with shame.'

'Wretch,' cried I, 'did **not you** meditate revenge, in a more horrible and more dangerous shape? **Silence, I** desire you, and add not to the torments I endure.'

Thus passed an hour; when, lo! the sound of footsteps above roused our attentions. 'They come! they come!' I exclaimed. 'What is to be done?' **A** groan from my companion was the only answer I received. **Two such** unhappy beings never existed. The trapdoor of **the** cavern opened, and the band, **one** by one, descended. The captain was the first to discover my deplorable situation. 'Ho, ho!' said he, 'we have caught the thief at last. **Our** noble Persian it is who has robbed us of our hard-earned gains. The trap has done its duty, I find. Release him,' he cried to one of his men, who immediately opening the treasury above, descended, and let go the chain by which the trap was secured.

Drawing forth my arm, I stood like an unhappy fool before the assembly, the trap dangling at my bleeding wrist. 'Seize them both,' cried the captain, 'and confine them.'

'Oh, mercy!' cried Peerbuksh. 'Save my life, and I will inform you where the money has been conveyed.'

'On those conditions, and that you name your associates, I will spare you,' said the captain.

Peerbuksh was about to confess all, when the stroke of a sabre on the back of his neck from one of our Mahommedan friends silenced him for ever. The whole cavern was now a scene of confusion; and the man who had sacrificed Peerbuksh was seized and confined in his stead, myself being his fellow-prisoner. My companion launched out in invectives against Peerbuksh, especially when he learned from me the treachery he had meditated. 'What will become of us?' cried I. '

' Death is inevitable,' replied my friend ; 'but I am ready to suffer a thousand deaths ere I confess where the money is concealed.'

' Our two remaining friends, then,' said I, ' may at last be the only gainers.'

' So much the better for them,' observed he. 'Had not I silenced that knave Peerbuksh, all of us but himself must have suffered, and the gang become repossessed of their money. But how in the name of wonder could they suspect us?'

' Nay, I know not,' I replied ; ' but most probably the last time we remained at home we helped ourselves rather too freely, and the plan of the trap was in consequence adopted to discover the thief. Alas! too well has it succeeded.' My wrist was extremely painful; but as I was sure of **suffering** death for my crime I was unconcerned about it.'

On the following day we were conducted before the gang, at the head of which sat **the** captain, who, without **any** harangue, sentenced me to be shot with arrows, offering my fellow-prisoner his life **if he** would inform them where the money was concealed. **My** companion, however, refusing, we were led away for execution, the place for which was fixed to be in the jungle. I **was** first conducted up the stone steps ; **and** the trap-door being **removed**, I breathed once more the air of heaven. It was a beautiful morning ; the sun had scarcely risen, and a refreshing breeze played through **the** forest.

Two of the sanguinary Kookies **led me towards a** tree, with **the** intention of binding me, to receive the deadly arrows of a **party drawn up** for that purpose. **In such a** situation a miracle alone could have saved me. I had nearly approached the fatal tree, when **an** enormous tiger darted from the thicket and sprang upon one of my conductors ; the other fellow fled, as did also the whole party, who were unprepared with musket and ball **to** encounter **so** formidable an enemy. **It** may be imagined **how** quickly I followed their example; **I** almost flew through the forest, fearing **to look** behind, **lest I** should behold the furious tiger or the bloodthirsty Kookie pursuing me. I fancy, however, the wild beast created too much alarm in the breasts of the valiant Kookies **to** suffer them to spare a momentary thought upon myself, for **when** I did venture to look around me all was quiet— not **a** creature was to be seen.

Thus **I escaped the fury of** the robbers. What became of the

unhappy man who was to have followed me to the place of execution I know not, but question if he was so fortunate as myself.
Finding I had preserved my life, I began to bestow anxious attention on my poor wrist, which was now dreadfully inflamed: my
first care was to bathe it in a small stream, where I sat and
refreshed myself. After two whole days spent in rambling through
the wilds and jungles, I arrived at Chittagong, where I applied to
a Portuguese doctor, begging him to cure my wounded wrist.
Alas! he assured me it was in a state of mortification, and that
amputation alone would preserve my life. I submitted to the
operation, and I and my right hand parted company for ever.
The few rupees I had in my possession began to dwindle away,
and I found myself once more a beggar in a foreign land.

CHAPTER XVII.

THE DYER'S STORY (*continued*).

MUTILATED and forlorn, I wandered from place to place, trusting to chance and charity for my means of subsistence, and thus have had many opportunities of witnessing **the** extraordinary customs and manners of the Hindús. At Benares I beheld many **of** their shocking sacrifices and self-inflicted penances; at Juggernaut I **saw** the ponderous **car, whose** wheels **are near** thirty feet **in** diameter, drawn by the eager multitude over numbers of the bodies of their infatuated brethren, who thus sacrifice their lives in honour of their god, hoping by these means to attain beatitude in a future state.

In some villages **I** have met with religious mendicants in a state of nudity, bedaubed with red paint and ashes, with their nails growing through the palms of their hands; others with one arm erect and immovable; others with one of their legs contracted; and many other horrid sights, which I shall have considerable difficulty in getting my countrymen to believe. Proceeding one day through a considerable town, I saw a crowd of persons gathered around **an** unfortunate man crying out, ' A Churku! **a** Churku!' Others were busily employed in undressing him, whilst many hurried onwards to prepare for some, no doubt, horrid ceremony. I enquired **of an** old man who stood **by me** the meaning of the exclamations I heard **and the scene** which I witnessed.

' Follow me,' said **he,** 'and you shall see.'

I did so, and beheld an unhappy object **led** from the town to the margin of a small river, where was erected a post about fifteen feet high, on the **top** of which swung a beam in an horizontal position, with a cord affixed to one extremity and a sharp iron hook **to** the other. To my surprise, the victim, placing himself immediately under the end whereon was fixed the hook, exclaimed, ' **I am ready!'**

The beam being lowered, a man advancing dashed the hook with violence into the flesh of the poor victim's back ; upon which **another** person, seizing the rope at the opposite extremity, raised the suffering creature from the earth, who without **a** groan was spun round and round for almost half an hour, swinging in a circle of nearly forty feet in diameter. 'What can be the meaning of this?' enquired **I.** **The old** man who had conducted me to the spot informed me that the man whom I saw swinging in the air had transgressed several rules of his tribe, and had lost caste, and was thus endeavouring to reclaim his rank and situation, such **a** method being the only one by which he could have any chance of success. 'Well,' thought I, ' it were better **to** be **an** outcast for ever than to be thus tortured.'

The ceremony concluded. The man, amidst the yells of the populace and maniac dancing **of** several misguided women, who had partaken of bhang[1] for the occasion, was gradually lowered,

[1] A preparation of opium.

and the hook extracted from his lacerated loins. He fell panting on the earth. Water being given him, and his back rubbed with some dirty-looking stuff, he, to my astonishment, arose and walked home as composedly as if nothing of the kind had taken place.

On the banks of the rivers Jumna and Ganges I have witnessed the sick brought by their relatives, and there left to be devoured by alligators or swept away by the waters of those sacred streams. Not unfrequently the mouth of the sick man is filled with mud, being considered highly beneficial to him to die with so agreeable a mouthful ; this, preventing his breathing, often produces death, where otherwise the patient might have a chance of recovery. Travelling near Allahabad, I was informed a suttee was about to take place. On enquiry I learned that a Brahminee woman had lost her husband, and that, according to the custom of her family, she considered herself bound to sacrifice herself on the funeral pile.

I obtained a sight of the extraordinary woman. She was young and handsome, surrounded by Brahmins and relatiyes. She walked with a firm and collected step. The pile was ready at a distance, whilst the wailing of the mourners, crying ' Rugoonath, Rugoonath!' (the name of the deceased) added to the terrors of the scene. I kept my eyes fixed on the unhappy widow, who, dressed out with the mogree[1] flowers, was employed in slowly divesting herself of her ornaments, giving them one by one to her female relations. Some there were who appeared anxious to dissuade her from her horrid purpose ; and she seemed, the nearer

---

[1] A species of sweet-smelling jessamine.

she approached the pile, to be less firm in her purpose ; but the wily Brahmins, who surrounded her, took care their victim should not escape : they sang hymns, yelled, **and** preached ; **and ere the** victim was prepared pushed **her** into **the pile,** which **was soon in** a'frightful blaze.

One faint scream **did** the hapless creature utter, and then of her I saw no more. **Nought** could be seen but flames and smoke, which, from the addition **of** oil and **ghee, now** raged furiously, shedding their **deadly** gleams on the unfeeling countenances **of** the murderous Brahmins, who still chanted their hymns **unmoved,** undisturbed **by** the awful sight which made me shudder.

Thus ended a ceremony which, had **I** not witnessed, **I never should** have believed ; many other sights did I see, but none so **horrid as** the suttee. Chance brought me to this city, and **I** was beginning to turn my thoughts **on Yezd,** when, in one of the public streets, I beheld to my amazement Yasmin and Yusoof, whose astonishment fully equalled my **own.** They related to me their adventures, **and I** also informed them of all I had undergone since we parted.

.**We** all agreed that **our ill** success was attributable to our own folly ; **and as** we must now subsist on charity, determined, when we received alms, **to** impose upon ourselves the tedious ceremony of prostrating ourselves thirty times **at** the feet of the donor. Our utmost wishes are to accumulate money sufficient to carry us back **to** Yezd, where Yusoof and myself intend to re-nounce Sufiism for ever.

The third beggar having concluded his history, Aurungzebe bestowed upon the unhappy men money sufficient to convey them back to Yezd; desiring, however, he might be informed **by letter of** their condition on their **arrival, and** whether their friends had received them. They promised obedience, received the money, and each prostrated himself before the mighty Emperor thirty times. **When** the beggars had quitted the city the Emperor amused himself **by** talking over with his Vizier the adventures of these singular men. He laughed at the vanity of Yasmin, and the troubles in which it had involved him, and expressed his belief that in the tale of that man the strict truth had been adhered **to ;** but, in commenting upon the blind **beggar's story, he would say,** ' I believe it **to be** all **a lie from** beginning to end, but the fellow deserves some credit for his talent of **invention.'**

' True,' observed the Vizier; ' though I **wonder his** experience did not suggest to him the danger of trying such an experiment before your Majesty. But **if** his tale strikes your Majesty as an entire fabrication, surely the history of the third beggar is no less so.'

' **No, truly,'** observed the Emperor. ' What he has stated it is very probable may have occurred ; it is evident the fellow has resided among **the** Kookies, **or** he could not have given **any** account of that singular race of people. And **it is also clear he** has wandered through the greater part of Hindústan. **At any** rate, as I demanded their histories, **I** must be content with what they have given me ; **but I** confess **I** am anxious to hear how the rascals get on in Yezd.'

In about a year after the departure of the Persians from Delhi **the Emperor** received **a** letter from Yusoof, the one-eyed beggar, wherein **he** mentioned having, **with his** friend Mohabet Ali, reached **Yezd,** having encountered great difficulties on the road owing to the treachery of Yasmin, who, in the plains of Belochistan, robbed them of the bounty of the Emperor and decamped, and they had never heard of him **since.** Yusoof proceeded to state that he had succeeded in inducing his father to become reconciled with him, and, having renounced Sufiism, was engaged as a partner in his father's mercantile transactions.

Mohabet Ali, having no father living, was unable to move the **hearts of** his cousin and other relatives, notwithstanding he had from his heart abjured the abominable doctrines the adherence to which had caused him so much misery. The letter concluded with expressions of heartfelt gratitude for the Emperor's beneficence, which, but for the avarice **and** wickedness of Yasmin, would greatly have facilitated their journey to their own dear Yezd, in which city having at length arrived, they determined quietly to remain.

'Here,' said Kuzl Bashee, the dyer, 'end my tales, which **I** trust have amused my illustrious hearers.'

The Nuwab confessed that the dyer had far exceeded his expectations, and dismissed him apparently well satisfied.

CHAPTER XVIII.

TELLS HOW THE STORIES **WERE DISCONTINUED.**

THE dyer received the congratulations of his **friends on his** apparent success; but the butcher felt a large portion of envy rising in his breast as he contemplated how he had been outdone, notwithstanding the aid he had received from the mysterious old woman, his relation. The course of tales **was** now interrupted **by** the approach of a grand festival, at which the Nuwab was accustomed to attend.

It was with displeasure he observed he was not so cordially received this year as he was wont to be. As he sat in his splendid howdah, on the back of a lofty elephant, he espied amongst the crowd a Persian; all his fears, all his doubts again crowding **on** his mind, he commanded the procession to halt. This order was, owing to the din of trumpets and drums, with difficulty obeyed, and ere the Nuwab could give orders for the arrest of **the** Persian he was nowhere to be found.

The disappointment vexed the Nuwab exceedingly, and he continued throughout the day thoughtful and melancholy, and in **a** very bad humour. Moye-ed-din ventured to propose the continuation of the tales **on** the following day, to which the Nuwab gave a sullen assent. In consequence the remainder of the story-tellers attended to **draw lots, and** Lalldass, **the** merchant, was the **man to entertain** the Nuwab **with** a history, **for** which he begged **three days' time,** which was granted.

At the appointed time Lalldass appeared at the palace, and **was about to** commence his tale, when an unusual **bustle in the court-yard of the** palace arrested the attention of the Nuwab and his minister.   On enquiry **it** was found that a noble Persian, notwith-standing the repulse **of the** guards, insisted on being ushered int : the presence of **the** Nuwab.   Jelal-ed-din, dreading he knew not what, sat motionless **and** silent; at last, signing to Moye-ed-din, he commanded that the Persian should be admitted immediately. Accordingly, a tall ferocious-looking man, habited in **the** Persian costume, walked boldly up the hall, and when at the foot **of** the Nuwab's Musnud **a violent** scream from behind the lattice com-pelled Jelal-ed-din to **arise to ascertain the cause.**   He found the **fair** Mheitab fainting, and the rest of the ladies endeavouring to revive her.   When somewhat recovered she widely opened her **eyes,** crying, 'Save me from that **man, oh, save me!'**

The Nuwab, astonished beyond measure, promised her his protection; **and** leaving her **to the care** of her attendants, com-manded **that the Persian** should be admitted to him instantly, in a private apartment.   The Persian appearing, presented a royal firman from Nadir **Shah,** King of Persia, the contents of which caused the Nuwab great agony, and almost despair.   To account **for this** mysterious intrusion of the Persian it will be necessary to **draw** the reader's attention to the following particulars.

Tehran, a city **in** Persia, was ruled by a Governor named Ghalib **Khan, a cousin of** the mighty king of the country, Nadir

Shah, who continued to shower **down** his favours on his relative with **a** generosity indicative of the respect and love which he bore him. The **Governor of** Tehran, therefore, was looked upon as the most prosperous and fortunate of men, and was approached **with a** submission and respect equal to that experienced **by** the sovereign himself.

So situated, it is natural to suppose the happiness of Ghalib kept pace with his honours, but, alas! this **was not** the case; for Ghalib, like other mortals, whether their brows are encircled by the glittering diadem, or covered by the coarse cap **of the dervise,** wished for **one** thing **more to** complete his happiness; **and this,** alas! was **not in** the power of kings **to bestow—it was a son,** who might succeed him in his government. Women and **wives he** had in abundance, but not one was kind enough to bear him a son; his wife, however, as if to make amends for the deficiency, produced **a** daughter more lovely than ever woman bore, more graceful and heart-alluring than the mind of man can conceive; she was named Zeefa, at whose birth her father summoned the astronomers and **wise** men from far and near, to pronounce her future fate.

What opinion these learned sages gave, or what they foretold, was never clearly ascertained; but whatever they might have said seemed in no way to affect the spirits of the Governor, who continued lamenting his unfortunate situation in not being blessed with a son, envying his sister who resided in Ispahan, married to **a man** of rank, by whom she had two beautiful boys. Whether this inordinate longing for a male heir or press of business occasioned him to fall sick is not known, but certain **it is** when Zeefa had attained her fourteenth year her father died, **and was soon** followed by her lamenting mother. **Zeefa was** then conveyed to Ispahan, where her aunt awaited her.

Zookma, the sister of Ghalib Khan, was a woman well skilled **in artifice** and every species of duplicity. No sooner, therefore, **had her** brother departed this life than she immediately urged her husband, Shamil Beg, to make interest to succeed to the vacant Governorship of Tehran; he did so, but was unsuccessful. Never despairing, Zookma, **on the** decease **of the** mother of Zeefa, planned **a union** between that unhappy orphan and her elder son, Zekey Khan, hoping thus one day to see him, her favourite son, Governor of Tehran.

Zekey Khan was at this period about eighteen years of age, **and Humza,** his brother, only one year his junior; the former **was a** youth of a vicious disposition, cruel, revengeful, and mean, whilst the latter possessed all the virtues of benevolence, openness, and candour. So blinded, however, were the eyes of the parents of these youths, that the real merits of Humza were seen by them to shine in Zekey Khan, whose wickedness was unjustly considered to be seated in his brother's heart. The art and cunning of Zekey Khan had contributed not a little to cause this defect of vision in the eyes of his parents. Humza saw and felt the decided partiality of his father and mother for his malevolent brother, and strove in vain, by attention and obedience to their commands, to obtain some portion of the favours lavished on his elder brother.

On the arrival of their lovely cousin Zeefa, Zekey Khan showed her the most marked attention, whilst Humza was constrained to admire in silence. It required but little penetration to discover that Zeefa lent an unwilling ear to the fulsome adulation of Zekey Khan, but it required the eye of one skilled in the soft mysteries of love to detect her partiality for the modest but fascinating Humza.   Faint is the language of the tongue compared to that of the eyes, for Zeefa, although seldom suffered to converse with Humza, frequently perceived his mild intelligent eyes bent earnestly upon her ; and if in return she raised her own, his were bent to the earth in modest confession of his presumption.

Zeefa at such times felt a blush tingle her lovely cheek, which escaped not the notice of her aunt, who, not dreaming the **real** cause, would attribute it to her real delight at the highflown compliments of her elder son, Zekey Khan.   Such speeches and so, to her, unintelligible a mode of conversation, especially when her thoughts veered in a contrary direction, often caused the lovely Zeefa to betray her insensibility to the attentions of Zekey Khan, and occasioned an awkwardness impossible to disguise.

One day in particular, when Zekey Khan was about to absent himself on business for a few days, previous to his departure he appeared before the fascinating Zeefa, and after a burst of rhapsody, and repetition of several worn-out similes and highflown compliments culled from the poems of Hafiz, stated he was about to proceed to Schiraz, and that every minute absent from her would be to him a year, and ventured to hope she would also feel a reciprocal inquietude, and anxiously look forward to his return.

' Yes, lovely Zeefa, I go from you for a short season ; but say, wilt thou not mourn my absence?'

At this moment Humza entered the apartment.   His eyes met those of Zeefa, who in confusion replied to the question of Zekey

Khan in the negative. The wounded pride of that aspiring youth took fire ; he turned round in anger to address his brother, to whose unseasonable intrusion he attributed the cold reply of Zeefa ; but Humza had withdrawn, and Zeefa alone remained to reap the consequences of her unguarded reply.

'Lady,' he cried, 'I fain would attribute the chilling negative which fell from thy beauteous lips to the intrusion of my brother Humza, and would commend the prudence which dictated it in the presence of a third person, could I divest myself of the idea that total indifference to me urged you to speak your real sentiments, for I have observed of late my visits give you little or no real pleasure.'

'My lord,' replied Zeefa, 'I much marvel that a man of your penetration did not earlier make the discovery, for——'

'Enough!' cried the exasperated young man. 'Haughty cousin, you may live to repent this day; and remember, if in future my visits should be less welcome than they now are, you have yourself alone to blame!' Thus saying, he burst from her presence, leaped on his horse, and was soon out of sight.

In his haste to depart, Zekey Khan, ere he proceeded far, discovered he had left behind him an important document, which his father, who was at Schiraz, had instructed him to be the bearer of; he therefore turned his horse, and arriving at the gate of his father's garden, secured the animal to a tree, and entered by a private way, intending to cross the garden and enter his apartments unseen by anyone. Passing through an avenue of cypress-trees, he fancied he heard voices ; he listened attentively, and was convinced he was not mistaken. The feelings with which he discovered **the** persons of Zeefa and **his** brother **Humza** may be better imagined than described. **It was** for him, then—for Humza—she had scorned his love ! That artful boy it was who had undermined him in his attempts, and dared in secret to thwart his ambitious views.

Zekey Khan felt more than half-inclined to sacrifice both to his fury. His hand already grasped the hilt of his sword, when he called to mind the relationship of Zeefa to the king, whose wrath he deemed it imprudent to rouse. Revenge in another shape, however, he determined upon, and for the present quietly withdrew, and gained his own apartment. Having secured the document, he repaired to his mother, to whom he unfolded his discovery, and related the subject of his parting conversation with **Zeefa.** The rage of his mother if anything exceeded his own, and **she** promised to have Humza removed far away from his fair cousin, beseeching Zekey Khan not to proceed to violence, or to prosecute any plan without her concurrence. He promised, and was departing, when Zeefa herself entered the room. Her surprise at beholding her angry cousin was excessive, and the mysterious expression of both his and her aunt's countenance greatly alarmed her.

In a haughty and commanding tone Zookma desired her to retire ; and when the trembling girl had obeyed the mandate Zekey Khan and his mother proceeded to discuss the important subject, when it was finally settled that a situation in the army should be immediately procured for Humza, between whom and Zeefa all communication should henceforth be guarded against. Dread of Nadir Shah alone prevented the adoption of harsh measures towards Zeefa ; and Zekey Khan, relying on the prudence of his mother, once more departed, and in due time arrived at Schiraz.

As soon as convenient Zeefa was summoned to the apartment of her aunt, who quickly commenced an examination as to how and in what manner the amiable girl had spent her time. In the most artless manner she assured her aunt she had only been walking in the garden with her cousin Humza. Zookma launched out in expressions of surprise at the impropriety she had been guilty of, magnified the act, and concluded with laying her commands against a repetition of the offence. Zeefa replied she was not aware of any great impropriety in conversing with Humza more than with his brother.

' There is, however,' said Zookma ; ' for knowing, as everyone does, that you are betrothed to Zekey Khan——'

' Betrothed, madam !' exclaimed Zeefa ; ' and who has conceived themselves authorised so to act ?'

' Those who know what is for your welfare,' replied her aunt.

' Surely, madam, you forget what the astronomers at my birth——'

' The King's commands,' said her aunt, ' cancel all astronomers' and soothsayers' predictions ; therefore, Zeefa, prepare to wed Zekey Khan.'

' Impossible, madam ; nor do I credit the King's commands being given on the subject.'

' This document, then, will perhaps satisfy you,' said Zookma, producing a paper bearing the royal seal, which the alarmed girl waited not to peruse, but fainted at the feet of her designing aunt.

When recovered she found herself alone, in her own apartment, and unmolested for the remainder of the day.

Early on the following morning, as she sat at her window to inhale the refreshing breeze, she perceived Humza walking in the garden, with his arms folded in a pensive attitude. He turned round and cast his eyes up to her window. Seeing the very person on whom his thoughts rested, he placed his hand upon his heart, and was approaching to converse, when Zeefa motioned him to refrain, which signal convinced the youth that their previous interview had been reported to his mother; he sighed, and withdrew, to plan some method by which he might once more, ere his brother returned, converse with his adored Zeefa.

In the presence of his mother Humza saw his beauteous cousin; but, under the restraint of her watchful eye, what could lovers do but steal glances such as lovers only can understand? Those only who have experienced what it is to be compelled by uncontrollable misfortunes to check the tongue which would declare the passions of the soul, and at the same time, although knowing the impossibility of a union with the object of their admiration, find a total absence utterly impracticable, can alone imagine the torture endured by the enraptured Humza. He saw before him a being rare in beauty and accomplishments, one whom, had he dared to have declared his passion, he felt would not have been quite insensible to his sufferings; and in confessing a mutual passion two fond hearts must nevertheless, owing to circumstances over which they had no control, be resigned to suffer eternal separation. Humza rushed into the shades of the lofty cypress grove, where he continued deep in meditation till midnight, his own sighs mingling with those of the mournful nightingale. Rousing himself, he exclaimed aloud, 'And can it be possible? Has the King indeed commanded my brother to wed Zeefa? If so, I durst not interfere. Without fortune, dependent on others; oh! misery unequalled! Could I dare to press my suit, obtain from her my heart adores a favourable answer, and then sigh and part for ever! Banish the thought! rather will I suffer her to imagine I am indifferent towards her; that her charms have not racked this heavy but devoted heart, rather let her suppose I detest her, than risk the chance of raising hopes which never can be realised. There is madness in the thought. I will leave her—will fly the abode which contains so much perfection, and in some secluded spot linger out my existence! Leave her, did I say? not even see her, because I cannot be united to her? Impossible! Life would be insupportable unrefreshed by the bright gleam of her cheering countenance. Oh! Zeefa! Zeefa! with thee I must not live, without thee I cannot!'

The broad streaks of day were now visible from the east, and the sun, rising in majestic splendour, found Humza the earliest of his adorers; and as the youth with religious zeal prostrated himself before the glorious orb he breathed a fervent prayer to the Great Controller of the heavenly planets for the safety and happiness of his beloved Zeefa. Another day elapsed, and Humza saw Zeefa only in the presence of his mother. The lovely girl with grief perceived his wan cheek and absent manner; she knew he loved her, and felt that powerful circumstances alone prevented a confession.

A younger brother, without fortune or situation, what could he do? The days **of** romance were gone by; and although Leila and Mejnoon[1] lived on air impregnated with the breath of their loves, **yet** in present times rank, situation, and prospects were obliged to be considered ere parents and guardians viewed love-sick youths with the same partial eyes as their daughters. Over Zeefa was the royal eye, and the more watchful one of her aunt, who favoured not Humza, but Zekey Khan; to indulge, therefore, in any romantic dreams **of** a union with Humza **she** felt was absurd; nevertheless she hoped the option was yet hers to wed him on whom she had fixed her affections, or not at all.

'I will,' cried she, 'retire from the world, nor dream of happiness, unless shared with Humza, whose love for me I cannot doubt; for although no tongue hath declared, yet from the eye hath beamed a language more explanatory of his feelings, more indicative of the workings of his soul, than words could have effected.' The circumstance of the youth having placed his hand upon his **heart** beneath her window was not forgotten, but treasured up in the memory of the amiable girl and engrafted on every feeble pulsation of her devoted heart. Hope would often steal amidst the shades of despondency and whisper, 'Humza may distinguish himself, may be deemed worthy the hand of Zeefa.' At such times the ardently devoted girl experienced a dizzy whirl of anticipated delight thrill through her perturbed brain, followed by a flow of spirits which **were** calculated to inspire hopes in the mind of her aunt that all would terminate as she desired.

It was late in the evening of a sultry day, when Zookma had

[1] The Romeo and Juliet of the East.

reason to believe Humza was from home, that she proposed to Zeefa a walk in the garden. The obedient girl complying, the artful aunt commenced launching out in praises of her elder son, and depreciating the merits of Humza so strongly, as to compel the maiden to request her to change the conversation.

'Well, well, my child, I shall say no more, save that Humza has gained a post of honour in the army, and has this day taken leave of me.'

'Humza gone!' exclaimed Zeefa; 'gone and not taken leave of me!'

'No, my dear, I thought you would not like to be disturbed so early; and as his orders admitted of no delay, it was impossible.'

'Oh, say no more, madam, say no more,' said Zeefa, vexed and angry at the conduct of Humza, and mortified at having expressed any regret on the subject. Her aunt continued by assuring her his place would be supplied by her dear son Zekey Khan, whose return she expected on the following day. They had by this time returned to the house, and had prepared to enter, when a rustling close by attracted the notice of Zeefa, who on turning her head perceived Humza in an attitude of supplication to herself, as if begging an interview. All idea of displeasure instantly vanished, and she determined to effect a meeting. Turning to her aunt, therefore, she said, 'With your permission I will continue my walk; my spirits are low, and the air exhilarating.'

'Do so,' replied Zookma, certain that Humza was by this time far enough off; 'but mind and stay not too long.'

Zeefa, with a hurried step, sought the sanctuary of the cypress grove, where she was soon joined by her admiring Humza, who thanked her a thousand times for thus giving him an opportunity of bidding her farewell. He then informed her of his appointment in the cavalry commanded by the Prince, and that his mother had hastened his departure, pretending his immediate appearance **at** Schiraz was indispensably necessary, the king being then at that place.

'Why, then, have you disobeyed?' said Zeefa. 'I fear this is a sad earnest of your future submission to orders.'

'Could I go, perhaps **for** ever, without one farewell from thy beauteous lips?' said the enraptured youth. 'To hear your wishes for my safety and success is necessary to stimulate me to deeds **of** valour. To know you are interested in my welfare will doubly nerve my arm, and render me a very lion **in my** sovereign's cause.'

'Enough, Humza,' said the maiden: 'that I am interested in your welfare you need not doubt, perhaps more so than I ought to be.'

'Nay, say not so, dearest Zeefa, **for** every act **of** mine shall prove me worthy of your regard.'

The cousins conversed in this strain for some time, until it ended in a mutual declaration of each other's passion, and solemn vows of eternal fidelity; and when the time of separation arrived, they parted with heavy hearts.

As Zeefa retraced her steps towards the house she fancied she heard a footstep. 'Heavens!' she inwardly exclaimed, 'have we been watched? Imprudent that we were to risk such danger!' She found her aunt, however, in her apartments, wearing a countenance dressed in smiles, which considerably abated her alarm.

Coffee being introduced, the conversation turned on subjects foreign to the thoughts of Zeefa, who soon retired for the night.

As soon as Zeefa had left her aunt old Sheik Abdoolah, the head-gardener, begged admittance, which Zookma immediately granted. As soon as **he** had made his obeisance he informed his mistress of the conversation between Zeefa and Humza which he had overheard in the garden. Zookma was enraged beyond measure, and felt inclined that moment to rush to her niece's apartment and **tax her** with duplicity and artfulness; but on second thoughts determined to feign ignorance of the fact, in order that a scheme might be effected, in the conducting which no share of suspicion might be attached to her.

This was no less than to have Zeefa actually carried away and placed entirely in the power of Zekey Khan, who might, most probably, at last induce her to marry him. This plan she unfolded to her favourite son, on his arrival the following day, detailing the information received from Sheik Abdoolah, the gardener. Zekey Khan was wild with rage and envy to hear how successful was his brother Humza, and with delight entered into the schemes of his mother. The great difficulty, however, was to avoid suspicion, and it was therefore necessary to carry the plan into execution at a time when Zekey Khan should be known to be absent. Nadir Shah's determination to invade India offered every nobleman in the country an opportunity of signalising themselves, and evincing their loyalty to the sovereign.

Shamil Beg and Zekey Khan were amongst the first to offer their services, which were immediately accepted; and Humza, as an officer in the cavalry, of course followed his commander to the field. Zeefa was thus to be left entirely under the charge of Zookma, her aunt. Here was the long-wished-for opportunity of conveying the girl away to any place which might be appointed. Humza determined once more to see his beloved Zeefa ere he departed, and to his surprise found his mother offered no objection to the interview, and more than once left the lovers alone. Little did he know the workings of his mother's mind. That artful woman had long determined to accuse Humza as the person who forcibly conveyed away his fair cousin; and this parting visit, therefore, she encouraged, in order to afford a colour to her accusation.

The lovers parted. It seemed an eternal separation; neither could dare hope to meet again. The time, the distance, the danger, all crowded on the mind of Zeefa; and with tears in her eyes, and an oppression at her heart, she saw her beloved turn in anguish from her side. Zekey Khan bade her a cold farewell; but Shamil Beg, her uncle, was so engaged in business as to be prevented from taking leave in person; he therefore in a letter informed her of his departure, and bade her consider herself entirely under the control of his wife, Zookma, in whom he had the greatest confidence.

Zeefa for many days confined herself to her apartment, indulging in the most bitter grief. About one month after the departure of the Persian army Zeefa was one evening walking in the garden in the very path where Humza had first declared his love, when the sound **of** voices, murmuring at **a** distance, broke upon her ear. The sound was so unusual that she felt considerably alarmed, and turned to retrace her steps to the house, when suddenly she found

herself seized by **four men, who,** unmoved by her screams, **con-**
veyed her **through** a low private door into a **wood** adjoining, where
one of the men, lifting her on **a** horse, and placing himself behind
her, galloped away, followed **by** his companions, well-mounted.

In **vain** she entreated and implored the men to release her;
they spurred their horses through woods and broken ground, **nor**
stopped **until** darkness impeded their progress. Food was offered
the sinking Zeefa, who, **alas !** could only partake of a cup of cold
water. A **shed was discovered, in which a bed,** composed of the
saddle-cloths of **the** horses, **was** made for the fatigued terror-
stricken **girl,** whilst the **men** stood as guards without the place.
What **could** be the object of these men? **Who** was the instigator
of the outrage? **Not Zekey Khan; he was far away.** Yet when
she called to mind his angry words, and **his** horrid expression of
countenance when **he uttered** them, suspicion deeply entered her
mind that he indeed it must be who thus dared to seize and con-
vey her from the protection of his mother. There was no help,
and the forlorn Zeefa resigned herself to her fate.

As soon as morning dawned the men prepared to proceed;
and thus they continued for many days, until they reached Busrah,
where, **in an** obscure **and** gloomy abode, they deposited their
lovely captive.

CHAPTER XIX.

CONCLUSION.

THE sanguinary deeds of Nadir Shah in Hindústan are too **well** known to require repetition; suffice it **to say** that Humza distinguished himself in battle so highly that the king was induced to **grant him any boon** he should **ask of** him. The youth on his **bended knee** demanded the sanction of the sovereign to his union with the lovely Zeefa.

' Your request is granted,' cried the king, ' provided Zeefa herself consent ; but her uncle has repeatedly informed me of her love for your brother, Zekey Khan, in whose favour **I** had nearly decided ; but, as bravery alone deserves the fair, be the prize yours, if you can win her.'

The delighted Humza arose amidst the congratulations of the surrounding courtiers. The news was soon conveyed to Shamil Beg and Zekey Khan. The latter swore a terrible oath never to permit Humza to wed Zeefa, or ever again to set eyes upon her, if he could help it. That his mother had executed the plan of removal he had no doubt ; but he dreaded the return of the king, who would doubtless, at the intercession of Humza, not only discover Zeefa, but learn who was the instigator of the outrage.

In due time the king, flushed with conquest, and satiated by acts of bloodshed and cruelty, returned to Persia. Humza on the wings of love flew to his beloved Zeefa, but he found her not. His mother, with well-affected grief, related her mysterious disappearance. To her husband even she durst not reveal the truth, so monstrous was her conduct in the affair; and to Zekey Khan she expressed her repentance of the part she had taken in the transaction, especially when she heard of the high favours showered down on Humza by the king.

Zekey Khan, by all the rhetoric he was master of, besought his mother to quiet her alarms, for that whatever might be his fate her name should ever by him be kept secret. Humza applied to his sovereign for aid to discover his fair cousin, and the King issued his royal orders throughout his vast empire. Zekey Khan, to avoid suspicion, set forward with a party of men, purposely taking the road to Busrah, where having arrived, he learned from his trusty hirelings that Zeefa was safe in the retreat in which they had at first deposited her. Zekey Khan, aware of the strict search instituted by the king, was at a loss what step to take to secure his fair cousin and at the same time to shield himself from suspicion.

Convinced no place in Persia was safe, he bargained with an Arab captain of a merchant vessel about to sail for India, informing him that his sister being about to form an improper connection, he was desirous, for a time, to remove her to a distance from the object of her affections, promising to follow himself in a short time. The captain consenting, the helpless Zeefa was conveyed on board his ship in the still hour of midnight, the captain having been directed to place her, on his arrival at Calcutta, under the protection of a respectable and wealthy Persian merchant of that city, to whom Zekey Khan penned a friendly letter.

Scarcely had the vessel weighed anchor ere Zekey Khan learned that his brother Humza was arrived in Busrah with a large party, having in vain searched in a contrary direction. The artful Zekey Khan immediately proceeded to his anxious brother, to whom he declared he had received positive information that Zeefa, or some lady answering her description, had been conveyed towards Bagdad. 'Let us hasten, then,' said he, 'to her rescue.'

Humza, delighted at the most distant prospect of once more beholding his beloved Zeefa, instantly prepared to march towards Bagdad, accompanied by the wily Zekey Khan, who, to all appearance, was no less anxious than his brother.

It was far from the intention **of** the crafty Zekey Khan to accompany his brother in what he too well knew was a fruitless search through the wilds of Arabia; and consequently, after the second day's march, feigned sickness, retaining only one trusty follower, directing the rest of his men to follow the footsteps of Humza, to whom he lamented the impossibility of his proceeding farther, at the same time promising to prosecute the search in another direction as soon as his indisposition would allow him. The unsuspecting Humza took an affectionate farewell of his brother, and pursued his route to Bagdad.

The sickness **of** Zekey Khan was but of short duration, and with his attendant he returned to Schiraz, where he learned the king then was. To his sovereign he reported his ill-success, but expressed the most sanguine hopes that his brother Humza would eventually discover **his beloved cousin**; at the same time offered his services **to** proceed **to** Hindústan, **if his royal master** would furnish **him with** his royal firman to the Emperor of Delhi.

Nadir Shah, anxious to do all in **his power,** granted a firman, **in which he** desired **every** exertion should **be** made **by** the **governors of** places throughout India **to discover Zeefa, and** that the bearer was authorised **to take** charge **of** her and conduct her to his court in Persia. This document **Zekey** Khan preserved, **little** dreaming **he should ever be reduced to** the necessity of making **use of it.** In due time Zekey Khan, accompanied by **his** servant, **who** was, he knew, privy **to most** of his machinations, **and** whom **it** would be dangerous **to leave** behind, arrived at Calcutta, **where in** breathless impatience he sought **out** the residence of **the** merchant under whose care he expected to find the lovely Zeefa.

How was he vexed and mortified, **however, on** learning that no such person had **been** delivered to him, nor had the captain of the Arab ship ever visited him! Zekey Khan was now quite at **a** loss to know how to act or where to go; **he cursed** the Arab captain from the **bottom** of his heart, and rushed through the city in the hope of meeting him, but learned that he sailed for Mocha many days ago. There seemed **but one step to** take, viz. to return to Persia in the same ship in which he had come, and for this purpose he agreed with the commander of the vessel, who promised to **set** sail as soon as his business should be completed.

Every day seemed a year to the impatient and restless Zekey **Khan.** At last the day was fixed **for** the sailing of the ship, and with a **favourable** breeze they bade adieu to the shores of Hindústan. Zekey Khan was, however, destined once more to visit some **part of this** country, **for a** dreadful gale compelled the captain to put into the port **of** Surat, in the Province of Guzrat, where some weeks would be requisite **to** repair the shattered vessel. Finding the inhabitants of the city beheld with aversion a Sheah, he **wisely** took lodgings in an obscure part of the city, near to the dwelling of Mhadeo Gúrú, the Brahmin astronomer, with whom he occasionally conversed.

From this man he learned the extraordinary circumstance **of** a Persian lady being in the Nuwab's palace, and on ascertaining the exact time of her sale by the Arab captain, doubted not but it **was** indeed his Zeefa, the lady he was **in** quest **of**. 'Now, **then**,' thought he, ' my firman will be highly necessary ; **let** this Nuwab disobey if he dare.'

Zekey Khan's suspicions were **indeed correct** ; it was Zeefa herself who was resident **in** the palace. The captain who had agreed **to** deposit her with the merchant in Calcutta having occasion **to** visit Surat, could not withstand the tempting offers made him **by** the Cotwall and the still more exorbitant ones of the Deewan, but parted with his fair charge, **and** sailed to Calcutta without her.

Zekey Khan in vain endeavoured to obtain **a** sight of the fair Persian lady. One morning he placed himself immediately before the palace, and was busy conjecturing how he could ascertain to a certainty if the mysterious Persian lady was indeed his cousin Zeefa, when he was accosted, as may be remembered, by the civil good-natured Buxoo, the barber, for which piece of good service he was knocked down, and Zekey Khan, in consequence of the imprudent outrage, was compelled to seek retirement more than ever, seldom venturing abroad by day. To his servant he had already unfolded his discovery and suspicions, and thus they continued a plan by which all doubts on the subject must be cleared away.

The servant became acquainted with one of the matrons of the Zenana, to whom a note was given, penned as if by Humza, to be delivered to Zeefa. This able matron soon brought an answer, which at once convinced Zekey Khan his suspicions were well-founded. Under pretence of deliverance from her imprisonment, the lady was induced to comply with, as she imagined, her Humza's request to procrastinate her final answer to the Nuwab, and thus, at the instigation of Zekey Khan, requested permission to visit the Mhamud-a-baugh palace, where, in conformity to the previously arranged plan, her palanquin was thrown open by a set of fellows hired for the purpose.

Zekey Khan had his reasons for not instantly claiming his cousin. It was necessary he should first learn how affairs were going on in Persia, as it was no part of his plan to quietly lead Zeefa to the throne of the King, and perhaps see her wedded to his detested brother, Humza. He therefore awaited patiently, in the hopes of some intelligence from that quarter, during which time the Nuwab was listening to the tales of his subjects. At last a vessel arrived from Busrah, from the captain of which he gleaned such information as determined him, without delay, to openly claim his fair cousin in the manner already related.

Scarcely had the Hindú merchant commenced his tale ere the imperious Zekey Khan demanded an audience of the Nuwab. The effect of his appearance on Zeefa has already been mentioned;

but the mortification and disappointment of the Nuwab it is difficult to portray. The firman, he had no doubt, was authentic, but he was quite at **a loss to** account for the abhorrence with which the fair Persian received the bearer of it. He therefore deferred giving **any** final answer until he should have enjoyed a conference with his adored Mheitab. From her he learned the particulars above-mentioned; and understanding her aversion to her cousin, Zekey Khan, determined on refusing to give her into his custody.

He was cogitating what plea he should urge for daring to disobey the imperious mandate of Nadir Shah, when he was informed that Moye-ed-din was desirous **of** an audience. The Nuwab instantly admitted him, and the zealous Deewan, having made his obeisance, begged his highness would give ear to what he had to unfold. Permission being granted, he thus commenced:

' May it please your Highness, **I am** aware of the nature of the Persian's business in this palace, and also of the reluctance which you feel to comply with the orders of the mighty Nadir Shah. A communication, however, has been made to me, which, whether true or false, I think will justify you in refusing to surrender the fair lady.'

' Ah, indeed ! what is it? Be quick, Moye-ed-din.'

' My lord, as I was about to retire for the night a message was delivered to me that a Persian demanded an audience that moment. Imagining it to be the man whom your highness had in the course of the day admitted to your presence, I refused; but the earnest entreaties of the man prevailing, I desired he might be admitted. The Persian, I soon discovered, was not the man who had presented the firman to your highness, but a short, stout, ill-looking fellow, who at once declared his name to be Ghuzzub Ali.'

' " I am come, my lord," said he, " to perform an act of justice and of revenge."

' I stared, but he proceeded to give me a full account of the mystery which has enveloped the fair lady to whom you are so strongly attached.'

' Which I know already,' interrupted the Nuwab, ' she herself having informed me.'

' Then, my lord, I need not repeat the tale, only I imagine there is one part which the lady herself is ignorant of, one circumstance she little dreams of, which is, that Zekey Khan has basely murdered his brother Humza.'

' Ah ! indeed, Moye-ed-din, that is an event I dare not communicate to her.'

' True, my lord; but it furnishes a sound plea for your disobeying the firman from the Court of Persia.'

' But, Moye-ed-din, may we rely on the information?'

' I think we may; the man who told me was the confidential servant of Zekey Khan, who most imprudently struck the man on the face, for which he has panted for an opportunity to be revenged. He swears he overheard his master give the murderous order to a fellow named Kummil Khan previously to his quitting his brother Humza, on the road to Bagdad, and that if the said Kummil Khan be closely questioned at the Court of the Persian monarch he will confess the whole transaction.'

' Enough! Moye-ed-din, seize this Zekey Khan the moment

he appears before me to-morrow **to** hear my answer; mark well my signal for his apprehension. He remains my prisoner until farther communication with Nadir Shah. Bring hither this Ghuzzub Ali, that I may first hear the tale with mine own ears, and take care he also is placed under safe custody.'

Moye-ed-din, bowing, retired to execute his orders, and soon returned with the Persian servant, who related to the Nuwab the whole affair, concluding with the directions for the assassination of Humza given by Zekey Khan to Kummil Khan, a notorious murderer; and that the news of Humza's death having only a few days since reached Zekey Khan, **by** means of a ship from Busrah, he delayed not openly to demand the fair Zeefa from the Nuwab. Ghuzzub Ali gave a detailed account **of** the insult he had received at the hands of his master, on whom he had determined to be revenged, and thought the present moment best suited to his purpose. **The** Nuwab dismissed the **man** from his presence, bidding him make up his mind to temporary confinement until he heard from Nadir Shah.

On **the** following day the haughty Zekey Khan appeared before the Nuwab and demanded the immediate delivery of his cousin Zeefa. To his utter dismay, instead of a ready acquiescence, he was surrounded and made a prisoner, the Nuwab not condescending to afford him any explanation for such proceeding. The next step was the selection of one of the most distinguished and wealthy persons in the city to proceed in the character of Ambassador to the Court of Persia, into whose hands dispatches, drawn up with the greatest care, were given, with orders to return with all due expedition. In the interim the Nuwab by degrees broke the sad news of **the asserted death of Humza to** the afflicted Zeefa, concealing, however, the supposed manner of his decease. Zeefa was at first distracted at the intelligence, and when the violence of her grief subsided sank **into** a melancholy from which nothing could arouse her.

Time rolled on, **and all** continued tranquil at **Surat.** The Nuwab was dejected but not morose; **whilst Zeefa,** in the expectation of news **from** Persia, **kept** entirely secluded, now giving way to fears, now **to joyful anticipations of the arrival of** some welcome herald bearing **a** report **of her** beloved being still in existence and perhaps on his way **to** claim **her.** Oppressed by these alternate feelings of despair and hope, her health declined, and it was with grief the Nuwab perceived the bloom on her lovely **cheek** gradually disappear.

The whole palace presented a gloomy and dismal appearance; one would have imagined it had been proclaimed treason to have smiled, so solemn **were** the countenances of all within its walls; **not that all felt in** reality grieved either **by** the disappointment of their master or the declining health of the fair Zeefa, but because it was ever customary with menials attendant in the palace of a Nuwab to mark well their master's countenance on his first appearance, and dress their own throughout the day in corresponding gaiety or cheerfulness, as the case might be.

Day after day passed, and still no news arrived from Persia. The Nuwab, from excessive anxiety, entirely neglected business, **and** shut himself up in his Anderun. Moye-ed-din, was one morning meditating how he could by any means divert his master's thoughts, when the idea of **an** aquatic excursion on the

broad and luxuriant Taptee struck him ; and proceeding to his
window, which overlooked the river, to ascertain the state of the
tide and weather, he descried a stately ship just passing the
second bar of the river, and was about **to** make enquiries from
his attendants, when Buxoo, that never-failing source of information, entered the apartment, exclaiming, ' He is come, my lord,
come at last ! '

' Who is come ? ' cried the impatient Deewan.

' Who, my lord ? Why, Humza, to be sure. So it is all **a** lie
about his being murdered. He is come, rely on it, to carry away
the Persian lady, and thus end all your troubles.'

' If this is true, Buxoo, I fear it will rather add to my troubles,
for if the Nuwab so despond at the idea of losing the lady, what
are we to expect when she is actually gone ? '

' Why, **my** lord, you must find him another beauty, unfettered
by any previous love-promises.'

' No, no, Buxoo, nothing should tempt me to provide more
ladies for the Nuwab ; I have had trouble and anxiety enough with
this one. Remember my beard, which yet bears the marks of the
accursed dye ; and remember—ah! you know.'

' Oh ! my lord, that was the most unfortunate circumstance ;
but indeed it was all a mistake.'

' Well, well, Buxoo, say no more ; but are you sure Humza is
indeed arrived ? '

' Certain, my lord ; quite sure ; saw him myself. Such a fine-
looking, handsome, long black-bearded Persian ! far superior to that
ill-looking cheat, his brother, whose ill-manners and uncourteous

behaviour I can never forget, for he it was who struck me for nothing, only because in the most civil manner possible——'

' Well, well, I know all that, Buxoo; pray mention it no more.'

An attendant now entered the room, saying the Deewan's presence was required at the **Nuwab's** palace.

Moye-ed-din, on his entering the Nuwab's apartment, perceived a noble Persian, whom he learned had been sent from Nadir Shah to take charge of the fair Zeefa, should she determine on returning to her native country. He confirmed the statement of Ghuzzub Ali, the servant of Zekey Khan. Humza was, indeed, no more; the agent of Zekey Khan had confessed the whole transaction; and the king in consequence issued his commands to the Nuwab of Surat to send the guilty Zekey Khan in chains to his court. The Nuwab expressed his readiness to obey the royal mandate, and gave orders that the ambassador should be sumptuously entertained during his sojourn in the city. The task of informing Zeefa now devolved upon the Nuwab, and with difficulty he performed it. Zeefa sat the picture of grief and despair, and for many days refused to take the least sustenance. As all grief must have an end, or is mitigated by the healing hand of time, Zeefa, on learning that the bearer of the sad news was a man who had formerly been a great friend of her father's, desired to have an interview with him. He obeyed, and at her request related the fact of Humza having closed his eyes on this world for ever. When she had for some time sat in mournful silence the ambassador informed her that he was commissioned to escort her back to Persia, if she determined on returning thither.

[' I am ready,' cried the afflicted Zeefa, ' and will intimate my intention to the Nuwab.'

' Ah, lady!' cried the ambassador, who had learned the great love Jelal-ed-din professed for her, ' will you thus deprive his highness of all hope, he who loves you to distraction ? '

' Forbear!' cried Zeefa, ' talk not to me of love; my heart is for ever——'

' Oh, lady! say not thus; allow his highness to visit you once more—once more give ear to his repetitions of everlasting fidelity.'

' I will see him,' cried Zeefa; ' it is my duty to thank him for his unremitting attentions to me, and to request a speedy preparation for my departure. Tell him I hope to be honoured by his presence.'

The ambassador, bowing, retired, and soon after the Nuwab entered Zeefa's apartment.

' I cannot sufficiently express my gratitude,' said the afflicted fair one, ' to your highness for the attentions received at your hands. I am now about to depart to my own country, where his Majesty Nadir Shah shall hear my testimony of your benevolence and kind consideration. I now request a vessel may be prepared with all due expedition.'

The Nuwab again declared the ardent love he bore her, and endeavoured to dissuade her from her proposed return. She waved her hand, and appeared greatly affected ; and the Nuwab, hoping a future opportunity might offer to urge his love, retired, promising to give orders for a vessel to be equipped with all due dispatch.

It may be imagined, however, there was but little haste made in the preparation; and in the interim the Nuwab redoubled his attentions to the amiable **Zeefa,** which he **with** joy perceived were received **with more and more** pleasure at every visit, and that she evinced less and **less** anxiety to leave Surat, although she **never** omitted enquiring when the ship **would be** ready to receive her.

'The ship is ready, fairest Zeefa,' said the Nuwab, **'and** my **arms are** also ready to receive you; why, then, are you determined to doom **me to misery** unparalleled? **My** whole **life and every** action shall be devoted **to you** and **to your comfort.** Say, then, will you abandon all **idea of** returning to Persia? Slight not my vows of everlasting love, **but by a word** make me truly happy.'

Zeefa could **not be** insensible to the ardent admiration **of** the **Nuwab, and she** continued silent, until again more earnestly **pressing his** suit, **she consented** to remain at Surat and become **his bride,** provided he allowed her **a period of six** months to mourn her beloved Humza. To express the rapture of the Nuwab baffles all skill, and with delight beaming in his eye he agreed to the required period.

Nothing now remained to be done but to allow the ambassador to hear the determination of Zeefa from her own lips, and for this purpose **a day** was appointed, when the Nuwab ushered him into the presence **of** the lady, who, on the question being put to her, with becoming modesty replied that the attentions of the Nuwab could never be forgotten; and that since fate had decided against **her** union with her first love, she had such confidence in the **Nuwab** as not to hesitate placing herself under his guidance and protection.

The messenger then took this opportunity of expressing his

joy on the **occasion, and of** extrolling the virtues of the **man to** whom she intended to link her destiny. The ambassador then took leave, having received Zeefa's instructions to express **her** gratitude to Nadir Shah for the interest he **had** taken in her welfare. The ship being ready, the once haughty, now downcast, Zekey Khan in chains followed **the** ambassador, accompanied **by** Guzzub Ali, his now amply avenged servant.

Moye-ed-din, although he could not get rid **of** the **Persian** lady, was as pleased as **his** master **at** the happy termination **of the** business, and **ventured to** represent to the **Nuwab that it was** owing to Buxoo the **existence of Zeefa was** ever known, upon which the Nuwab settled on **the loquacious shaver a** pension for life, **and** bestowed **on** Moye-ed-din **a rich** khilaat, **or** robe of honour.

The six months required **by Zeefa to mourn the** fate of Humza having expired, the day was fixed for the nuptials; but **as it was** not an early one, and much preparation being requisite, **Moye-** ed-din ventured **to ask the Nuwab whether the stories should be** continued.

' No, no!' said the Nuwab, ' release the story-tellers; tell them I am well satisfied, and present each with one hundred rupees, as a reward for their trouble and loss **of time.'**

The preparations for the wedding now commenced, **and for** splendour and magnificence could not have been exceeded **by the** Emperor himself. Beggars were **fed and** clothed, prisoners released, honours conferred, and injuries forgiven. Fireworks and rockets and salutes resounded through the air, whilst drums, trumpets, and cymbals drowned all care throughout the city. The wedding itself was conducted with solemnity and magnificence, and the happy pair retired to the Mahumed-a-baugh palace, there to breathe their loves amidst silvery fountains and shady groves.

Buxoo appeared once in every month before the Nuwab to make his salaam for his pension, and sometimes the Nuwab would require from him an amusing tale; but the syren voice and exquisite beauty of Zeefa now chiefly engrossed his leisure hours.

THE END.

LONDON : PRINTED BY
SPOTTISWOODE AND CO., NEW-STREET SQUARE
AND PARLIAMENT STREET